GANGLAND
3

A Real Chicago Love Story

A NOVEL BY

LEO SULLIVAN
PORSCHA STERLING

Leo Sullivan Presents
P.O. Box 924043
Norcross, GA 30010

Cover Designer: Marion Designs

JOIN OUR MAILING LIST!

Join our mailing list to get a notification when Leo Sullivan Presents has another release.

Text LEOSULLIVAN to 22828 to join!

To submit a manuscript for our review, email us.

SYNOPSIS

In the series finale of Gangland, there is a deadly stand-off between Kato and Polo, forcing Star to make a decision. With both men demanding her love and loyalty, she has no other option but to figure out which one is worthy. With her sister missing, she is also racing against time to find her but when she does, it may be too late.

This tragic story of Chicago gang life comes to a close and just like in real life, many don't make it to the end. Does Star have what it takes to survive or will love and gang lead her to the last days of her life?

WARNING

This book contains bad language, violence and some explicit sex scenes. This is a work of fiction. Names, characters, business, events and incidents are the products of the author's imagination. Any resemblance to actual persons, living or dead, or actual events is purely coincidental.

This is a cautionary tale. In no way do the authors promote or condone acts of violence, rape, gang activity or any criminal activity that may be illustrated within this novel.

GANG CULTURE

"The gangs filled a void in society, and the void was the absence of family life. The gang became a family.

For some of those guys in the gang that was the only family they knew, because when their mothers had them they were too busy having children for other men.

Some of them never knew their daddies. Their daddies never look back after they got their mothers pregnant, and those guys just grew up and they couldn't relate to nobody.

When they had their problems, who could they have talked to? Nobody would listen, so they gravitated together and formed a gang."

— GEORGE MACKEY

CHAPTER 1

STAR PANICKED WHEN SHE SAW POLO STANDING IN *THE SPOT* WITH about fifty Disciple crew members. Each one looked even more rowdy and thugged out than the next; bouncing around like something was about to jump off. Her heart pounded in her chest when she read Polo's lips as he turned to her and frowned.

"I'm gonna violate you, bitch," he mouthed, pointing at the car.

She quickly ducked down in her seat as her heart somersaulted in her chest. Paranoia was overwhelming her, and Kato wasn't making matters any better.

With his hand reaching for his strap, he glared at Polo and sneered.

"If this nigga rap slick on some disrespectful shit, I'ma have to check his ass, viciously."

"No, please. Just keep driving," she pressed apprehensively.

At that exact moment, she happened to glance across the street in time to spot Tonya walking out of the entrance of her grandmother's apartment. Something about her demeanor caught Star's attention, although it wasn't uncommon seeing her there. In their hood, the vestibule area of apartment buildings was used for all types of functions; stashing money, drugs, rolling blunts and a list of things.

Still, there was something suspicious about her activity. Star's fear took over as she turned back to Polo and his legion of Disciples standing around him. She squirmed in her seat, feeling a sharp sensation in her chest like she had to pee. It only happened this way when she was scared.

"Well, what will we tell him?" Star asked Kato, surprised at the tremor in her voice. She couldn't help but take a look up at her grandma's apartment window, expecting to see Ebony looking down at all the activity on the streets.

"What the fuck you think we supposed to tell him? We ain't gotta tell that nigga shit!" Kato responded as he pulled next to a car. "As far as he knows, we ain't done shit so he better come at me correctly."

As he was about to park, Star stared at the large gathering around them, thinking of how much they reminded her of a nest full of aggressive bees. Some of the Disciples started moving around preparing for their attack; others even pointed at the car. She didn't know what Polo had told them, but they were angry and alert while internally bubbling with the excitement that came about when somebody was about to be violated.

She looked over at the other side of *The Spot* and saw Tonya quickly walking over to join with a few of the other Gangstress. Brenda and Kee-Kee were among the group as they all stood attentive, wondering what would become of their leader. Kevia stood to the side of the group, appearing anxious, terrified and devastated all at the same time.

"Get da fuck outta that car, Star!" Polo raged.

His facial features were cast in stone as he glared through the windshield. His ego was bruised; seeing Star with Kato, his closest friend and now primary foe, wasn't something he would take lightly. Regardless of his past actions or his reasoning for being with her in the first place, in his mind, he loved Star and couldn't see her with anyone other than him. Especially not the man he'd so suddenly come to hate.

With bated breath, Star watched as Polo's lips continued to move. She couldn't tell what he was saying but she knew it wasn't good. Her thorax began to heave; she could never remember a time when she was as scared as she was now. Except maybe the time when she was trying to escape Kato's wrath on the night that she shot him. She reverted her eyes over to him and briefly wondered which of the two she was more afraid to be the enemy of.

Definitely Kato, she thought, watching his poised, deadly-calm exterior. *He's too comfortable in the midst of this shit. His ass is crazy for real.*

There was no way he would consider backing down, but Star wanted to avoid a shoot-out in the streets at all costs.

"Can't you just tell him that you found me and gave me a ride here?" she managed to ask in a small voice, as her heart continued to beat like a bass drum. Kato had just finished parking across the street from *The Spot* and all eyes were on them.

"Not when he got that fucked up look on his face like he can't wait to tell them boys to light my ass up. I ain't feeling this shit!"

Kato's face twisted up into a hard scowl, like he was fighting his demons. His anger would always be his worst enemy. It wasn't until the moment that Star looked down at his hand and saw that he was holding a pistol in it that she began to feel like she might be living in her last days.

"Oh, God! Can you put that up?" she groaned, petrified, but it was no use because he had his door open and was halfway out.

"Fuck nah! This nigga got me fucked up like I'm one of them other mark ass niggas."

With that said, he was out the whip with the quickness and moving fast, walking right into the fire. That took Star completely by surprise as she watched in horror.

With no other recourse, she sat in the car with her fate undecided; her reality probably about to be a distant memory and her life right on the perils of self-destruction. Or would it be Polo's destruction?

Breathing hard, she watched Kato walking with a purpose, his sagging pants slightly revealing the handle of another pistol that he had stashed at his waist. He walked with a slight bounce, his feet bouncing on the balls of his toes, as he headed across the street. Star inhaled a large dose of courage and then exhaled her fear before grabbing the door handle and stepping out into the unknown.

With his pistol at his side, Kato dodged cars as he walked right into the fray of thugs. This was the entire clique of Disciples that he had broken bread with and ran the city with but now, ultimately, the tables could turn making friends become foe.

Star stood at the curb waiting for cars to pass before she crossed. Moments seemed to stall until she heard Kato's voice roar like a lone lion in a concrete jingle.

"Nigga, I know you not out here tryin' to confront me 'bout no bitch!"

By the time Star looked up, Kato was already in Polo's face; they were toe-to-toe. With a quick pivot, he then turned around like something suddenly occurred to him and grilled the entire crew with his pistol in hand.

"And what the fuck you niggas waitin' 'round for? Some shit 'bout to pop off that I need to know 'bout?"

A wave of disgruntled chatter came from the crew as they all gave Kato their full attention, but none were foolish enough to step to him. That was suicide in their minds. Well, in every mind except Polo's.

"Bruh, you doin' too much. First off, I only asked what she was doin' in the car with you. And second, are you callin' Star a bitch?" Polo said with grit in his voice as Sloan walked up beside him, his expression offering proof that this was the last place he wanted to be.

"Nigga, I ain't call Star a bitch. What I said is, don't be stepping to *me* 'bout no bitch. You was the one who brought her into it when you asked what she was doin' in the car."

Confused, Polo couldn't help but frown. Like, what the fuck kind of dumb ass answer was that?

Before he could respond, Kato continued, "It's obvious I gave her a ride up here but what ain't obvious is why all these niggas posted up on the block like y'all was waitin' on my ass or somethin'. Y'all tryin' to get some shit started?"

"Nigga, you trippin'," someone commented, an anonymous voice in the crowd.

"It's better for me to be trippin' than to put a bullet in ya head for being a nosy ass fuck boy all up in my business," he replied with a subtle threat.

There was silence from the other Disciples as Polo continued speaking.

"All I asked was one question and now you're on one. You need to tone that shit down!" Polo fumed as his hand reached for his strap, in preparation for whatever.

Both gangstas had a short fuse for patience and a strong propensity for gun violence. Things were getting ugly and fast.

"Tone it down or what!?" Kato challenged, edging closer into Polo's face. "I'll tone it down when you can explain to me why the streets been talkin' 'bout you double-crossin' Jimmy Johnson."

Star stepped up as a gentle breeze pushed a tuft of curly hair on her forehead and an ominous black cloud formed directly overhead. Before her, Polo and Kato stood glaring at each other, hate smoldering in both of their eyes. The moment was volatile as the battleground filled up full of goons, the two titans in the Disciple organization standing dead center.

"Bitch, I'm fuckin' violating you!" Polo said, flipping the script as he turned and pointed a finger into her face.

"For what?" Star snaked her neck with an attitude and hand on her hip, playing it bold.

The worst thing you could do was underestimate Polo's conniving, street savage ways and she didn't want to show weakness which would only make him certain of her guilt.

"For takin' the money that you stole from me."

"All that fuckin' money you makin' and you're worried about the little bit I took? I took it to get my own place but if it's like that, I can give it back."

She grabbed her purse and tried to keep her hands from trembling as she pretended to go inside to get money that she knew wasn't there. She was trying to sound stern but inside, she was as fragile as an autumn leaf.

"Nah, you should have thought about that before you took it. Now I'm ordering that you get violated," Polo said. "Matter of fact, I should let Tonya do the shit."

Her lips parting slightly in shock, Star stole a glance over at Tonya. Her face was stolid like a blank sheet of paper; she was hard to read. Again, Star was catching the most terrible vibe from her. Something wasn't right but she wasn't sure what it was.

Parting the group of Disciples into two, Sloan stepped up with his head lifted high and spoke with authority, hoping to be the voice of reason amongst the crew.

"This is not organization related. Your domestic dispute with Star isn't worthy of calling a violation. Nowhere in the bylaws says that you can have a Gangstress violated for a situation like this," Sloan spoke with diplomacy in his voice.

"In other words, you can't throw a pussy fit and violate somebody just 'cause y'all was fuckin'," Kato sneered, chuckling a little under his breath. "You punk ass sucker for love ass nigga."

Polo wasn't buying it.

"Fuck outta here! Me callin' for her violation ain't got shit to do with us fuckin'."

"Oh, really? I left you and now you want me violated for some petty ass money that I said I could give you back. So, tell me, what's really good?" Star said with an attitude.

Before Polo could answer, Kato chimed in as well.

"Yeah, and like I said, I been hearin' that organizational funds been coming up short. Word is that the old man fightin' for his life and havin' trouble payin' his appeal lawyers because you ain't been sendin' the money out. What's up with that?"

With that said, the Disciples standing behind Polo all began to shift uneasily, no longer as willing to stand behind their leader if what Kato was saying was true. The fact that he'd even openly voiced it told them that Kato believed the rumor to be valid because, if false, he could be subject to deadly consequences for even making the statement.

"Nigga, that ain't got shit to do with what's going on now," Polo replied, keeping his eyes forward, although he heard the shuffling behind him.

"It's more important than you bein' in your feelings over some bitch—"

In broad daylight, Polo reached for his strap just as Sloan stepped in between the two men and other gang members rushed up. Star gasped, seeing several shotguns and AK-47's being brandished in broad daylight. There was a lot of pushing and shoving from the crew as spectators, who had been merely watching at first, took off running. Bullets didn't have a name on them and any innocent bystander could get shot.

Lines were drawn as the Disciples split, some siding with Kato and others with Polo.

"There you go with that 'bitch' shit again." Polo held his gun by his side while glaring threateningly at Kato. "You know I'm not gon' stand by and let you disrespect mine."

Under the bylaws, no Queen Gangstress was to be disrespected and called a bitch. The thing was, Polo was being petty and looking for a reason to check him, but it was backfiring terribly because Kato, being Kato, didn't give a fuck. He'd done it deliberately. He never meant any disrespect towards Star, but he was using any opportunity to get under Polo's skin in all the ways that he knew how.

"Let's not take it there," Sloan spoke up once again. "Star said she'll give you your money back so let that shit go. We don't need no heat out here, especially not over this small shit."

"Right! So tuck that pistol back in your waist, you soft dick ass nigga," Kato gritted with his jaw clenched.

That was it!

Before anyone realized it, Polo eased his strap up and took a big swing at him, barely missing. The second Kato registered what had happened, he looked at his former friend with empty eyes as a permanent shift took place between them.

Polo had committed a cardinal sin by pulling a pistol on Kato and, even though he was not trying to shoot him, it didn't matter. In Kato's mind, he should have done it when he had the chance because he came up from the hip with his pistol and cocked it, fully prepared for a head shot. Just before he could get his shot off, Sloan and about three other gang members grabbed onto him, saving Polo's life in just the nick of time.

While Star looked on in sheer terror with her heartbeat like a sledgehammer in her chest, nothing could have prepared her for anything happening before her eyes. Absentmindedly, she took several steps back in trepidation and just happened to glance up at her grandmother's building. A familiar figure through the third-story glass window made time freeze around her. It was her grandmother, watching her with her hands covering her mouth. Star's legs nearly went weak as her entire world began to tumble to pieces around her.

Then, out of the blue, a caravan of police cars swooped in like black predators. Five unmarked sedans and one blue and white patrol car pulled up with marked precision and cops expeditiously hopped out their cars. In total, there were about eleven cops, all of them members of the heavily armed GIU, Gang Intelligence Unit.

Each cop wore a scowl that illustrated their hate for this community and they each carried weapons that were unimaginable: AR-15's and Mossburg shotguns. These were veteran cops with hairpin trigger fingers and no patience for Black people. The very people they were paid to serve and protect were the ones they didn't hesitate to kill, maim and imprison without impunity.

All Disciples and Gangstress looked on, none wanting to do anything to be granted unwanted attention, but their expressions and body language making it clear that the GIU weren't welcome at the same time. Like oil and water, gangs and the GIU never got along. Both groups were ruthless and wouldn't hesitate to use deadly force when necessary; the only difference between the two was that the GIU had a license to do so and exercised that right daily.

"There she is right there!" yelled a cop, who was dressed from head-to-toe in all black army fatigue, that almost made him look like a ninja. He appeared to be nearly seven feet tall with muscles that bulged, like he spent most of his nights and days at the gym.

The Gang Intelligence Unit was comprised of huge, mammoth men. They donned an arsenal of other crude weapons too, that were lethal and legal, like the steel prods that had electrical shocks for the unruly or to force a confession, once placed on the private areas of men and women.

"She's there!" another cop shouted.

He was bald headed, wearing dark shades, and his bald head gleamed in the sunlight. There was an earpiece in his ear. The metallic sound of all the paraphernalia rattled louder as cops moved in on Star.

"Come with us," the bald head cop said in a deep baritone voice as the other cops surrounded Star.

"Where I'm going?" Star asked in a high pitch tone, that gave away her terrified frame of mind as she looked up at the cop in horror.

"With us," the cop said impassively.

Star looked at Polo, then Kato, her fear palpable. Polo looked over at her and the cops like this was the last scenario in the world he wanted to be in. He, along with his entire crew, were strapped with guns and drugs hidden on them. It was apparent just from his expression that Star would have to be the proverbial sacrificial lamb.

None of the Disciples wanted to have anything to do with the GIU. As far as Polo was concerned, the GIU were the biggest gang in Chicago. He had seen more than enough so-called accidental deaths caused by them. Like guys falling down a flight of stairs, while hand-cuffed, and breaking their necks dying or simply killed for allegedly resisting arrest. Directly opposite from him, Kato wasted no time speaking up; his gun was back under his pants and concealed by then.

"Man, y'all got a fuckin' search warrant or some shit? Keep runnin' up on a nigga like y'all Rambo, you might fuck 'round and get shot," Kato said, stepping to a cop wearing a uniform. He was the only cop that was driving a blue and white patrol car.

A gloved, white cop toting an AR-15 and wearing some type of Star Wars looking shades that Darth Vader wouldn't get caught dead in, spoke up. Star narrowed her eyes at him, recognizing him immediately as the cop she'd seen at the hospital the first day she went with Polo to see Kato. The one with the mohawk.

"Yeah, we got a warrant. Here it is, right here." He patted his assault weapon with his black-gloved hand.

"That lil' ass pop gun? We got cannons in this bitch that'll flip you and them putt-putt ass cars y'all drivin'," Kato raved. He was upset as he pointed an angry finger at the cop.

"Oh, yeah? How about we start shaking a few of you down and see if we need to take a trip downtown?" the cop retorted and took an aggressive step forward.

Instantly, bodies moved like a tidal wave of thugs regressing backward.

Polo cut his eyes at Kato, looking at him in great disdain. His temper was going to get them all jammed up or worse.

"Chill, nigga!" Polo shouted, and his voice carried like a tempest wind.

All of his men were strapped with enough heat to give out life sentences because some of the weapons the Disciples were carrying had bodies connected to them, including Kato's. With no other recourse, they all fell back and watched Star get kidnapped in broad daylight by none other than Chicago's very own notorious GIU.

Would she snitch?

Paranoia ran rampant through the hood. It was blind and suspicion held no rules in a land where people died just trying to survive.

As soon as Star was carted off, Tonya rushed over to Polo.

"That bitch probably snitching. You know she ain't thorough. The second she thinks she's in trouble, she's gonna tell every fuckin' thing she knows."

Polo paid her no mind; his focus was on Kato. With grit in his voice and loathing eyes intensely glaring at his target, he spoke with a tight jaw.

"Dig my nigga, you was out of pocket with what you said and we still need to handle it. Let's go have a meeting and you can get whatever you need off your chest."

"Bet. 'Cause I don't like the fuck shit I'm seein'," Kato replied with ease. He was ready for whatever.

Although he was fresh out the hospital and in no condition to fight, his trigger-finger was more than able. When Polo turned, he seriously thought about shooting him in the back of his head, but Polo was 'Folks', and their named leader, so he exercised self-control. The violation for killing him without showing cause was death.

Helpless, Star watched them as the two cops led her away. As soon as she sat in the backseat of the police car, sandwiched by two huge, massive cops, she knew something was wrong. *Terribly* wrong. Devastation would wreak havoc on her life like nothing she had ever experienced from this day forward.

THREE HOURS EARLIER

CHAPTER 2

"In every crisis there is a message. Crises are nature's way of forcing change."

EBONY LAY ON THE FLOOR WITH HER FEET AND HANDS TIED, HER mouth had been taped shut and she had been blindfolded as the rancid stench from something terrible enveloped her nostrils; the smell was like a dead animal. She had been stripped of all her clothes, except her panties and bra.

There was no doubt in her mind. She was going to die, and it might not even be due to intentional homicide. All her life, she had asthma and a series of bad sinus infections. All it took was for her sinuses to get clogged up and she wouldn't be able to breathe. With her mouth taped shut, she would suffocate and die.

Ebony cried hard as she squirmed and twisted on the cold, dilapidated floor as her captors plotted.

"Are you sure this shit is going to work?" Tonya asked quizzically, as she squatted down inspecting a box.

It looked like a small, makeshift casket with a long breathing tube of some type attached to it. Assassin furtively glanced at her ass while she was bent over, wearing black legging pants. He quickly shifted his eyes to his cousin, Jazmyn, who was standing on the other side of the shed, wearing a brown, dirty restaurant uniform. She was eating a left-over hamburger she had stolen from her place of employment.

"Jaz, get yo' fat ass over here and explain this shit one more time!" Assassin yelled, trying to look confident with a meek smile that faded as soon as Jazmyn's nineteen-year-old ass waddled over.

She was three hundred plus pounds, and black as night with smooth, even skin that would have guaranteed her the status of a beauty if she only took care of herself. She was so heavy that when she walked, her feet never left the ground; they slid like she was walking on ice. She wore a long, blond lace-front wig that looked atrocious, as if it had been crocheted in with cloth made from an old mop. She smelled of restaurant grease, nicotine and funk that emanated from her so loudly Tonya crinkled her nose. Jazmyn always smelled terrible and she knew it but had stopped caring long ago.

"Alright but don't forget about what you promised me. A bitch need something to smoke." Jazmyn smiled, showing off caked up food in her teeth.

"Chicken head ass girl, didn't I tell you I got you? Now tell me how this works."

"Nigga, didn't I tell your ass to stop calling me names?"

To his surprise, she balled her fist and pulled back like she was going to hit him, so he had no choice but to ease back.

Tonya took a hesitant step to the side away from Assassin, in case big ass Jazmyn did explode and things popped off. Trying to stop her would be like a trying to stop a Mack truck rolling downhill, out of control and without breaks. You didn't want to get hit.

"Cuz, can't you take a joke? But anyways, my bad. Now tell us how this shit works." Assassin smiled and pointed down to the box.

Jazmyn continued to hold him with contempt in her eyes as she went on to explain.

"It's simple, we shut her in the box and bury it. This breathing tube and that container has fresh oxygen in it for seven hours or more, depending on if she holds her breath or don't breathe too much. I wrote the directions down in my diary a long time ago when my grandpa told me about how he used to use this for animals and shit."

"Animals? What the fuck? Who bird brain ass idea was that?" Tonya said and stood up suddenly.

Assassin didn't answer. His eyes were locked in on the phat coochie print in her tight leggings. Tonya also wasn't wearing a bra and the nipple piercings in her luscious double-D breasts protruded visibly like infant fingers pointing through the sheer, satin, white blouse she was wearing.

"It was my idea," Assassin said finally and walked up close on Tonya.

"But why couldn't we just tie the bitch up and leave her somewhere?"

"Because who the fuck gon' watch her all day? I can't! Can you? Especially if she starts movin' around, screamin' and shit or manages to get loose?" he said.

Tonya exhaled out a heavy breath and glanced back at the box.

"But still, this shit looks crazy as fuck. I mean, like how she gon' piss and shit? And what is that fucked up ass odor in here?" She frowned, first looking around and then back at Jazmyn like the smell might've been coming from her.

"She'll be alright. As soon as I get off work in a few hours, I'll give her a bucket to go," Jazmyn spoke up.

"This shit sounds crazy as hell," Tonya snapped.

"Well, take this bitch to your house then. It's the best I can do," Jazmyn huffed; her attitude was spreading like the plague across her face.

"She got a point," Assassin reasoned, staring at Tonya's breasts. His dick was starting to get hard.

Tonya looked around the shed. There was an old ancient tractor, the kind that you drive for farming, and a bunch of other miscellaneous things like boxes, crates, shovels, lawn equipment, big ass spider webs.

"One question, how the hell you come up with this idea anyway?" Tonya asked looking at the big girl.

She shrugged and pulled out a hamburger from some unknown place, biting into it before she began to explain.

"It was simple. My granddaddy, Elmo, used to work for this white man that was a poacher. They would steal exotic animals, like monkeys and big ass snakes and shit, that they had to pack in that box and sneak them past the custom agents. They used these boxes with the breathing thingamajigs."

"Did any of them die?" Tonya asked looking at the small, casket type box.

"I'on know." The big girl rolled her massive shoulders and took another bite out of her sandwich and chewed, smacking.

"You don't know?" Tonya screeched.

"I mean, not that I know of and besides, you only need the box a day or so, right? So, it ain't like she gon' die if she don't get a little bit of air."

Tonya rolled her eyes at the repugnance of it all and glanced over at Ebony. She continued to writhe on the floor, making all type of awful noises like she couldn't breathe with the tape covering her month. But Tonya felt no sympathy for her. The only reason she didn't want her to die was because, if she did, they could kiss their big payday away.

"Fuck it, y'all right," she agreed. "This shouldn't take too long. I'ma hit that bitch Star's grandma house up for the ransom money and we gon' bounce. It shouldn't take more than twenty-four hours because Polo will pay it."

"Then what?" Assassin asked her. She frowned.

"The fuck you mean, then what? Shit, we get the money and we good."

Assassin shook his head in dismay.

"Nah, shawty, what I'm sayin' is, then what we gon' do with this chick? If we get the money for the ransom, we can't just turn her over to Star and Polo. She seen us so that would be a death sentence."

Tonya pondered what he said for a second as Jazmyn dug deep in her pocket and pulled out one lone weathered French fry, then bit into it. Tonya looked at her in disgust, then replied to him.

"Let me handle the small stuff. I got this." Then on a second thought, she added, "I gotta go, a G.D. meeting is in a few hours. Polo called one, so I know it's gonna be something important."

"Okay, and I have to be at work in a few hours," Jazmyn said, still munching on something.

With an arched eyebrow, Tonya asked, "Where you work at?"

"White Castle, I just got promoted to hamburgers." The girl beamed and Tonya tried hard not to roll her eyes once more.

"Make sure you handle this right and I got more money for you," Assassin said, handing Jazmyn a couple bills. She glanced down at them, checking the amount before stuffing them into her greasy pants pocket.

"Okay, I get off work at four o'clock, she has enough oxygen to last for about thirty minutes after. It only takes about fifteen minutes for me to catch the CTA bus to work. I could walk, but I wear a size eleven, these shoes is a size eight. I got my toes balled up and shit, feet be killing me."

Tonya glanced down at her feet and her eyes almost bugged out of her skull at what she saw. Jazmyn had on the most raggedy shoes she had ever seen. Her big toe had nearly worn a hole in the fabric in both shoes and was about to burst out. Both shoes were covered in dirt and grease, severely leaning all the way on the sides and looked like splashes of paint were on them.

And this is the bitch Assassin chose to take care of this shit with Ebony? she thought, feeling like she'd made a mistake in trusting him to help her carry out this plan. J-Rock may have been a better choice.

"Dammmmnn," Tonya droned, pathetically.

A DOG BARKED in the distance and the sun moved behind dark clouds, resulting in a fuchsia-colored sky. The footfall of feet moving could be heard on the mushy, wet grass as they carried the casket sized box, to a hole in the ground; a place that once used to serve as an old school barbecue pit, three feet deep and six feet long. It was perfect for what they were doing. Once they had the box in the ground, they covered it with shallow dirt. Then something dawned on Tonya as she watched

Jazmyn rig up the tube and oxygen tank above ground, while Ebony violently kicked and thrashed inside the box to no avail.

"Suppose it rains or gets cold outside?" she asked, glancing up at the cloudy sky.

"Shit, we will just move her out of there but, hopefully, we would have gotten the money by then."

Jazmyn grunted as she stood back up, covered in dirt and mud. She was suddenly moving in a hurry as she wiped her hands on her dirty uniform and dug into her pocket for something, then took off in a trot, wobbling all the way, late for work.

"I'm out. I can't be late again. I just got promoted," Jazmyn said over her shoulder.

Assassin and Tonya both vaguely heard Ebony screaming inside the box, as overhead, the clouds continued getting darker. With Jazmyn's grandfather dead and her grandmother in an old folk's home, there was no one around to hear the young girl's cries for help.

"So, what's the plan now?" Assassin asked, while reaching into his pocket removing Backwood cigars to roll up a blunt.

The entire time, his eyes roamed from Tonya's breasts to her luscious thighs. She was watching him too, looking at his fat pockets full of cash.

"Easy, I'ma go plant the ransom note at Star's granny's apartment then play it close right there with the gang so I can hear what's goin' on. I'll act like I'm trying to help find her sister, all sad and shit, but in reality I'm the bitch that kidnapped her ass."

Tonya chuckled, causing him to glance over at her and smile slyly as he licked the blunt. He didn't even know that her conniving ass was trying to figure out how she would get rid of him next. He looked over and blew a plume of smoke at Tonya while giving her a seductive stare.

"A nigga still tryna smash. Let me hit that ass and see what that mouth do."

"Smash?" Tonya jerked her neck.

"Hell yeah! 'Specially after all this shit you done took me through."

He grabbed her arm roughly and pulled her onto his groin. She could feel his hard dick, placed against her leg. It took everything in her power not to look down.

"What you doin'? Stop!" She tried to pull away.

"What it look like? I'm tryin' to fuck somethin'."

She twisted her face up in disgust. He was gross but he was also aggressive in what he wanted. Her only resort was to try one of the oldest tricks in the book to assuage his thug nature.

"My period is on,." She shrugged. "I can't do shit."

"Ok, that's cool," he replied without missing a beat. "My dick don't discriminate. I'll fuck that fat ass or your tits. A nigga be liking that wild shit."

"Boy, you trippin—"

Before she could finish her statement, he yanked her hard by her arm and pulled her toward the stanking ass shed. She resisted, but not much. Assassin was a true to life hood nigga; he was about to take the pussy whether she wanted him to or not. But what he didn't know was Tonya had a pistol in her purse, the same pistol she had killed J-Rock with.

For a second, she was tempted to pull it out and shoot him but that would have been foolish because he was an ally that, for the moment, she needed more than life. Without him, she couldn't pull off her plan, and time was running out like an hourglass running out of sand.

Finally, she stopped and planted her feet down into the dirt.

"Damn, you 85th street niggas be wild as fuck. I'll do it."

"Do what?" he stopped and asked. There was no humor in his voice; he was nearly devoid of emotion like a cave man.

"I'll give you some but I ain't going in that stankin' ass shed," she scowled.

Something about her facial expression made him smile as he held the blunt dangling between his lips. In the distance, a police siren blared two houses down and a dog barked voraciously.

"You know what? I think it's time for us to make this shit legit. I already called my niggas over and we gon' set that ass out. Make you part of the crew for real. We need to make sure you loyal."

Tonya's neck jerked and her entire body was overcome with the icy feeling of dread. 'Setting that ass out' was a term that was commonly used in gang culture. She had gotten herself in too deep and knew it.

Crazy ass Assassin was about to hand her over to his gang to have their way with her once he was done.

She suddenly stopped and reached for her purse to get her gun, but Assassin snatched it away and slapped the shit out of her, twice. She was dazed and disorientated when she felt him take her arm and drag her to the old decrepit house.

As soon as they were inside, she heard a roar of voices, and saw a bunch of Four Corner Hustlers inside. They had to be at least 20 deep with the melodious smell of loud, musk and mildew. Music was coming from somewhere in the house; clothes, garbage, empty bottles and trash were everywhere.

"Take them fuckin' clothes off, bitch!" Assassin yelled with blood-red eyes as Tonya stood there with about twenty pairs of eyes peering at her.

However, defiant and dignified, she held her chin high as her eyes rimmed with tears.

CHAPTER 3

"SO THAT'S HOW IT IS? YOU NOT GONNA TELL ME WHERE SHE IS?"

Pressing her lips into a tight line, Kevia crossed her arms over her chest and turned away from Sloan. Standing over her, he took one look at the stubborn expression on her face and knew that there was no use in asking her about Star's whereabouts. Kevia wouldn't betray her friend.

"This shit can get real nasty, Kee, and I don't want you to be part of it. It ain't no secret that Polo ain't really feelin' you like that so don't give him another reason to try and come at you." Reaching out, he rubbed her growing belly. "Especially not when you got my shorty growin' in your belly. I need to keep you safe."

Running her hand across her brow, Kevia balled up her lips into a frown, both loving and hating the fact that Sloan was mentioning their child. She loved to hear the words 'my shorty' fall from his lips but hated the fact that the baby she was growing felt like anything but. So far, Sloan hadn't even made it to a single doctor's appointment.

"If you're so concerned about me bein' safe, why don't we move in together somewhere? Then when I have our baby, we can be a family," she said with a small smile. "Under one roof. All legit and shit."

In spite of the seriousness of their present situation, Sloan couldn't help the smile that nearly covered his face at the thought. There was a lot about his life that Kevia didn't understand and even more that he couldn't tell her at the present time.

"I'll have to see 'bout that," he said, not giving her a straight answer. He didn't want to disappoint but also didn't want to make any promises that he couldn't keep.

With a sour expression, Kevia leaned back into the worn, brown leather couch that her mother had purchased before she was born. The same one that, apparently, she would be sitting on while nursing her new baby as well.

"Let me guess... we can't move in together because your main bitch won't like it."

"Kevia..." Sloan warned, his tone raising only slightly. He hated to argue with her and, since she'd gotten pregnant, she only seemed to get more and more argumentative every day.

"Why won't you just be honest with me? If I'm your side bitch, I'm your side bitch. I'm a big girl, you can tell me."

"You ain't no fuckin' side bitch!" Sloan gritted, annoyed to even have to be addressing this. Especially when there were other pressing matters he needed to deal with.

"If anybody is the side bitch, it's her. I'm not fuckin' her, I don't tell her that I love her. I don't give a damn about her outside of makin' sure she does right by my daughter."

Kevia sniffed, wanting to believe him but not being able to see through all of her unanswered questions.

"But why do you stay with her then? Why can't she have her own shit?" she argued. "Plenty of people are parents to children without being together. What makes you two so different?"

Sitting down in a worn recliner chair across from Kevia, Sloan sighed and ran his hand wearily over his face. This wasn't the time for this conversation. His phone vibrated in his pocket and he grabbed it, knowing who it was before he even got a chance to look at the screen.

What's good?

Looking up, Sloan placed his focus on Kevia once again, knowing that he had to get some answers from her and he needed them fast.

Polo was on one and the last thing he wanted was for him to try to bring Kevia into his madness.

"Kee, listen. You're 'bout to be a mother now. You're in charge of a life so forget about me and my bullshit, think about our child. Star is makin' her decisions based on what's best for her and her family and you need to do the same. Now, where is she?"

Pursing her lips, Kevia turned away from him as thoughts ran rampant through her mind. He was right; Star always did whatever she had to in order to look out for her grandmother and her sister because she felt like she was responsible for them. Kevia had a child that she was now responsible for and she had to make sure no harm came to her or her unborn child. Still, Star was her best friend. She would never betray her in any way that could cost Star her life.

"Will you make sure that he doesn't hurt her?" she asked, staring at him doubtfully.

One thing Kevia knew about Sloan was that he was a man of his word. He took his role as a Disciple seriously and followed all the laws of the organization to the letter. If Polo called for Star to be harmed, Kevia couldn't say that she was certain he wouldn't see to it, as was his duty as Polo's right hand.

"You know I will always look out for Star. She's your girl and she's the Queen G."

"But if Polo asked... if he commanded it, you would have to. Would you go through with it?"

Sloan chose his next words carefully. "I won't allow anyone to harm Star as long as she is not going against the laws that I stand for or betraying the leaders of our organization."

Biting on the corner of her lip, Kevia thought about what Sloan was saying and realized that was as good as it was going to get. For a brief moment, she wondered if he knew about who Star's father was. Knowing that might give her leverage over Polo as far as Sloan's loyalty was concerned. But then she also remembered that Star made her promise not to tell anyone because of what Kato told her about Jimmy Johnson's enemies.

"She... she left to go see a family member. In another city," Kevia stated, deliberately being vague. "She told me that she'll be gone for some hours."

Sloan raised a brow. "She rode the bus?"

There was a brief pause as Kevia swallowed hard, suddenly feeling her temperature rise the more that Sloan stared at her. He made it hard for her to lie.

"Nooo, she..."

Her eyes darted around the small living room as if she were trying to read the answer on the wall. Her younger siblings were in school and, in that moment, she wished that they'd been home to give her an excuse to make a quick exit.

"Did Kato take her?"

The question caught Kevia by surprise and she froze in place. In the next instant, she tried with all her might to loosen the tension in her muscles and frowned deeply, doing her best to play it cool.

"Kato? Why would he, of all people, take her anywhere?"

The pointed look that Sloan gave her said that he knew more than what she thought he did, and he also knew that she knew more than what she was admitting.

"Since you wanna play it this way, I'ma level this shit with you. But we gotta be quick because I don't have a lot of time," Sloan said, clasping his hands together. "I'll answer every question you have 'bout what's goin' on in my life... I'll give you the full truth and in turn, you gotta tell me what the real deal is with Star, who she's goin' to see and who took her there."

Her eyes narrowed. "You'll tell me everything? The full truth with absolutely no lies?"

Without saying a word, Sloan gave her a tacit nod and Kevia took a deep breath before saying another thing.

"If I tell you who she went to see, you can't tell Polo."

"Kee, I—"

"Promise me!" she shouted, cutting him off. "You can't tell him or I won't tell you *anything* at all!"

His jaw tightened as he sat, thinking to himself.

"Fine. Just tell me who she is with and when she'll be back," Sloan finally said. "You can keep the rest of it to yourself."

His vow to gang and duty ran deep, Kevia realized after hearing what he'd said. He would rather not know than to know and be put in a position where he would have to go against his word.

"And you'll still uphold your end of the bargain?"

He nodded; his eyes pointed at some distant spot on the dingy apartment wall. Kevia looked down at her stomach, only slightly rounded from her young pregnancy, and sighed.

The bait was out, and she was aware that she wasn't strong enough to resist. There wasn't any point to it anyways, because the truth was that she was a terrible liar. All that she could do from this point on was hope that Sloan stayed true to his word and would make sure that he did everything in his power to keep Star safe.

CHAPTER 4

TONYA WAS IN A SITUATION THAT WAS IMPOSSIBLE TO GET OUT OF. She had been tricked and it wasn't abnormal for young, Black girls to be murdered after being set out, their bodies discovered in trash cans. She would be another statistic that barely made the news reports. It occurred to her Assassin could have just been using her to get back at Polo, setting her up for revenge. He probably didn't give a fuck about Ebony or the kidnapping money.

Slowly, she began to take off her clothes. Her blouse was the first to go. She wasn't wearing a bra and as soon as her large, pendulous breast were exposed, her nipple piercings were on display, causing salacious 'uhhs' and 'ohhhs' from the crowd.

Someone said, "I'ma hit that ass from the back!" and she flinched. Then more voices rang out, all of them letting their plan for her body be made known.

"I'm going in from the front, long dick style."

"Well shit, I'ma fuck dat mouth. Deep throat them tonsils!"

They all laughed at her expense.

Tonya wiped her face with the back of her trembling hand and just when she was about to take off her panties, Assassin said, "Hold up!"

He grabbed her arm. For some reason, there was more jovial laughter. Tonya would have been humiliated but she was in too much fear for her life. She was all too familiar with situations like this. There was no way she would walk out alive. It was the unwritten code of the streets; dead bitches don't talk after they have been raped and brutalized.

She glanced up as he held her arm, her eyes sparking with tears as she looked at him questionably.

"Come here," was all he said with a slight pull on her arm, leading her through a door right next to the kitchen.

The room was trashed as well but not as bad. There was a picture of an old man with a huge hunting rifle, with a lion trapped in a cage in the background. The man was Elmo, Jazmyn's grandfather. He was Assassin's grandfather too, but he refused to claim the old deceased man. Since Elmo had dedicated his life to a white man instead of his family, and the two never got along.

As soon as the door shut, Assassin cracked a devilish grin and then reached out to pinch Tonya's nipple hard, tugging on the ring attached to it.

"Ouch!" she cried out in pain.

"Guess what? You passed the test," he said, still grinning, and tossed her purse on the bed.

He then unzipped his pants and took his dick out. It was hard and long, thick as a Coke can, but stunted in size with a fat pink head. He was also not circumcised; his dick looked like a truncated elephant trunk that had been burnt in a fire.

Tonya did a comical double take with her eyes gaped wide. He had the fattest, ugliest dick she had ever seen. But, at that very moment, she would suck the skin off it if he would let her walk out the house alive.

"What test?" she asked finally, still trying to hide her fear and balance her composure as she absentmindedly covered her breasts with her arms.

She seemed calm but she was actually petrified. The thought of death and being gang raped by a house full of Four Corner Hustlers was horrifying and she knew without a doubt they would do it.

"It was a test to see where your loyalty lies. You was down and that was dope as fuck. 'Cause if you would've bucked, my niggas may have done something terrible."

He pulled her close, as he stroked himself wantonly, the blunt smoldering in his month.

"I told you I was a down ass bitch. Whatever you want, I'ma do it. We in this shit to win and I know how this shit works with gangs and girls. Niggas wanna test a bitch loyalty and they should," she said with fake bravado and held his gaze.

"Cool, that's why I'ma make you my bitch, exclusively."

He squinted with the smoke from the blunt burning his eyes as he reached out and pulled her by her neck forcefully and placed the blunt on the dresser to his right and reached for his throbbing dick in hand.

She looked up into his slanted eyes and saw his attraction for her. She wanted him to cling to it like a drowning victim lost at sea.

"I'm down with whatever," she cajoled and poured a heavy dose of seductress all over him as she pushed her breasts forward and tried to smile.

The entire time, she plotted in her mind that when the time was right, and after she had gotten her money from Star, she was going to kill him. He would die a most horrible death. She wanted to put sleeping pills in his drink, slice his throat with a razor then cut his mule dick off.

"Good, that's what I'm talkin' bout," Assassin said in a deep baritone, then took a long toke from the blunt, nearly choking.

"Can I hit it?" she asked in a small voice, trying to show him she was on chill mood but in reality, she was scared as shit.

"Hit this dick first," he said and aimed it up at her and pulled the skin back as he grabbed the back of her neck.

She got down on her knees and began stroking his dick, feeling slightly disgusted but it was better than dying.

Assassin sneered with a sex face as he caressed her head like she was his new pet.

"I want you to suck me real good. Then I'ma hit you in the ass, just like we talked about, and then bust all over them big ass tits and pretty face."

She looked up, her hand instantly stopping its jerking motion as she grimaced. Trying not to offend him, she tried to smile.

"I was just playin'. I ain't on my period so I can just give you some."

She tried to charm him with a grin. His dick was less than an inch from her mouth, and he smacked her with it, right across her eye.

"Ouch!"

"See, you play too much, so I'm still gonna hit that asshole and teach you a lesson tho," he said with a lascivious grin. He began stroking her head faster, and she instantly saw his dick grow bigger, with veins spreading out and pulsating.

She shuddered as she looked at him and was about to complain when he shoved his dick in her mouth. With no other recourse, she sucked on his dick like a starved Ethiopian, hoping she could make him cum fast.

She pressed her entire face on his dick and down her throat, where she heard him suck air like he had fallen into quicksand. He palmed the back of her head, guiding himself deeper down her throat, fucking her face.

"Fuck!" Assassin winced in pleasure.

It was like her lubricious lips and mouth had suction cups on them, pulling at the seed deep in his loins. He was fighting the battle of control and then she stopped to spit on his dick and then jerked him off at jack hammer speed. When she looked up at him with jaundiced eyes that he mistook for lust, he felt his loins tighten.

"Shit!" he yelled when she took him back into her mouth again. He rose on the tip of his toes, his body seismic like he was about to have a seizure. But still, he humped her face, forced himself deeper down her throat, making a loud whooshing, slurping sound that resonated in the room in the backdrop of loud music and the cacophony of voices coming from the other room.

In the background, Tonya heard what sounded like a loud clap of thunder, resonating in the distance.

Is it about to rain?

For a fleeting second she thought of Ebony, buried in the shallow earth. There was no sympathy; she needed the money so she couldn't let the girl die.

She sucked harder, faster, feeling his body going rigid. He was about to cum. Tonya deep throated him and allowed her hot mouth to turn into a sink hole as saliva spilled from her mouth, intentionally giving him that SuperHead experience.

Afterwards, both were winded. The sound of them breathing was like two prize fighters that had gone 15 rounds. They were both covered in a sheen of perspiration.

Assassin stroked his dick that was shrinking by the second and said,

"Shawty, you can truly suck a dick. That was the best I ever had."

Tonya glanced at her phone, it was time to go. She needed to get out the house and make the meeting, so she ran game.

"Wait 'til you get some of this good ass pussy," she said in a breathy voice and stood.

She began to put back on her clothes, not even thinking about cleaning herself up. She didn't have the time.

"You in a hurry?" he asked and fired the blunt back up as he admired her body.

"I need to go place that ransom note like we agreed on," she said winded, still breathing hard. "I can probably even set Polo up for you."

She was trying to entice him with the allure of setting the head Disciple up, so she could get out the house faster.

"Yeah, you do that," he said, watching her intently.

She spied his pockets and asked in a sensuous voice while she leaned so close to him that her breast were against his chest, as she tried to kiss him. He ducked his lips away.

She said, "Right now I need a place to stay. Can you give me some money? I'm living with my girl, Brenda, in her little as fuck crib."

"Yeah, sure." He pulled out a knot of money. "Here you go," he said passing her some money. She frowned.

"I'm going to need more than this," she said.

"Bitch, you asked for a place to stay like a room or some shit. I can't pay for no damn apartment right now."

She suppressed the urge to roll her eyes. This is what she got for messing with a broke ass nigga. More than ever, she needed to get Polo back.

"Fine. I gotta go so I'll hit you up later."

Assassin nodded, puffing on his blunt without a care in the world.

"Don't make a nigga come looking for you. Just hit up my phone when it's time for me and my niggas to roll up. You tell us where that Disciple money and product at and we might not even need ole girl out back," he said, referring to Ebony.

After Tonya finished getting dressed, she began walking out the door. She was happy to be alive, to just see another day.

The clouds were threatening rain, and Ebony was stashed in a shallow grave. Tonya really didn't give a fuck; she was just happy that her plan was coming together. Once she got the money and revenge on Star, she would be the happiest bitch on Earth.

PRESENT TIME

CHAPTER 5

STAR SAT WEDGED IN BETWEEN TWO COPS IN AN UNMARKED POLICE car as she looked up and saw what looked like an army of cops storming into her grandmother's house.

Startled, she asked, "What's going on?"

"You tell us, princess. Or should we say 'queen' since you're the new leader of the Black Gangstress?" one of the cops said, eyeing her with disgust.

His blue eyes seemed to be too close together and too deep in his sockets. His head was nearly bald, shaped like a bullet, along with a beak nose that reminded her of a buzzard. Under Disciple laws, she didn't have to tell her status with the organization to the cops. Let them do their own damn job.

"I don't know what you're talkin' about, but what is going on? If you're not arresting me, then let me go! I know my rights."

"You know we can take you down to the station and hold you for up to twenty-four hours for questioning, right?"

"Questioning for what?" Star asked.

The entire time, her head jerked around to scan her surroundings. There was so much going on. The police were running into her grandmother's apartment and on the other side of the street, Polo, Kato and the entire crew were rushing into The *Spot*. Star knew firsthand nothing good was going to come out of that. With Polo and Kato being alpha males and beefing with each other, there was a serious chance that death would follow. She was instantly concerned for both men.

"We could take you in for murder," the opposite cop, on her right, said as he jabbed a finger in her face.

For some reason he was very angry. He had brunette hair, dark, beady eyes and a bad attitude.

"MURDER! For what?" she asked as her heart beat faster. The first thing that came to her mind was Mink, Polo's brother, who she had shot. Could, somehow, they have heard about that? The other problem was that she was holding a banger in her purse, an ounce of loud and a couple of pills. Percocets that Kato had been prescribed for pain but the cops knew her history and wouldn't give a damn.

"You let us ask all the questions and you just fuckin' answer. You hear me?" the cop with the brunette hair yelled, spraying her with spittle. It took everything in her power not to go off on him once his spit hit her face.

"Yes, sir," was all she said, trying to keep her composure.

"Now, your sister, Ebony, is about to be wanted for murder, so I suggest you tell us where she is—"

"My little sister wouldn't harm nobody. There has to be a mistake," Star said, suddenly feeling claustrophobic, sandwiched between the two irate cops.

"The only mistake is if you don't talk to us. Tell us what's going on."

Just then, his police radio erupted with a chirring sputter, as a staticky voice came on.

"The suspect, the young girl by the name of Ebony, is not in the apartment. Just some old lady, and she damn near had a heart attack when we came in. We called the paramedics to attend to her. Other than that, all clear!"

Star thought she heard a cop snicker over the radio.

"All clear!"

"All clear!"

The police units responded over the radio in unison.

That's when she looked up and saw a S.W.A.T team van, more police cars and trucks moving in the neighborhood and looking like a small army about to engage in war.

"What the hell?" she droned aloud.

"Yeah, right, what the hell. Like where the hell is your sister at? You tell us something or we run your ass downtown so fast your fat nose gonna bleed!" the bald-headed cop said. They were doing everything in their power to strike a nerve with her and doing a good job of it.

Star gestured sincerely with a wave of her outreached hands like a silent plea.

"Honest to God, if you tell me what's going on, I can help, but I don't know where she is at. Honest! And I need to go see 'bout my granny."

Just then Star saw Tonya walk out front from The *Spot*. The police vehicle that Star was inside had dark tinted windows, making it so Star could see her but she couldn't see Star. Tonya was on the phone, talking to somebody, and Star's gut feeling was telling her something wasn't right.

The brunette cop leaned in close to Star's face, his breath smelled just like horse shit.

"I'm going to show you a picture to identify a person and if you lie to me, you're going to jail for obstruction of justice, accessory to murder after the fact and a laundry list of other charges, you understand me?"

She winced and nodded her head, he was shouting in her ear like a drill sergeant. Absentmindedly, she watched Tonya like she was in a bad dream.

"Do you know this guy right here?" the cop with the bald head asked and shoved a mugshot picture of J-Rock in her face.

"Yes, I know him. His name is J-Rock. He used to try to talk to my sister, but he was too old for her; she is only fifteen."

"Fifteen?" both cops repeated and exchanged glances. Star had their full attention.

"Yes, my little sister is only fifteen and never been in trouble, not in a gang or nothing. She's not even allowed to stay out late past ten o'clock. That guy, J-Rock, he would have been a child molester as far as I'm concerned if he would have touched her."

"Why would you be concerned? You're a female gangbanger and a drug dealer."

Star lifted her chin in the air and frowned.

"No, I am not, I just got accepted to a major college—"

BAM!

The cop slammed his meaty hand down on the car headrest in front of him.

"The moment you start lying is the moment you go to jail and we place you in a nice, cozy cell with Bubba, a six-foot-eight dyke. She gon' wanna fuck you with a twelve-inch dildo made from an old mop handle and rubber gloves. So your best bet is not to lie to me. We got snitches out here who say you pick up drugs for the Disciples and you snatch money too, so stop fucking lying!" the cop yelled again, and again, Star wiped spit from her face.

Star winced as she shrunk in the seat between them.

"J-Rock, known to the police department as Jamel Thomas, is dead, as in murdered and ran over by a vehicle, closed casket. Your sister's I.D. was found in his pocket and the school says she never showed."

"What?" Star's eyes shot wide. "I'm telling you now, my sister wouldn't do no shit like that. J-Rock was an asshole that used to rob and shoot people. Even with the truce between the gangs, he was robbin' and killin' like it was a sport. Anybody could want him dead. My sister ain't 'bout that life, period."

"Are you certain?" the cop with the bald head asked and took out a small notepad and began to jot down things on the paper.

"Yeah, I'm certain. This dude, J-Rock, had everybody on the south-side of the city wanting to kill his ass for all the wrong he did. I don't know where my sister is but when I find her, I'ma bring her to the station," Star said honestly and watched medics run up in the building her grandmother lived in.

"You do that and also, if you want to make some extra money or have some enemies you want taken out, we can do that. All you have to do is work with us as an informant."

Star chuckled disdainfully, wanting nothing more than for them to let her go.

"I find it interesting that cops don't snitch on each other even when it's on video and y'all done beat a Black person to death, but you expect for me to snitch. Nah, I'd rather be skinned alive and tossed out the hundredth floor of the John Hancock building, butt ass naked before I turn on one of my friends," she spoke solemnly with her chin high.

The cops smiled as if they admired her truthfulness. The reality was, no one really liked a snitch, not even the cops, even though their help was invaluable.

With that said, the cops let her leave. As soon as she stepped out, a tempestuous clap of thunder ricocheted throughout the sky. Star noticed Tonya glance her way before ducking back into The *Spot*. Instantly, something unnerved her, pulling at her gut strings.

Star dodged cars as she took off across the street and was nearly ran over as it began to rain hard. She stared up in the sky as water pelted her face, feeling like something was terribly wrong. She could sense it.

CHAPTER 6

THE MEDICS WERE LEAVING, CARRYING AWAY AN EMPTY GURNEY. Star was happy her granny wasn't lying on top, wrapped in a black bag on her way to the morgue.

As they passed, she took to the stairs two at time, in a hurry.

The moment she walked into the small apartment, she knew something was wrong. She could hear the syncopated whir of her grandmother's breathing machine reverberating throughout the house, along with labored breathing, panting and moaning. Star just happened to look down and see a piece of paper. It looked like it had been shoved under the door and trampled on with footprints.

She unfolded the paper as she walked to the living room looking for her granny.

The ransom note read, **"We have your sister. If you want her back alive, we need $100,000.00. If you contact the cops, we will kill her and you next. You got three days."**

Star stared at the note as she walked with her heart racing; she was near panic driven. She folded up the paper and placed it in her pocket when she heard her grandmother cry out in pain.

"Granny!" she shouted and took off for the front room.

She found Geraldine lying on the couch with her arms plastered over her chest as it heaved like she had just run a ten-thousand-mile marathon.

"Grandma, you okay?" she asked, rushing over.

"Hell no, I ain't okay. Do I *look* like I'm okay?" she said in a snarky voice as her mask fogged up intermittently. The T.V. blared loudly in the background.

"What's wrong? Why you breathin' like that and holding yo' chest?"

Her grandmother swallowed hard before speaking with trembling lips.

"Baby, I feel like the end is near. My heart hurts something terrible. I ain't never felt nothing like this before in my life."

"You just hold it right there. I'm going to call the ambulance back." Star rushed toward the window.

"No, not that kinda pain. My heart is hurtin', chile. The police just come in here looking for Ebony, like she was a common criminal. She ain't come home yet and I'm scared somethin' wrong."

Geraldine began to cry poignant sobs that rocked her thin, small shoulders as she began to wave back and forth as if she was wrestling with her own demons.

"I don't like this... I had a dream. I saw death. That chile ain't never did nothin' to nobody but I'm scared something bad done happened to her."

"Granny, everything gon' be alright," Star said sympathetically and fell to her knees on her grandmother's side on the floor.

She rested her head on Geraldine's leg, just as she used to do when she was a little girl. She wiped away tears of sorrow, careful not to let her grandmother see them.

"Granny, she gon' be alright. She's just late coming home," Star lied.

The truth was that she had a feeling that everything wasn't going to be alright. She needed to find her sister fast, and just the thought of her coming up with $100,000 was daunting. Star had a little money saved but nowhere close to that amount.

"How the police gon' make the victim look like a criminal? They was lookin' for that baby like she was a killer, like she had something to do with a murder. Them white folks talked mean to me. It just hurt my spirit... my soul, deep down inside."

"Gram, everything is going to be alright. I'ma go look for her now. You just be sure to take your meds and call me if you need anything. Everything will be fine."

"I hope so because—and I pray I'm wrong—but I feel something terrible happened."

Geraldine cried harder and Star stood and embraced her grandmother as the two cried together.

MOMENTS LATER, Star left her grandmother's apartment. There was a light drizzle coming down, and the sky was dark like the bottom was about to fall out the clouds as she jogged across the street to The *Spot*.

The lookouts that were strategically positioned around the area saw her coming and all showed respect. A few then looked at her with suspicion because of the amount of time she had spent in the back of the patrol car but Star didn't care, she had other troubling things on her mind.

K-9, one of Polo's loyal assistants, opened the steel door on the side of the building as she walked up. Before being pulled into the gang life, Star and Kevia in their girlish nature jokingly gave him the nickname Mandingo because of his appearance. His skin was swarthy jet black, he was about six foot six in height and built like a professional body builder. Even his muscles had muscles; at 280 pounds, he was huge. He had an ugly, deep scar on the top of his nose, and brawny African features with more cuts on his arm and neck, like he had been to a knife fight.

"Hi, Star. Come in," he said in a deep baritone voice as he peeped both ways looking out the door.

Instantly, she could sense something was wrong. Her instincts told her to turn around, but she was like a chick on mission. She needed to talk to Polo, even though this was not the right time. He was in the process of waging war on her for some stupid shit but the good thing is he had no idea where she'd been or that there was something going on between her and Kato.

Truthfully, she wasn't yet sure herself what was going on between the two of them but she had no time to figure that out. Although Polo was the last person she wanted to go to, right then, she needed him badly, to help find her sister. She was stuck in between a rock and a hard place.

Her phone chimed as soon as she walked inside. She could hear loud voices: Kato's and Polo. They were arguing about something and she only prayed that it wasn't her.

She glanced at her phone and it was Kevia calling. Star sent her a quick text.

I can't talk now. I'll hit you back!

She placed the phone back into her purse and walked into hell on Earth as she described it later. She stepped into a smoked-filled room in the basement. There were at least a hundred Disciples packed tight and crowded, and along with that was the murmur of many voices. The tension was so tight you could cut it with a dull knife. It took a moment for her vision to clear, but on the other side of the room, she saw her clique of Gangstress, including Tonya. They all showed love by throwing up the hand gang signs, the pitch forks. They were also looking very apprehensive like something serious was about to jump off.

And it was.

"So, what I'm saying is, there is a code of conduct and a chain of command. You violated that, my nigga. You're the Chief Enforcer. You enforce shit, you don't call shots. I do!" Polo raged as he turned and looked at Star with what looked like pure hatred and then turned back to Kato who began to speak.

"First off, let's get this shit straight, my nigga. I fear no man but God Almighty. As for my position, my ranking don't mean shit if the structure is corrupt. If niggas out here fillin' their pockets with the organization's money and then calling bogus violations on bitches 'cause they in they feelings, I ain't gotta abide by that bullshit!" Kato exploded.

"Fuck you mean? I know gotdamn well you ain't tryin' to say I'm stealing' shit 'cause I built this hood up with blood, sweat, and murder!"

"Murder?" Kato snorted disgusted. "What fuckin' murder? Oh,

'cause you callin' shots and gettin' niggas killed? I'm the muthafucka doin' the killin'!" Infuriated, he pressed a pointed finger into his own chest. "So let's keep that shit trill, my nigga. I dropped over fourteen bodies in one year, so who doing the killin'? It damn sho' ain't you. Ain't a nigga in this fuckin' city put in more work in than me, and you know it. I even caught a fuckin' bullet in my head over dedicating my life to this shit. So you need to respect my muthafuckin' gangsta. I ain't like none of these soft ass niggas, includin' you."

Kato's temper was uncontrollable, he was on one.

"What you just said?" Polo squinted; his eyes were tiny dots of optic terror about to erupt.

"You heard me, nigga! I made an oath, fuck what you got to say. My oath is to Jimmy Johnson, so I ain't got shit else to say to you or no other nigga at this point."

Polo reared his head back, with his eyebrows spread wide across his face, incredulously. Then a devious smirk spread across his face.

"Alright, slick talkin' ass nigga. I'm having you violated, right fuckin' now. Today!"

This time it was Kato's turn to laugh, a dry cackle that was as sinister as the devil's prologue to death's calling.

"Nigga, I wish you would. Now tell me how the violator gets violated? That would be like Jesus reprimanding God. It just ain't happening, bruh," Kato spat and took a step back, looking around as if he was evaluating the room, its occupancy and his next move.

Star's heart was beating out of control just like most of the people in the cramped basement. She just happened to look over and Tonya was watching her like she was daydreaming, thinking about something.

"What you forgot is Jesus was crucified for runnin' his big ass mouth when he was in the presence of a room full of goons, just like you are right now," Polo shot back. "It's a hundred niggas in here. They all take orders from me or die. Right now, you are outnumbered and outmanned. If I wanted to, I could call a 'treason violation', kill you and stuff your body in that furnace over there then call it a day. Instead, I'm generous. So I'm just goin' to take you off count, strip you of your rank and status as a Disciple and call for you to receive a

Pumpkin Head Deluxe. A hundred punches, straight to yo' ugly ass face."

"Nigga, you got me fucked up! You can't call no 'treason violation' on me. That's for niggas that worked with the other side, or turned rat and snitched to the police," Kato said, and looked around the room, searching for any face that wanted to agree with him.

He happened to glance over at Star, and their eyes locked for an infinite moment in time. Her heart throbbed for him. She knew deep down inside this was nothing more than politics for Polo and that more than likely, Kato's life was doomed. There was no doubt that if Polo gave the word, every gang member in the basement would follow his every command.

Silence followed and Kato shuffled his feet anxiously before casting a long glance at Sloan. The two had a great relationship. Sloan, the second in command to Polo, was the only one who could stop the madness before it began.

"Yo Sloan, tell this nigga that treason shit don't apply to me."

All eyes then strolled over to Sloan. He gave Kato a weary shrug and threw up both his hands helplessly with a look of despair.

"I'll read the bylaws again, but the as the first in command, Polo can call a treason violation if and only if he deems it a risk to all nations governed under the G.D. organization," Sloan spoke with his eyes cast down at the concrete. It was easy to tell he didn't want to have nothing to do with Kato being violated.

"That is some bullshit and you fuckin' know it!" Kato shouted.

Polo ignored him. He was looking uncertain and with good reason because everyone knew Kato was not about to take this punishment without a fight.

Looking over to the biggest men in the room and the only ones who might be able to handle Kato, he began to speak.

"I need four hittas. K-9, Nate, Junior, and Rock, relieve this nigga of his banger and his clothes. Place him against the wall right over there for everybody to see that when Folks get outta line, they get fucked up and carried out in an ambulance, or worse."

With the word out, the men prepared to move and Kato calmly pulled out his pistol. There was a rippled stir of disgruntled voices throughout the basement as the four hittas, men that normally would have been Kato's right-hand men on a mission, men that Kato had killed with on many occasions and broke bread with like brothers, were about to be his attackers.

As if practiced and rehearsed, K-9, Nate, Junior and Rock stepped to Kato. To them, this was business without empathy. The reality was, in a kill or be killed society, one soldier's fallen position was another man's way to level up in rank. Kato's position was admirable, the only ones with more power were Polo and Sloan. All of the hittas were hungry to be his replacement, knowing that one of them would be next in line for the prestigious position.

"Let me get your banger, Kato. Man, don't make this difficult," K-9 said standing close to him, attempting to appear intimidating. He was nearly a foot taller and seventy pounds heavier. His demeanor was overbearing to most.

"Yeah and strip so we ain't gotta make you. Let's just get this over with," Rock added and cracked his knuckles as Junior and Nate came up behind Kato.

Kato mopped sweat from his brows and sighed as if he were about to give in. When he spoke, it became clear that wasn't the case.

"The only thing I got in this life is my pistol and my balls. I'd rather be dead than let some clown ass nigga take my gangsta from me over some fuck shit."

"We can arrange your death if that's the way you wanna go," Polo cut in, his voice as edgy as the moment.

"Give me your pistol, Kato. You my nigga and I hate it had to come to this, but I ain't gon' ask you no more," K-9 said and inched closer with his hand on the gun concealed in his pants. Junior and the other hittas followed suit.

Kato knew the drill—hell, he was the one that trained them. They would steal on him the second he wasn't looking, take his weapon, stomp him out to the point of being unconscious and then give him a Pumpkin Head Deluxe. That was the ultimate punishment, so severe that almost all who received it suffered brain damage afterwards. With Kato just coming back off a severe head injury, receiving more trauma to the head would send him to his grave.

Kato turned and Star could see it in his eyes, almost read his thoughts. He was going to buck and possibly get killed.

"No, Kato, don't!" she shouted. Her voice echoed like they were in a subway station tunnel.

Frowning, Polo turned to look at her in dismay along with several other gang members. Kato seized the moment with perfection.

With his top lip pressed tightly across his teeth, Kato said menacingly, "You niggas want my banger? Well, here is. You even get the bullets for free!"

Without warning, Kato pulled out and shot K-9 in the face, cheek and neck. Then delivered a head shot to first Junior then Rock, and fired at Killa. hitting him square in the ass when he tried to take off running in the small confines. It was pure pandemonium as audaciously, Polo rushed forward and started letting off shots. Kato tried to return fire, but he found himself at a disadvantage; Polo was upon him quick. The first shot hit him in his mid-region, another shot hit him higher up, just as a violent stampede started. Gang members began moving like startled cattle in the cramped space. Kato nearly fell as Polo rushed over to finish him off.

Star stood by witnessing everything like a horrific horror movie then, suddenly, she too was swept up by the tumultuous tide of people in a violent upheaval. The worst thing that could happen was gunshots in a small basement that was crowded with people; it was a sure recipe for disaster.

Fighting through the crowd of people, she gasped when she saw Polo aim his gun for a clear shot at Kato's head.

"Nooooo!" she yelled out, pushing through the people around her, struggling to exit out of the small door. When she saw Polo's finger push against the trigger, she knew it was too late.

BLOCKA! BLOCKA!

The shots echoed loudly in the small room as Polo let more shots off, forcing Kato's body to jump as he keeled backward.

As he dropped to the ground, Star screamed to the top of her lungs.

CHAPTER 7

JAZMYN LOOKED AT HER WATCH AS SHE TRIED TO FRY TWENTY-SIX hamburgers on the grill even though her supervisor had warned her not to fry more than twenty. The thing was, six of the scrumptious, juicy burgers were hers. As time ticked on, she felt slightly panicked. She needed to be off work and get home soon. It was already 3:15 and the place was packed. Hearing what seemed like a crack of thunder, she glanced out the window and noticed that it had started to rain. Ebony was buried in a shallow grave, barely three feet deep, with only enough oxygen for seven hours.

Or is it six? Jazmyn pondered.

Still thinking on Ebony, she looked up and flinched when she saw her manager coming her direction.

She had been warned twice not to cook extra burgers on the grill because it could cause a fire but she couldn't help herself. She even managed to start a side business after she discovered how to steal some of the patties and sell them to clients that she'd gathered in the hood. Business was booming because she had a system. She would load all the burgers up from the freezer and place them in the trash when no one was looking and then take them out to the dumpsters.

The only chink in her system was old ass Wilcox, her manager. He was a racist old man who hated Black people, hated his job and everything remotely related to it, including Jazmyn. In his late 50s with a hump back, big nose and sunken eyes to match, Wilcox was evil as hell.

Jazmyn looked up and, sure as shit, he was glaring at her and walking with urgent and purposeful intent.

"Jazmyn," Wilcox called her name as he hobbled over, walking with a bad limp like he had been kicked by a horse. He was within ten yards of her as employees scattered like the Red Sea getting out of his way.

Frantically, Jazmyn looked for the spatula to grab the extra hamburgers and for the life of her, she couldn't find it. She started to panic; Wilcox was too close and she knew that if he found out what she'd done, she would get fired.

With no other choice, she grabbed the flaming hot burgers, saturated with hot grease, and used her bare hands to shove them down her pants, experiencing excruciating pain that made her scream out loud. The hot grease from the burgers burned her thigh and by the time Wilcox walked up, her face was beet red. She was sweating profusely as she did a two-step. The grease was seriously hot!

"Hey, Jazmyn, I need you to work an extra shift," he said like an order and for some reason, he furrowed his brow at her.

"I—I... I can't. Not today. I gotta go," she said, stepping from one foot to the next, like her pants were on fire; actually they were, kind of.

"Janet couldn't make it in so I'ma need for you to stay until seven until we find a replacement."

"Replacement? Uh-uh, I gotta go! Nope, not happening," Jazmyn said and squirmed, pinching her eyes closed.

The midriff of her body was experiencing pain like she had never experienced before. She actually considered dropping her pants and taking the sizzling hot burgers out. No job was worth second-degree burns.

"This is extremely urgent. We need you to work late until Janet arrives, or another replacement," Wilcox said sternly.

By then, Jazmyn could feel one of the burgers sliding down to her crotch, stinging her with hot grease all along the way.

"Oh, shit!"

The pain was too much. She stuck her hand down her pants to move the burger to the side. Her boss took a step back, bug-eyed like he was shocked and appalled.

"Sorry, I gotta use the bathroom really bad," she said and rushed off.

"You don't have to worry about working overtime. I'll find somebody else," Wilcox threw his words at her as she rushed off.

He was disgusted by what he saw and even more determined to write her up.

FOUR O'CLOCK FINALLY CAME AROUND AND Jazmyn was ready to leave the job in a hurry. She threw up the deuces to all her co-workers, especially the cute chick she had trained about a week ago. Jazmyn liked women more than men. For some strange reason that she couldn't understand, men didn't seem to find her attractive.

As she approached the front door exit with a backpack full of burgers, she looked out the huge picture window and her heart sank. It was pouring raining and she couldn't help but think of Ebony buried in her grandparents' backyard.

She needed to get home fast.

Just as she stepped to the exit door about to open it, she heard her name called.

"Jazmyn Donald!" She didn't even have to turn around to recognize the voice. It belonged to Wilcox, her manager. She heard his footsteps rushing up behind her and took in a sharp breath, thinking fast. She was cold busted, standing with a backpack full of stolen hamburgers on her back.

"I got you now!" he said with riveting enthusiasm.

"What?"

She turned around, and the entire staff was watching, including a few customers. Wilcox loved to make a big show of firing people or belittling them. Even though Jazmyn didn't want to lose her job, she most definitely didn't want to go to jail for stealing.

Or for murder, she thought, thinking back to Ebony.

"Jazmyn, can you come over here?"

"For what?"

She stared at the door and thought about making a mad dash for it. She just happened to glance outside and groaned heavily when she saw her bus leaving.

"Come over here and sign these papers," he ordered her.

"What papers?" she asked, and shifted on her feet nervously.

"I'm writing you up for bad personal hygiene and poor job quality at your station today," he said.

As crazy as it may sound, Jazmyn actually felt a sense relief. She would have rather been written up than arrested and embarrassed any day. She strolled over and signed the papers, feigning like she was upset, but in reality, she was excited. Now she only needed to make it out of there in time.

She stared at the clock on the wall. It was 4:14 when she finally made it out the restaurant. She was already late being that she needed to get back by 4:15 and, thanks to Wilcox, she had already missed her bus. Taking off quickly into the rain, her mind was filled with dread and despair because she knew that Ebony was either dead or dying.

As she walked, she checked for a bus coming as the rain pelted her face, but there wasn't a single one in sight. Then, suddenly, she had an idea. Reaching into her backpack, she pinched off one of the delicious burgers and called her cousin, Assassin.

He picked up on the second ring.

"Yo, fuck you calling me for? Ain't you 'posed to be at the house? It's already after 4 o'clock!"

"I almost got fired from work and missed the bus," she said just as she stepped over a puddle of water, but it didn't matter; a car sped by through a puddle, completely dousing her with muddy street water.

"Yo' ass was probably stealing food. I told you to stop that shit. You see what happened to your aunt, my mom. She doin' 10 years for some dumb shit. Yo' fat ass tryin' to be like her?"

Jazmyn stopped walking and mopped at the water on her face with her hand; she was enraged.

"Nigga, didn't I tell you to stop calling me fat! The only reason I called was because I need for you to slide this way and scoop me up right quick."

"Man, sounds like yo' ass is 'bout to be part of a murder. That girl can't breathe and you late as fuck. I'm in Quincy, Indiana with my plug and you out here doin' stupid shit."

"It ain't my fault that—"

"I won't be back until late night, around seven," he cut in. "You better hurry yo' ass up and get to that girl, if ain't already too late."

"You on some bullshit. This wasn't my idea in the first place and if she dead, I ain't taking the full blame so you better come get her."

Jazmyn trudged through the rain shouting into the phone and just happened to look up. Her entire mood shifted when she saw a bus coming her way. It was about a block away, and the next bus stop was a long way down the street. In Chicago, if you were not standing in front of the stop, you could forget it because the bus wasn't stopping.

"Shit, I gotta go."

Jazmyn rushed to hang up the phone and took off running, something she hadn't done in years. It was a sight to behold; her mammoth body rumbling down the pavement splashing through puddles of water and, just when she got to the bus stop, she tripped and fell. The weight from her body propelled her forward down the steep pavement, and she nearly did a cartwheel twice as the bus came to a halting stop.

All the people on board looked on in shock; most laughed, others snickered but none came off to help her. Fortunately for her, she only suffered what felt like several bruised ribs and a lot of cuts and bruises, some on her forehead and nose.

She limped onto the bus, and the driver had a smirk on his face when she showed him her pass. The bus was packed and unusually quiet, except for a few snide whispers as people openly stared at Jazmyn hobbling down the aisle.

An old lady, who was for some reason looking at Jazmyn as if she had just pulled off some miraculous feat, stared at her as she began to talk with a jovial tone.

"Chile, are you okay? You flipped like two or three times and then went airborne twice. Did you used to do gymnastics?" she asked with glee.

"Did you? Yo' old ass need to mind your own damn business!" Jazmyn shouted then gave everyone on the bus repulsive scowls as she labored to the back.

As soon as she got off the bus she tried to trot as best as she could, but her legs wouldn't obey the command to move as she urged them to. The pain was too great as she urgently walked as fast as she could. Instead of going into the house, she cut through the back gate littered with trash and debris and rushed straight for the makeshift grave. The rain had nearly subsided to a trickle at most, even though swarthy clouds bellowed overhead deep in the gray eminence of the sky. The sun was nowhere in sight.

She padded across the mushy, wet grass, and she could see the oxygen contraption and the tank. She bent down and read the time gauge. It read 'empty', but for how long?

"Hey! Hey! You okay in there?" Jazmyn shouted, and was instantly rewarded with sounds of dogs barking in the distance. No response from Ebony who was buried alive.

Frantically, she looked around. She saw the shovel to her right and began digging until she felt it hit the wooden box. With a heavy exhale, she then fell to her knees and removed the rest of the dirt and mud with her bare hands as her body raged with pain; the fall down the steep hill at the bus stop was brutal and she still felt the effects of it.

Finally, she had removed enough dirt and struggled to open the box; it was stuck, as if the rain water had made the wood swell into place. Grunting heavily, she decided to call out to Ebony once more.

"Hey! Hey! Are you okay in there?"

No answer.

Jazmyn worked harder until she could pry her fingers into the opening of the box. She pulled with all her might, and the top made a loud screeching complaint when it finally opened. To Jazmyn's horror, Ebony was lying there with pale skin, purple lips and gaunt, sunken eyes.

She was motionless.

Is she dead?

Just as Jazmyn reached into the box, a large black snake slithered out. Terrified, she screamed and jumped out the way as the snake slithered away, winding across the wet grass, leaving a trail. She shuttered and looked back at Ebony, noticing for the first time red markings that looked like snake bites on her skin. It was a horrific sight. Swallowing hard, Jazmyn reached down and pressed her fingers against Ebony's wrist, checking for a pulse.

"Oh my god," she said solemnly, dropping her head in grief. In the distance, the howl of police sirens sounded off in her ears.

Unsure of what to do as she sat, kneeling in the rain, she broke down and cried pungently.

CHAPTER 8

IN THE CHAOTIC UPHEAVAL OF VIOLENCE, MAYHEM, MURDER, AND gunplay, Polo stood over Kato and fired at his head, causing Kato's body to jerk like he had been hit with a stun gun.

Before he could get off another shot, a stampede of bodies knocked him over. He let out a grunt as he hit his head on a table, which instantly dislodged his gun from his hand. With his teeth clenched, he moved in between the many feet running around him and reached out for his pistol, spinning swiftly back towards Kato once it was back firmly in his grasp.

But Kato was gone.

The only thing left of him was a large puddle of crimson blood on the floor where his body should been. Polo jumped back up on his feet desperately looking around with his burner in hand, wild-eyed and crazy. Then he spotted Star, huddled next to a table that they often used to cut dope. She was bent over, cowering and nearly trembling with fear. She also had a pistol in her hand, as he did, but his was much bigger.

"Bitch, get yo' muthafuckin' ass over here!" he shouted above the upheaval.

Star dropped her pistol back into her purse and stood, shivering all over. She, too, was mystified that Kato was gone, as if he had evaporated like air. She never even saw him leave. Before she knew it, Polo had grabbed her arm tightly as he waved the gun around. She trembled in his grip, wondering if he would shoot her next.

"You're hurting my arm!" Star cried out in pain and instantly regretted placing her gun back in her purse when Polo looked her in the eyes.

"Where did that nigga go? I know you saw!" Polo shot his words out with manic eyes as he whirled her around to face him.

"I—I—I don't know. I swear I didn't see him leave. A--Are you okay, baby?" she asked in an attempt to assuage his rage.

Polo didn't falter and kept his lips pulled back tight across his teeth like a raving lunatic. There was no doubt in her mind that he was going to shoot her.

All of a sudden, Sloan and a few other remaining Disciples walked over to them with ease now that many of the others had already left. Standing next was Tonya, and she too looked disheveled and dirty.

"I don't know where Kato is but it looked like you wet him up pretty bad. I have to mention that ain't neither one of you niggas functioning within G.D. protocol."

A deep frown formed on Polo's face.

"Fuck you mean, you take orders from—"

He was interrupted when both men heard a salvo of shots ring out!

BLACKA! BLACKA! BLACKA! BLACKA!

BOOM! BOOM! BOOM!

KA-BOOM! KA-BOOM!

Out in the middle of the streets, it sounded like the war in Vietnam. Gunshots rang out in the air, accompanied by the sound of human anguish and suffering.

With Star in tow like she was his hostage, Polo dragged her to the door and looked out.

The ground was littered with bodies as unbelievably, some moving and some not. Polo watched as Kato audaciously held Lil' Banks by his shirt collar as he walked backwards, using the man's body as a shield as he was being fired upon by at least four Disciple hittas. The scene was taking place in the middle of the street, like something right out of a mob movie. Star had to do a double take. She couldn't believe her eyes. It was as if he had been dipped in red paint, twice.

"Oh, my god..."

Star was petrified and clasped her hands over her mouth to stifle a scream. This was too much to bear. She had never seen anything like this in her life.

It didn't take but a second for Polo to step over the bodies in front of them and run over with his gun blazing too, firing blindly, but not before Kato fired a shot and hit one of Polo's hittas in the face. The back of his head exploded like a grapefruit, spewing Polo's face and clothes with blood and bone matter.

As soon as Kato reached his car, he spun Lil' Banks as the man flailed his arms, pleading for his life.

"Fuck nigga, you 'bout to learn not to ever try me," he said with his top lip snarled and then lifted his hand to shoot Banks in the neck and chest. Before the body could drop, Kato was halfway in his car with the door open as bullets riddled the vehicle.

Fortunately for him, shots were being fired from only one direction and he was able to pin them down with his expert shooting. The one thing that Polo hired him for, to be his Chief Enforcer, was the thing that hurt Polo the most: Kato was a brilliant shooter, the best, even when he was leaking blood and severely wounded.

As soon as he hopped into the vehicle, he lost his marksmanship shooting advantage. If he didn't work fast, the car would double as a casket. A hail of bullets rained on the vehicle as shooters boldly ran into the middle of the streets taking aim, firing at him as he started the vehicle, ducked down and mashed the gas and took off like a bat out of hell.

Suddenly there was a crunch of bodies; human flesh and metal collided as Kato's windshield splattered with shreds of glass like sharp metal.

"Shit!" he cursed just as he plowed right into three shooters that couldn't get out the way quick enough. The gut-wrenching sounds of agony, bemoaning and carcasses of bodies stewed in the streets.

More shots fired as Kato was able to speed off in the Dodge Challenger SRT Hellcat with the motor roaring like a demon, wheels screaming, burning rubber making gray smoke as it moved at high speed, with a fusillade of shots firing upon it. It wasn't until the vehicle fishtailed, side-swiping two parked cars, that everyone noticed a body trapped underneath the car's tires. Its victim was still alive, screaming for his life as he was being dragged underneath the speeding vehicle.

In Kato's wake there was a trail of body parts for miles, but he couldn't think of what he'd done. He was forced into it; he'd only been trying to escape with his life. Bending a corner, he gritted his teeth in anguish while doing nearly a hundred miles an hour with the car nearly on two wheels.

For the next few miles he topped speeds up to 120 miles an hour and soon after, his vision started to get blurry. Suddenly, he had an incredible throbbing headache so bad that he grabbed his forehead and grimaced in pain. There was a gaping scar on the side of his head, leaking blood badly. He had been shot once in the hip and another in the shoulder.

Lucky for him, the bullet from Polo's kill shot to his head only grazed his skull, not killing him but it was bad enough to show gory pink and white flesh and bone from the wound. Simply said, Kato was in terrible condition as he sped down State Street running lights, zig-zagging in and out of traffic. The entire time he pressed his bloody palm against his head, trying to stop the throbbing, the pain. At the same time, his lower extremities hurt too from the gunshot wounds. For the first time in his life, he wondered if it would have been better to die.

The seat was covered in blood, along with the dashboard and the steering wheel. As he fought with the pain, with his gun on his lap, he closed his eyes, just for a second. He couldn't help it; the inertia from losing too much blood combined with the pain was a cocktail of hurt.

Just as he opened up his eyes, the speedometer read 110 miles an hour. Kato looked up and blinked. He was dizzy, sweating profusely and his vision was still blurry, so he had no idea that he was headed straight for the rear end of a school bus full of four-year-old preschoolers. In just a nick of time, he punched on the brakes and the car jerked and then began sliding.

Kato was losing control.

He fought with the steering wheel and managed to turn on to 39th West Pershing Road. The section of the city was teeming with hustlers, gangbangers, Gangsta Disciples and more. The ironic thing was, this was familiar territory to Kato. He once hustled out this same trap with his Tony, the young hustler who he'd personally mentored.

The Charger drove right into a huge oak tree at a high speed, crashing. Instantly, the motor under the hood burst into flames right before the airbags in the vehicle engaged. The old heads and the foot-dragging hood rats, that had been trying to relieve the old men of their money, took off running as the fire engulfed the car.

None of them knew that Kato was stuck inside the flaming car, unconscious as the fire started to spread. Then about six or seven hustlers, a few junkies and one gang member rushed up. They were not heroes, or people looking to help; they were looking for anything they could steal.

A dope fiend, with an afro like steel wool and ashy black skin like burnt coal, rushed up and peered inside the car as the flames roared. She knew it would be just a matter of time before the gas tank exploded in a ball of inferno hell, engulfing the man inside and possibly harming people in close proximity. As it was, the heat from where she stood was too hot for her to bear as her eyes looked at what she was certain was a dead body covered in blood. He might have a pocket full of money, but still... she wasn't sure she could risk it.

"He look like he dead, y'all. But he do got a gun in his lap," the dope fiend scowled and took several steps back just as other people ran up.

Suddenly, something made a loud popping sound from under the hood causing people to run back from the burning vehicle. Only one man walked back up, hesitantly, and glanced in the car just as police sirens could be heard coming in the distance.

The car was starting to fill with smoke, but his eyes were locked on it. Something about the vehicle felt so familiar to him. Looking closely, he squinted hard when he saw the body inside move slightly but what caught his attention was the six-pointed star with pitchforks on his bloody arm. The man's brow knotted in recognition and then his eyes widened.

"Yo! Folks, this Kato trapped in this bitch!" he clamored and then shouted again with urgency, "Dirty and T-Bone, come over here and give me a hand!"

The guys all rushed over as the dope fiend shouted, "It's about to blow up! Don't do it."

Still, the guys reached in the smoke-filled, burning car. They managed to pull Kato from it and dragged his body out before they took off running. It wasn't three yards they had traveled before the car exploded. The velocity of the impact knocked down one of the guys, T-Bone.

As he stood, he happened to see Kato's gun on the ground and picked it up just as police cars came screaming into the hood with their lights blaring. By then, there were at least a hundred people gawking in awe at the burning wreck that had suddenly exploded causing havoc, when the police stormed the neighborhood in search of the occupant that was missing from the burning automobile. Just that fast, the place was surrounded by cops, angry cops. The block was hot!

Dirty and T-Bone posted Kato's body up against a wall and wiped at the never ending blood that ran from his body as the police searched the street. The throngs of congested people served as a camouflage and confusion would act as a subterfuge.

Ace was the name of the Gangster Disciple that had discovered Kato's identity. He continued to attempt to wake him but he was in bad condition, however, semi-conscious at least. Then Ace had an idea. He dug in Kato's pocket and removed a wad of cash covered in blood. The nappy head dope fiend that had first approached the car was standing from a distance, watching. She peeped the loot when Ace pulled it out and cursed her dismay.

Ace placed the money back into Kato's pocket and reached into the next pocket, just as several cops walked up. They were young, barely in their 20's with blond, buzz haircuts and funky ass attitudes.

"Any of you seen the Black man that got out that car?" the cop asked, shoving his hat back on his head like he was John Wayne.

Everyone standing around scowled at him, no one willing to give Kato up. Ain't no love in the hood between racist cops and impoverished Blacks living to survive.

"Get the fuck outta here!" someone shouted.

Another person cut in, "It was a tall white midget who jumped out the car. And he was with yo' mama."

The crowd erupted in giddy laughter. The cops were standing three feet away from Kato with his head open to the white meat and leaking blood like a river. All they had to do was look to their left and he'd be discovered.

So close but so far.

After briefly harassing Black people and getting harassed, the cops decided to move on and Ace let out a heavy breath of relief. He continued to search through Kato's pockets soiled with blood until finally he found what he was looking for, a phone.

Ace quickly searched through the phone, struggling to hold up Kato as he looked for a name or a number to someone who Kato may have trusted. Everything seemed coded because the phone was a *burner*, intended for illegal purposes. Kato was a Gangsta so that was usual.

He scrolled to the text and saw that the last one had come from someone with just in initial: 'S.'.

Ace dialed the number. The phone was so caked with blood, he wondered if it would even work.

He let out another heavy breath when the call began to connect. A female picked up on the second ring.

"Hello?"

"Do you know Kato? He fucked up bad. I can't take him to the hospital because the police looking for any dude who comes in burned up."

"Yes... I gotta go but somebody coming in a second. Text me the address."

CLICK!

CHAPTER 9

AFTER KATO SPED OFF, LEAVING BEHIND A CARNAGE OF BODIES, blood trails and burnt rubber, silence lulled. It was as if the place was a graveyard as everyone stood around in shock, looking at the destruction scattered in the streets.

Star heard the wails of several people crying; it was Ki-Ki and several other Gangtress. They all had been friends with some of the dead Disciples. Feeling someone watching her, she happened to look up and caught Tonya staring right at her.

The fuck is up with her? Star thought eerily.

Then they heard it all at the same time—the sound of police sirens, ambulances and maybe even the fire department.

Polo was the first to act. With his rigid face spotted with blood, he issued his command, his words carrying like thunder over the top of a mountain.

"Get ghost, move out! Move! I'll send an order by Sloan for the next meeting. Don't show up at *The Spot* until I say so. It's a wrap; this place gon' be hot for weeks."

As Polo yelled orders, he was moving fast back peddling down the street. He still held on to Star's hand, squeezing it tight as he drug her along with him.

Once he was at his whip, he shouted for her to get in and she wasted no time obeying, eager to escape the scene. His pistol was still in his hand, just as an ambulance pulled up, followed by a caravan of cop cars.

As soon as she saw them, she bent down in her seat to hide. Unconsciously, so did Polo. Pulling dark shades over his eyes, he frantically wiped at his face to remove spots of blood. Star couldn't help but notice his sudden changed demeanor.

Niggas played hard, especially niggas like Polo, but he was doing everything in his power not to get cased up by the notorious Chicago Police Gang Task Force. No man alive was hard enough to take a life-long prison term with ease and if the cops pulled them over they would find enough forensic evidence to lock both of them up and throw away the key.

Driving fast, Polo moved through the throngs of congested streets hidden behind tinted windows in his sleek, black BMW. A vein protruded in his neck showing off his anxiety as he tried not to get pulled over by the cops.

It wasn't until they managed to make it to 59th Street that Star heard him take a deep breath as he removed his shades and then glared at her with contempt. His eyes were blood-shot red and the scowl on his face was riddled with apprehension. Though he would never admit it, he was feeling something that was probably the closest thing to fear. With Kato on the loose and the two of them warring, he had a whole, big ass problem to deal with that he wasn't ready for. He'd been trying his hardest to put a bullet through the man's skull but, once again, he'd managed to hold on to his life.

"I saw the police put you in the car and they held you there for a minute. You ain't workin' with them, are you?" Polo turned and looked at her with a dead-serious expression.

"NO! Hell fuckin' NO!" she exclaimed. He stared at her for a moment but could see in her eyes that she was being truthful.

"That was fucked up what you did back there. You and Kato got some shit goin' on that I don't know 'bout? Is there somethin' you need to say?"

"Polo, my sister is missing—might be even dead—and you're sittin' here questionin' me 'bout some bullshit. That was why the cops put me in the car. J-Rock was killed, and they think she had something to do with it," Star said, throwing her head back.

She was mentally exhausted, stressed out and terrified. Frustrated, she closed her eyes.

"What? See, that fuck nigga Kato probably behind that shit. He ain't never liked J-Rock," Polo said and drove faster.

Star noticeably flinched as she said timidly, "It wasn't him. Whoever it was wants $100,000 to get her back."

Polo pulled the car over on 49th and Calumet and reached into his pants, pulling out his pistol.

"Bitch, you fuckin' the nigga or somethin'? The fuck you mean, it wasn't him? That nigga just damn near slaughtered my whole fuckin' team and you tryin' to tell me that he wouldn't pull no shit like this just to get in my pocket? All he talk 'bout these days is my money as it is. Why you always defendin' him?"

Reaching over, he grabbed a hand full of her hair, yanking it back with his gun up like he was about to pistol whip her. All of a sudden he was acting like a maniac.

"Noooo! I'm not doin' anything with him. I just want to find my sister!"

She cried as he twisted his fist in her hair, determined to get a good grip to knock the shit out of her.

"The reason why I say it ain't him is because somebody left a note at my granny's apartment demandin' the money. You know Kato don't work like that."

She winced in pain and then tried to pull away. Polo glared at her but didn't say anything right away. He knew that if what she was saying was true and there was a ransom note, Kato definitely wasn't behind it. He was a gorilla Gangsta so he took shit; writing notes wasn't his forte.

"Lemme see the fuckin' note," Polo growled, releasing his hold on her hair and placing his pistol on his lap.

She passed him the letter and as she watched him read it, her mind plotting on how she could convince him to help after he'd, just moments ago, been fixated on violating her for stealing far less than she needed now.

Then, suddenly, her phone rang. She looked at the caller's name and her eyes bugged out; it was a call from Kato's phone. She started not to accept the call but Polo was still focused on the ransom note. He was reading it over and over studying it, as if he'd be able to find some clue as to who left it. Lowering the volume, she accepted the call. The entire time her heart raced in her chest as she kept her eyes on him. This was past being bold, this was suicide.

"Hello?" she asked with her eyes cut, watching Polo from the corners.

"Do you know Kato? He fucked up bad. I can't take him to the hospital because the police looking for any dude who comes in burned up."

"Yes... I gotta go but somebody coming in a second. Text me the address."

CLICK!

"Who was that?" Polo asked, looking up suspiciously at her.

"My granny," Star lied. "She's just worried 'bout my sister. She's waitin' for a detective to come ask questions so I told her they would be down in a second."

Polo stared at her suspiciously from under one lifted brow.

"And what she textin' you an address for?"

Star paused.

"No, I said I'll text *her* an address. To my new place."

When she saw his forehead knot up into a frown, she almost thought that he was going to call her out on her lie until he began to speak again.

"So you got you a new spot already? You really tryin' to just move the fuck out?"

She rolled her eyes looking at him, adjusting her hair back in place as she responded.

"Did I have a choice? You're not ready for a committed relationship and don't forget that just a few hours ago, you were in the process of gettin' me violated," she said acidly with her phone in one hand. "Plus... you been puttin' yo' hands on me and I can't deal with that shit."

At the mention of the abuse, Polo dropped his head shamefully. It was crazy but, in some twisted way, Star had his heart like no other woman ever had before. He did crazy shit, put his hands on her, abused her physically and mentally but it was all done to ensure that she wouldn't leave. He didn't know how to give love any other way.

"Man, you had a nigga in his feelings. I'd rather do all that shit than to see you walk away," he said earnestly and turned his head looking out the window.

His thoughts were riveting. He wanted Star back with him but he could see that forcing her wouldn't do any good. She was a boss ass chick just like he'd thought she was. The fact that she was able to move out and find her own place in the matter of a few hours, showed him that he had to come at her differently to get her back.

"I gotta make a call right quick," he said, looking down at his phone.

At that exact moment, Star's phone began to vibrate as a text came through. She surreptitiously sent a text to Kevia, giving her the address to where Kato was, along with his phone number and instructions for her to take him to her new apartment. Kevia had gotten her a place in her same building, only a few floors up from hers, and she also had a spare key.

I can't believe I'm doin' this, Star thought, looking out the window.

This was dangerous—No, *crazy*. Why was she even trying to help Kato and risk her own life in the process? If Polo found out, she could also be risking Ebony's life because there was no way he would help find her then. Star started to text Kevia back and tell her to ignore the other text, but her fingers wouldn't oblige. The truth was something she was still in denial of; she was in love with Polo's most hated enemy and, no matter what, she couldn't stand by and not help him.

"I want all Gangstas in every borough from the Southside to the West to be on the lookout for Ebony," Polo said, speaking into his phone. "The Queen Gangstress' lil' sister is missing. I am issuing a reward of twenty grand to whoever finds her and another twenty grand for finding whoever abducted her. I want them dead. Be sure to check the El Rukn's spot on Woodlawn first because I don't trust them niggas. And I don't trust the Four Corner Hustlers, or The Blackstone

Rangers either. If we gotta go to war with either of them again, so be it!"

Once the call was ended, he turned to Star, expecting to see anything but the somber expression on her face.

"What's wrong with you now? I got every Disciple in the area lookin' for your sister."

She shook her head and wiped tears from her cheeks.

"But what if they don't find her? Can't you just loan me the money to get her back? I don't want to risk her losing her life."

Polo let a gush of air out of his mouth and ran his hand over the top of his head, pulling at his long dreads.

"They ain't going to kill her. Trust me, they want the money just as bad as you want your sister back." Reaching out, he squeezed her thigh. "Plus, I'm tryin' to spend some quality time with you."

Her skin burned under where he touched it but she tried to keep her composure. On the inside, she was screaming for God's mercy. Going back to Polo's place and being forced to have sex with him was the last thing that she wanted to do.

"Listen," he started speaking again, trying to appear more sympathetic. "I'm tryin' to help you. You askin' for a lot of money and you in a fucked up situation. I know earlier I was about do some crazy shit to you, but I'll make up for it, if you let me. Just promise that you'll help me too. If that nigga, Kato, contacts you, I need you to help set him up for me. Prove that you love me like you say you do."

She fixed him with a stare full of love and hate; her emotions were all over the place. She was vulnerable. As Polo pulled back onto the road and began to drive, she began to feel hopeless for another way to fix her situation. Polo held all the power and she was only a pawn by circumstance. With her head bowed, she lowered her eyes and walked her fingers over to his side, caressing his hand affectionately as he drove.

"I'll do whatever you need me to," she vowed, swallowing hard to force down the lie.

Polo's brow shot up as he glanced her way.

"So I guess it's safe to say we drivin' to my crib?"

She didn't answer. Instead, she gave him a subtle nod, something that conveyed yes, because her mouth wouldn't utter the word.

At the end of the day Polo was a man, a king that ruled his dominion on the streets with a cast iron fist. Being alone, young and naïve on the cruel streets would make anyone conform or die, love or lie.

Star was confused, she was desperate, and time was a clock with too many hands moving in all the wrong directions. She was willing to sacrifice herself if it came to it. Until she found her sister, she would do whatever it took.

CHAPTER 10

Moments later

As she quickly washed her body, Star's mind whirled with all types of thoughts and plots on anything she could do to avoid this moment but still have a way to get Ebony back. By the time her bath was finished, she was still clueless on what to do.

While she rubbed lotion over her body, staring at her reflection in the bathroom mirror, her female curiosity suddenly got the best of her and she opened Polo's medicine cabinet, wondering what he kept in there.

What in the world? she thought as she looked at all the prescription bottles of medication. *Is this nigga a low-key junkie?*

Reaching inside, she grabbed one of the bottles and read the label before grabbing another.

Lithium... Depakote... Ziprasidone, she read. Another bottle read Trazodone 300.

She quickly searched the names in her phone and her out dropped open when she read what came on the screen. The first three medications were for bipolar disorder and the last was for schizophrenia.

"Get the fuck outta here!" she mouthed. She was in utter shock.

Moving fast, she went to place the bottles back inside the cabinet but one fell over, causing a few others to come crashing down behind it.

"What the fuck you doin'?!"

The door ripped open and when Star turned, Polo was standing right behind her. She nearly passed out as her eyes darted from his angry face to the open medicine cabinet that he was now glaring at. Her legs got wobbly as her heart slammed against her ribs.

"I...I...I was looking for some mouthwash," she stuttered, taking a tentative step back.

"There is some fuckin' mouthwash right there on the sink!" he yelled at her, his forehead knotted with exasperation as he pointed behind her.

"I... I can't use that kind because I'm... allergic."

She was trying to appear convincing and was doing a terrible job.

Polo took a step closer, towering over her, then shoved her out the way with his shoulder as he picked up the bottles and placed them in the cabinet before eyeing her suspiciously.

"You goin' through my pills?" he asked.

She couldn't help but notice that his right eye had started twitching uncontrollably like he was trying to fight his anger. She was certain he was about to hit her.

"No, why would I do that? My mind is just all over the place. I can't stop thinkin' about my sister and I'm frustrated. Please forgive me."

She ambled over and placed her head on his chest affectionately. She felt his heart beating like a drum as she spoke passionately.

The entire time Polo stood unemotional as he stared at her reflection in the mirror; gazing lustfully at her round backside.

"Hurry up and come out of here. I'm done waitin'."

Closing the door, Polo picked back up the phone to finish his call after making sure that he was far enough away so that Star couldn't hear him speaking.

"Hey, B, my bad, man. My chick in here actin' weird as fuck."

The man laughed. "Say less, nigga. I understand."

"Anyways, I need a favor. But you can't tell anybody I asked. Feel me?"

"Whatever I can do for you, man, you know I got it," the voice on the other line returned.

With a smirk, Polo nodded, feeling like he was one step closer to getting a lot of questions answered.

"Listen, how long will it take to send me a list of people that Jimmy has been callin'? Also the list of people that have been visitin' him?"

There was a brief pause.

"Shit, it might take a minute. At least a few days. Why, is anything wrong?"

"Nah, not really," Polo lied with a coarse chuckle. "You know how we do. I'm just in the process of trying to exterminate some rats, if need be."

The person on the other line laughed and then replied jovially.

"Okay, I'll hit you back at this number in a day or two, maybe longer. But I got you man."

Polo nodded and then glanced back across the room to the closed bathroom door.

"Okay bet."

WITH TEARS IN HER EYES, Star stood naked in front of Polo's bed as a placid ambient light from the overhead window cast a radiant glow on her body. In the large wall-to-ceiling mirror, Polo stared admiringly at the gap between her legs, like an eclipse of the sun. He licked his lips hungrily as he observed all of her voluptuous body, her tangent curves, and her round breasts that seemed to arch upwards as if in defiance of gravity, a salute to the heavens above. Between her legs was a manicured nest of hair, shaped like a heart. Polo liked her pussy shaved bald with a small tuft of hair, about the size of a dime.

"I want to taste you. Let me eat some of that sweet pussy," he said in a husky voice, thirsty for her sex.

Star mired, her pupils rotating around the room as she tried to find a way to delay the moment. She'd already wasted time so that she could text Kevia, telling her that she was with Polo and begging her to stay with Kato until she was able to get away. She was all out of ideas on other ways to waste time.

"How 'bout I heat up some oil so I can rub you down?" she suggested.

Polo frowned. "The fuck? Do it look like I'm in the mood for all that cheesy movie shit? I'm tryin' to fuck."

Just then his phone began to ring and Star closed her eyes, sending up a prayer that whoever it was would cut this moment short. Frustrated, Polo reached out and snatched up the phone.

"Fuck, it's Sloan calling. The hell does he want? He gon' have to wait," Polo muttered under his breath and then placed the phone back down.

"You—you should answer it," Star said, licking her dry lips. "It might be somethin' about Ebony. Or Kato," she added, hoping that would be enough to persuade him.

For some reason he was watching her intensely.

"You're right," he said, finally.

The second he dropped his head to look at his phone, Star turned around and grabbed hers. The first thing she saw on her screen was a message from Kevia.

This nigga trippin'! He's wide awake. I went to the liquor store and got him some Hennessy and some Backwoods cigars. Then he asked me to drive him so he can pick up an AK-47 and a submachine gun. Bitch, you need to put his ass the fuck out!

She quickly read and then deleted the message as she'd done all the others. She couldn't risk Polo finding out.

"Aye, I gotta go. Sloan just hit me up 'bout some shit I gotta deal with," Polo said, all of a sudden.

With her back to him, Star closed her eyes and thanked God for this small miracle. She didn't know it but she was about to get another one.

"And I'ma give you the money, too. Actually, I'ma give you two hundred grand that I need you to hold for me."

Whirling around on the balls of her feet, Star squinted her eyes in confusion, knowing that she couldn't have heard him correctly.

"What?"

He stood as he pulled on a pair of shorts.

"It's good you got yo' own spot because I been needin' a spot to stash some cash. You know... just in case some shit go down. *The Spot* is hot and I never know when them boys in blue might come lookin' for me. I gotta watch my back."

Star had no idea what he was talking about. No one knew where Polo lived, even this condo wasn't in his name, so what could possibly go down? However, she didn't ask any questions and chalked it up to his constant paranoia.

Or his schizophrenia, she thought, thinking back to the pills she'd found.

He left out the room and when he came back, he was holding two duffle bags of money in his hands. Star's jaw almost dropped as she eyed the bags. She had no idea that he'd kept that much money stashed in there.

"If it comes to it, you can use one of these to get your sister but I don't think it will. Hold the other for me and I'll let you know if I ever need to use it."

Reaching out, he stroked her cheek gently, in a loving way that was not his norm. Star bowed her head, feeling thankful to him as well as guilty because she knew that she would never be the girl he wanted her to be. She could never love him the way that she used to.

"I gotta get out of here but you can use one of my cars to drive to your place. Make sure Ki-Ki and Brenda tail you."

Star agreed but she had no intentions of using anything that belonged to him. It was risky but as soon as he was gone, she was going to call a car to take her home. The last thing she wanted was for him to be able to trace where she laid her head now that Kato was there as well.

CHAPTER 11

UNKNOWN TO POLO, STAR HAD BEEN PLANNING FOR MONTHS TO GET her own place. As a matter of fact, the first time he laid his hands on her, she and Kevia spoke to the manager of her building about reserving her a spot. Once that was taken care of, all that was left was for her to find the courage to move, which she did after Polo had decided to bring Kato's ex home.

The first day she walked into her new one-bedroom apartment on 54th and Ellis Ave, she knew it would take a lot of love because it was in poor condition, but it was better than not having her own. The only bit of furniture that she'd been able to put in there during the months when she was living with Polo and plotting her departure was a bed, a dilapidated couch and a few kitchen chairs, minus the table. But as soon as Ebony was found, she would use some of the money she had saved to make the place feel more like home.

As she stood in front of her apartment door, she took a deep breath and eased the key in the lock. Though she already expected the worse, nothing in the world could have prepared her for what happened next.

When she pushed the door open, there stood Kato, looking like a disheveled Egyptian mummy with bloody gauze bandages wrapped around his head, chest, arms and stomach. In his hand, he held a large, chrome-plated Desert Eagle .44 aimed right at her head. The barrel of the gun was so big she could have sworn she looked inside and saw a bullet pointed at her eye. In his other hand he held a .9 mm, but due to his shoulder injury the gun was not as high.

"Kato, what the hell?" Star exclaimed, startled, and jumped back flailing her arms. She almost punched him in the face.

"Man, you need to knock next time," Kato said, fatigue riddled. "I almost shot you in the head." He sighed and dropped the guns to his side before leaning against the wall in the entrance of the apartment.

"What I'ma knock for? This *my* place!"

"What is goin' on?" Kevia asked standing at the end of the hall.

"I almost shot your girl for trying to creep in on a nigga," Kato said with a tang of humor as he leaned off the wall and attempted to walk.

"For creeping into my *own* apartment."

"My bad, Star, I didn't even hear you comin' in the door. I was in the bathroom," Kevia said, throwing up both her hands for emphasis.

"I hear everything," Kato spoke, running his hand over his face. "A nigga like me can't get caught slippin'."

Star eyed him before walking fully inside and closing the door behind her.

"From the look of it, you done got caught slippin' way too many times already. I swear, it's like you have a hundred lives. God really looks out for your crazy ass."

He didn't respond and she glanced over at him again. He looked pathetic; sweating like a Hebrew slave and wobbly on his feet like he was about to fall as he stood with both pistols in his hands.

"Let me help you," she offered, placing the duffle bags on her arms in the coat closet near the door.

Stepping to his side to help him walk, she tried to steady him but as soon as she reached for one of his weapons , he pulled it away and turned to her, his eyes flashing with rage like she was the enemy.

"Kato?"

Her voice was like a soft plea sent straight to his heart. Recognition shined in his eyes and in the next moment, his body went limp and he nearly collapsed against her.

"I'm sorry, Star. They tryin' to kill me and I..."

He didn't finish his sentence and she didn't press him to. Instead, she allowed him to lean against her and when she pulled the pistols from his hands, this time, he didn't fight her.

Together, they managed to walk down the small hallway into the living room. To Star's dismay, the living room was littered with Hennessy bottles, cigars and drug paraphernalia. On the side of the couch was a large bottle of 'lean', nearly a half cup of the purple drink.

It suddenly dawned on Star what Kato was using for pain. The codeine in the drug was potent but not just that, she noticed about an ounce of Kush on the floor right by a big ass roach that waddled right by as if it was part owner of her new apartment. Kevia rushed over and disposed of it as Star got Kato to the couch.

The moment his body hit the cushions, he rested his head back, mouth all the way open. As he slept, he was a sight to behold as his haggard, bandaged chest heaved, breathing. His body was a battle-ground of scars, with scars on top of scars and tattoos.

At some point, Star fell asleep watching him and only woke up, the next morning, when she heard movement in the kitchen. Standing up, she greeted Kevia who was busy making a bowl of cereal for breakfast and then slipped in the bathroom to wash up and brush her teeth. When she came back out, she sat down in a chair next to Kevia who was watching in awe as Kato slept peacefully.

"His ass been shot so many times, you think he kinda immune to pain?" Star said, bemused, as she looked at him.

"No, what I think is you are crazy as fuck," Kevia said. They were both sitting in the dining room chairs that Star had pulled into the living room.

"You're my girl and all, but this nigga right here is *a lot*. I had to drive his crazy ass to get lean, weed, drink, and then his crazy ass wanted me to drive him to 85th so he could get a missile launcher—"

"My crazy ass also gave you two hundred dollars for your help too, right?" Kato raised his head, speaking with a slight slur.

Both girls jumped, shocked that he wasn't asleep.

Before Kevia could answer, he dropped his head and, once again, appeared to be out cold.

All of a suddenly Kevia turned serious and she grabbed Star by the arm, tugging her into the bedroom.

"I heard 'bout your sister. Sloan told me when I called him to ask if he could make up some shit to get you away from Polo—"

Star's eyes widened. She had no idea that Kevia was the one who had helped her. Her girl always came through.

"—Anyways, he also said that Polo put a bounty on Kato's head. He wants him dead or alive. You've got too much goin' on right now, you need to make that crazy-ass-maniac-menace-to-society-ass go!"

Star glanced up at the ceiling for a minute before she spoke. Instantly she was a bundle of nerves. As she spoke, she wrung her hands together.

"I know what you're sayin' but I can't just let him get caught up in this shit."

Kevia wasn't trying to hear it. Not only was Star in over her head, but now she was involved and she had a child of her own to think of.

"You do know this is the same nigga that you shot—"

"I think Polo set Jimmy up for murder," Star said, interrupting her before she could finish her sentence.

"Get the fuck outta here!" Kevia droned with her mouth forming an incredulous 'O'. With her hand on her stomach, she turned and walked over to the bed to sit down, making the bed springs squeak.

"Does he know Jimmy's your father?"

Dropping her head, she nodded.

"Yeah, I think so. I think that's why he even looked at me in the beginning. I also found out today that he's on medication for schizophrenia and bipolar disorder but he gave me the money I needed to pay for Ebony's ransom."

With a blank face, Kevia sat in front of her blinking.

"So on one hand, you got the craziest muthafucka in Chicago in your living room sippin' lean, bandaged up like a fuckin' mummy. And on the other hand, you got a certified crazy nigga, who thinks he's in love with you, out here ready to set off World War III when he finds the crazy muthafucka that you're hidin' in your living room?"

Just then there was a hard knock at the door.

Horrified, both Star and Kevia took off running for the door as

Kato grabbed both his burners and struggled to put on his shoes. The pain was still unbearable. Even though the wounds were superficial and the lean numbed most of the discomfort, he was still in poor condition.

Star peered out the peep hole, gasping when she saw an army of men all dressed in true blue, Disciple colors. Then a large finger covered the peep hole.

"Who is it?" she asked through the door, her voice quivering.

She was so frightened that she didn't know what to do and when she looked down the hall, she saw Kato with both pistols leveled. His back was against the wall, leaning on it for support, and his eyes glazed with mania.

"Yo, we lookin' for Kato. Open the door!" a deep voice bellowed.

"That's Polo?" Kevia whispered with her eyes wide, blazing with fear.

Star took off running and quickly returned, this time with a .9 mm of her own in her hand. She had shot and killed Polo's brother before, so there was no doubt in her mind she would shoot and kill Polo if it came to it. She didn't really have a choice.

At this point, she had too much to lose and everything to gain. It was either kill or be killed. This was Gangland.

"Kevia, go into the other room."

"No!"

"I'm not *askin'* you, I'm *tellin'* you. You pregnant and I'm almost certain this ain't goin' to turn out well."

Kevia's shoulders slumped, but she abruptly turned and walked through the living room.

"Kato, you gon' come out or you want us to come in?"

With a 'fuck it' attitude, Star began unlocking the door. In her mind, just like last time, she was just going to start shooting. Behind her, Kato was ready to blast as soon as he saw who was on the other side.

They were like Bonnie and Clyde, both ready for whatever.

CHAPTER 12

JAZMYN HELD EBONY'S LIFELESS BODY TO HER LARGE BOSOM AS SHE cried. There was no pulse. As soon as she pulled the tape from Ebony's mouth, she saw that her lips had turned deep purplish, her body was ashen and cold to the touch.

Jazmyn panicked even more and shook the girl like a rag doll in her massive arms, then attempting CPR—the hood version—she hit her chest several times before placing her lips against her mouth, blowing air like she was blowing into a tire.

Overheard the sky erupted with tempestuous thunder as Jazmyn sat perched on her knees in the mud, crying her heart out. She'd tried her hardest to attempt to revitalize the young girl but to no avail.

Then, suddenly, Ebony's body went into some type of convulsion; she spit up mucus and began to cough and shiver. At first, her eyes rolled to the back of her head like she was having some type of seizure as the rain pelted her pretty face, then they rose up, focusing on Jazmyn. The moment she recognized the person holding her, Ebony screamed to the top of her lungs.

Holding her as tight as she could, Jazmyn clamped her hand over Ebony's mouth and nearly stumbled over her own feet as she took her to the shed. Thankful that her arms were still bound, she then placed

Ebony on a makeshift cot and put a dirty blanket of some type over her shivering body.

Instantly Jazmyn was overcome with the stench of urine and feces. The smell was overwhelming. With no other recourse, Ebony had to relieve herself and the stench was toe-curling.

"Please, let me go. I can't breathe. I can't breathe, I almost died... Please, don't place me back in that hole, please!" Ebony begged and pleaded so loud that Jazmyn was tempted to place the tape back over her mouth and shove her back into the hole in the ground.

"Shut up before you get me caught! I saved your fuckin' life. If it wasn't for me, you would be dead."

"Nooooo, please, lemme go! Please, lemme go!" Ebony wailed.

"Bitch, didn't I tell you to shut the fuck up?!" Jazmyn snapped and bent down closer.

It was at that moment when she saw the gold chain on Ebony's neck with the cute little medallion, the one Star had given her. Jazmyn's eyes bulged with greed. She reached down and unclasped the chain from around the girl's neck, thinking that, if it came to it, maybe she could exchange it for weed.

"I'm so cold. I need a drink of water. Help me, please. My sister will pay you what you want, I promise."

"Shut up!"

"I almost died! Just, plea—"

Before Ebony could get the sentence out, Jazmyn slapped the tape right back over her mouth and stood up and walked over to the shed window. It was covered with spider webs with dead bugs entangled inside.

She pulled out several wet burgers from her pocket until she found what she was looking for: her phone.

As she called Assassin, she took a bite of the burger while she held the line. The meat and soggy bread was like ambrosia to her taste buds.

Finally, Assassin answered with loud music in the background along with the chatter of voices.

"Hey, Jaz, you gonna have to be still. Shit lookin' crazy out here," he shouted with urgency in his voice.

Instantly, Jazmyn's heart dropped. She knew something was wrong.

"Fuck you mean 'be still'? I got this little shitty bitch in here. She almost died in the box."

"Them Disciple niggas got a mad reward for her. I wasn't prepared for this but they got the entire city lookin' for that girl. You need to lay low for a few days."

Jazmyn sucked her teeth, ready to clean her hands of the whole thing. They hadn't promised to give her a big cut of the ransom money anyways and here she was doing all the work. If anything, she should give them up and collect the reward.

"That ain't got shit to do with me. I need some fuckin' money. I ain't got no weed or food. You ain't done shit for me and now you tellin' me to lay low with this bitch for some days."

"I know. We 'bout to send another note today. We gon' have to figure out how to do this shit so we can get the money without it bein' traced or havin' to meet up with them niggas. Shit... I ain't think this shit through."

"That Tonya chick act like she got it all figured out, ask her ass to do somethin'," Jazmyn suggested and then cut her eyes over to Ebony with her nose curled up. "What I'm 'posed to do with this girl until y'all get back? She stinks!"

"Yo' ass stink!" Assassin barked back. "And I don't give a fuck what you do. Bathe her... throw a bucket of water on her. Do whatever the fuck you want, just keep her safe until tomorrow!"

"Okay," she agreed with a roll of her eyes. Then, looking back at the chain she'd taken off Ebony's neck, she began to speak once again.

"Oh wait, since I ain't got no money, I was gonna take the neck—"
Click!

He hung up in her face before she could even ask him about keeping the necklace.

"I'm owed this shit anyways," she said as she roped the necklace around her chubby neck. It almost fit like a choker.

"I'm going to take you in the house and give you a bath. I'm only doing this because I care about you," Jazmyn lied.

Reaching out, she grabbed the tape and tried once more to pull it from her mouth. As soon as she took it off, the girl began to yell like a rape victim.

"Help! Somebody please, help me! They gon' kill me!"

Instantly Jazmyn regretted removing the tape and slapped it right back on her mouth.

"I'm going to take you inside to bathe you and feed you. I hope you like hamburgers. They a little wet but I like them that way. But you gon' have to keep your big ass mouth shut or you gon' be rat food."

Jazmyn sniggered at her own sordid humor and reached down to scoop Ebony's body up. In some way, she was enjoying taking care of her. It brought a small bit of excitement to her otherwise dull and pointless life.

AFTER JAZMYN HAD BATHED Ebony's body in the tub, she placed her on the bed and couldn't help but admire the young girl's body as she dabbed at it with a dirty dish towel. She was tempted to touch her in an inappropriate way, but her only concern was that. Ebony would tell on her, so instead she tried a different tactic. As she looked at her tiny breasts, her mouth watered.

"Have you ever been with another girl before?" she asked in a seductive tone.

Ebony's eyes spread wide. She couldn't talk because her mouth was still taped shut but, somehow, Jazmyn took her behavior as a sign that maybe she would be game.

"So if I untie you and give you some food, you promise to behave?" With a coy look, she added. "And... maybe we can hold each other. I can touch you and make you feel good?"

Thinking fast, Ebony nodded her head and Jazmyn was overcome with joy. She stood up from the bed, excited, and then winced in pain. Her body was still aching from the fall. She began to take off her dirty clothes, and when her panties hit the floor they were so crusty they stood up by themselves.

The bottom of her feet were caked black, like she had been walking barefoot for miles. Ebony's eyes crinkled with disgust and horror as she looked at the huge naked woman, then the potent smell of rotten fish that emanated from her body hit Ebony in her nostrils.

She would have vomited had it not been for the tape covering her mouth.

Next Jazmyn dashed out the room, her body jiggling like a heap of jelly. Just as quick as she had left, she returned with an assortment of items in her hand; a stepped on Black N' Mild cigar, a partial blunt and bottle of Hennessy that had less than a quarter of alcohol left inside. All courtesy of Assassin's Four Corner Hustlers. They had been there drinking and smoking earlier, leaving her with a treasure trove of left-over goodies.

"You smoke?" Jazmyn asked with glee as she lay on her back looking up at the crooked ceiling.

With the Black N' Mild poised in her lips and a butt of a blunt wedged between her fingers, she waited for Ebony to respond. She could barely contain her happiness. She was elated to be with another woman—any human being that shared her passion and need for another.

Again, Ebony wiggled her head as she narrowed her eyes into tiny slants, looking at Jazmyn butt naked like a beached whale lying next to her. Her body odor was the worst.

"Oh shit, I forgot to take the tape off your mouth. My bad." She chuckled and eased the tape away.

With the tape gone, Ebony looked at her with her eyes wide open as if in suspense of it all. A lone tear slid down her face.

"You wanna smoke? Or drink?" Jazmyn asked in a raspy voice as she held the partial blunt in her hand.

"No," Ebony's voice croaked as she look around the room.

There were pictures of an old man with animals and another with a lady about his age.

Jazmyn rolled onto her elbow causing the bedsprings to squeak a complaint like they wanted to snap and break, her three hundred plus pounds nearly too much for the queen size bed.

"If I untie you, will you promise to be nice and don't try to escape? You don't have to. Once the ransom money is paid you are going to be returned."

The entire time Jazmyn talked, her fetid breath smelled like cow shit. It took everything in Ebony's power not to duck her head away when she answered.

"No, I will not try to run... and thank you... so much for everything you have done," she managed to say, her tongue feeling like sandpaper.

Her mouth was dry, she was tired, fatigued and determined not to go back to the hole, the makeshift grave. She would rather be dead or die trying not to go back there.

"Good, that is what I want to hear," Jazmyn said, enthused, and began to untie her.

Her big, bulbous body was pressed on top of Ebony's as she untied her hands and feet. As soon as she was finished, Jazmyn lay back down next to her, winded and breathing hard. Ebony couldn't help but notice the many fresh new scars, blue and angry red marks on Jazmyn's body from the fall at the bus stop.

Jazmyn, still breathing hard, fired up the blunt and inhaled deeply, then blew a plume of smoke up at the crooked ceiling and, instantly, she became talkative. In her mind, she thought about all the many things she'd fantasized about doing with a woman; things she'd only mentioned in her diary.

"Like I said, if you never been with another woman before, it's a lot of things I want to teach you. I got sex toys, big ass twelve-inch dildos, strap-ons, nipple clamps, G-Spot vibrators and butt plugs. You going to love it."

She had a smirk on her face and was bubbling with excitement. Ebony was about to be the sex slave she'd always wanted. She didn't have any choice, she had to do whatever Jazmyn told her to.

"Can I sit up?" she asked meekly. "My back hurts from all that time in that cramped box."

"Yeah, babe. Sit that ass up."

Jazmyn delighted in seeing Ebony's nubile body sitting next to her, and her perky breast, along with the young girl's slim, sensuous figure. She was in pussy heaven, and the girl was being so confident and sweet and polite. One day, Jazmyn had read an article about something called Stockholm Syndrome. She was certain that was what Ebony had. According to the article, Stockholm Syndrome was when the hostage developed a psychological alliance with the captors, sometimes even falling in love. It was a survival strategy but Jazmyn would make it work in her favor in more ways than one.

Puffing on the blunt, she closed her eyes, imagining what she was going to do. Life was finally good. She would have sex with Ebony and rock her world, fuck her with a ten-inch strap-on then eat her pussy until she screamed, thus turning her out. Jazmyn couldn't help but smile through the haze of gray smoke as she began to finger herself in anticipation of what was to come.

Unknowing to her, Ebony was about to make her move as she moved slowly out of the bed...

"Hey, you wanna hit this blun—"

CRASH!!

WHAM!

WHAM!

WHAM!

Before she knew what happened, Jazmyn experienced excruciating pain as a Hennessy bottle exploded upside her head. Then she was struck violently with a three-piece, extra crispy, right to her face. Instantly, she felt a tooth dislodge and move to the other side of her mouth as Ebony, in a fit of rage, rolled on top of her and began to pummel her face, raining blows. Jazmyn tried her best to ward off the blows but the young girl's fists moved fast, whirling at jack-hammer speed. The next punch was delivered directly to her eye, and she saw red, white and blue stars ignite in the back of her brain as she howled in agony.

"Ouch! Shit!" Jazmyn cried out in pain.

She figured she must have left the door unlocked and three people came in, all of them whooping her ass. There was no way this could be an attack coming from one person. All she could do was try to flail her arms in an attempt to fight back, but it was useless. With one good eye and the other filled with blood from the nasty gash she had suffered from the Hennessy bottle, blood was gushing from her head like a spigot.

Then the bed bounced and Ebony took off running. Jazmyn could hear the frantic footfalls as she made a mad dash and ran out the room and to the front door.

Dazed, she was barely able to wobble out the bed. She slipped and stepped on broken glass, hopped on one foot but was still moving. She made it out the bedroom and saw Ebony down the hall desperately trying to get the many deadbolt locks on the front door open, but there were too many as she tried with all her might to fumble with them.

Suddenly Jazmyn was upon her. The door was still locked as Ebony desperately clawed at it with her hands. She turned and screamed for help just as Jazmyn grabbed her.

With one hard kick in the solar plexus, Ebony caused Jazmyn to reel backward, a loud whooshing sound came from her lungs as she nearly fell. Ebony then rushed back on her with her arms swinging, connecting with more solid blows as the other girl cried out in pain. Even though she outweighed Ebony by more than a hundred pounds, she was too fast, too agile. Fear would make a person do miraculous things and Ebony was a testament to that as she fought for dear life.

Then it happened. Jazmyn's bloody foot slipped and she fell, coming down on top of the raggedy living room couch. Ebony was on top of her pounding her face severely at rapid speed, going even harder when she saw Jazmyn's eyes ripple as if she were going to pass out. She couldn't get up, the blows were too much as Ebony sat on her chest and pounded her face with her fists, the brutal sound resonating like a cow being beaten with a wooden two-by-four.

Jazmyn keno that she was about to lose consciousness, and maybe even her life, if she didn't do something fast. With all her meager strength, she arched her back and leaned off the couch. Together, they both toppled onto the wooden floor with Jazmyn falling on top of Ebony, nearly knocking all the wind out of her as she struck her head hard on the floor. She was dazed, badly, and incoherent.

It was the perfect time for Jazmyn to seize the moment. With her meaty elbow, she slammed into Ebony's face, not once, not twice, but five times, knocking her out cold.

Afterwards, she laid on top of the girl as she panted, breathing hard, struggling to catch her breath. They were both covered in blood, it was a sight to behold.

When Jazmyn rose, staggering, leaking blood, limping badly, she could hardly get her bearings. She bent over gasping for air, and then grabbed Ebony by her ankle, dragging her back into the filthy bedroom. It was a long, arduous walk, leaving a trail of blood across the floor like an animal had been slaughtered.

Once in the room, she was able to tie the unconscious girl up again.

The next day the rain had, thankfully, stopped.

Still battered and bruised, Jazmyn rigged the oxygen tank back up and placed Ebony back in the makeshift grave, but that time it was not easy because the girl was fully awake and fought back as much as she could.

Even though her nose had been broken and her face was slightly fractured, she fought like a champion not to go back into that grave. By the time she was finished, Jazmyn had even more marks and scratches on her face and neck, not to mention a purple and black eye that was swollen shut, nearly the size of a baseball.

"You lil' bitch!" she cursed as she stood over the grave.

She then tried to call Assassin but no one picked up the phone. With no other choice, she headed to work, late, not knowing that this was going to be the worst day of her entire life.

CHAPTER 13

As soon as Jazymn hobbled out the old house, she was met with incredulous looks from everyone who saw her. There were patches of her hair missing, and her face looked like it had been stepped on by a giant, twice. Her face was black and blue and even with a pair of her grandfather's old sunglasses that she'd found in the tool box, she couldn't hide the enormous, grisly purple and black eye that was fully closed and, by then, the size of a fist.

As soon as she got on the bus, she heard a chorus of voices making crude comments as she made her way to the back of the bus. She did everything in her power to play it off, to act like she didn't have an uncanny resemblance to some character from *The Walking Dead*.

She sat down next to a scrubby looking fat thug, with a toothpick in his mouth, Chicago Bulls hat turned sideways, and there was some type of tattoo on the side of his face that looked like a submachine gun. She sat on the edge of her seat and just looked straight ahead. She could feel eyes staring at her and saw in her peripheral as the guy took the toothpick out his mouth to shout at her.

"Damn! Whaaaat daaaa fuck? What did you do, use your face to block punches from a baseball bat?"

Several people began to laugh heartily, others chuckled. Thank

God, she was only two bus stops away from her job. She ignored the clown but then he cracked on her again.

"Must have been a whole tribe of hood niggas stomp that ass out."

That time, he laughed along with everyone else.

Jazmyn turned to him and balled her fist up tight.

"Mind your own fuckin' business, nigga."

"Or what?" He shifted in his seat, facing her.

The bus was approaching her stop next. She kept her mouth shut, only glaring at him before she got up.

"Just what I thought. Get your hump back, Big Foot lookin' ass off the bus."

She took several steps, the bus stopped, the door opened, and she was emboldened as she turned and looked at him.

"Fuck you, asshole!" she shouted, waving her middle finger.

He got up like he was going to chase after her but she took off running, hobbling badly. The occupants on the bus roared with laughter as it drove away.

As USUAL, the restaurant was jam packed busy. When Jazmyn walked in, the delicious aroma of frying burgers whiffed into her nostrils. She already had a plan: she was going to steal a record number of hamburgers that day. As she looked up at the clock, she needed to be off work at 3 o'clock. That would give her enough time to get home at 3:30 and get the girl out the ground before she ran out of oxygen.

There was a group of girls at the counter ordering food when she walked up and stood at the door to the kitchen, waiting on one of her co-workers to let her inside. She noticed the hood rat chicks staring at her, but she was used to that. All one of them hoes had to do was jump at her and she would beat their ass like a man.

One of the girls was named Myia. She was a Gangstress, assigned right under Brenda. She looked over at Jazmyn, wincing at the sight of her battered and bruised face, as everyone around did, but what caught her attention was the gold chain and medallion around her neck. She nudged her girls, and they all stared.

"That looks like the chain Star had," she whispered to them. "I remember it."

Her friend, Andra, responded with a wad of blue bubble gum in her mouth.

"Girl, maybe she sold it or some shit." She blew a bubble and let it burst.

"No," Myia shook her head. "She told me she gave it to her sister, Ebony."

"You talkin' 'bout her sister that's missing?" one of the girls asked just as Jazmyn walked through the door into the restaurant kitchen area.

"Yeah," another chimed in. "I remember seein' it on one of Ebony's Instagram photos. The one Polo sent to all of us."

"Let's bum rush that hoe then. She already look like she been attacked by a hundred niggas with sticks," Andra said, eager for some shit to get started.

"Wait. This could be serious and we don't want to lose her by startin' some bullshit that will get the cops involved. I'ma call Brenda first and let her know. Then we can move from there," Myia said.

"I think we should just beat that fat bitch ass and see what the fuck the business is or whateva," Andra said, her mouth poked out as she sulked.

Andra shook her head and then turned to call Brenda and inform her of what they found, following the chain of command.

CHAPTER 14

"THAT'S SO SAD 'BOUT STAR'S SISTER MISSIN'."

Brenda raised a brow. "Really, bitch? Who you think you foolin'? You don't even like Star."

"No, but that ain't got shit to do with her sister. She's just a kid," Tonya replied with a shrug before getting to the real reason for her comment. "You heard anything from Star 'bout what she gon' do? I heard somethin' 'bout her findin' a ransom note."

"How you know that?"

"The streets be talkin'. I may not be queen but people still be tellin' me shit."

Brenda gave her a look. "I don't know who because I didn't even know 'bout no ransom letter. The only thing Star told me was 'bout the reward he was offering to anybody who knew anything about who had Ebony."

Shit! Tonya thought once she realized that she'd just put her foot in her mouth.

It never occurred to her that Star wouldn't have told anyone about the ransom letter, especially not Brenda who was her second in command. Clearing her throat, she struggled to fix her mistake.

"That's what I meant—the reward. I got the words mixed up."

Dropping her phone to the side, she pulled at her crop top, making her heavy chest bounce around in front of Brenda's eyes. She didn't even have on a bra, which was obvious, being that her hardened nipples showed through the thin material of the top like beaded chocolate chip morsels.

"That ain't the only thing you got mixed up. Why don't you go put some fuckin' clothes on? You damn near naked and you know my nigga home."

Sucking her teeth, Tonya made a huge show of dramatically rolling her eyes.

"Girl, please! It's only Kush. Ain't nobody worried 'bout that nigga but you."

"Whatever," Brenda replied, letting the issue go.

Her pride stopped her from admitting that she wasn't worried about whether Tonya was checking for Kush but whether Kush was checking for Tonya. He was a known cheater and when she thought about all of the girls she'd caught him with, it was clear that chicks who looked like Tonya were more his type.

With her phone in her hand, Brenda thumbed through Instagram, pretending to catch up on the latest gossip and happenings in their hood when really her thoughts were elsewhere. With Polo keeping tight reigns on Star, Brenda was home with some downtime today—a rarity since she'd been appointed as Star's Second in Command. But what was also rare was the fact that Kush was home as well. In fact, the second he saw her walk in the door behind Tonya, he seemed shocked, almost disappointed that she was there, and it immediately made Brenda think back to the warning Ki-Ki had given her.

From what I been hearin', the bitch you need to fight might be right in front of your face.

The exact moment the thought hit her mind, she lifted her eyes in time to see Kush emerge from the hall and step into the living room. His eyes went to Tonya, who was sitting across from Brenda, and when she lifted her head, he caught her glance. In that brief moment that they connected, Brenda saw a collection of unspoken words pass between them before Tonya cut her eyes to Brenda, dropping her eyes when she saw her watching.

"What da fuck y'all got goin' on?" Brenda snapped, looking back and forth between the two of them.

A boyish grin covered Kush's face, but she was not amused. With her lips pressed tightly shut, she watched as he walked over to her side and slid onto the couch next to her, wrapping one arm around her shoulder. She had half a mind to pull away but simply crossed her arms in front of her chest and frowned.

"What's that stank ass look for?" Kush said, pulling her closer into his body. Brenda resisted.

"Alright, keep it up. I got somethin' to knock that attitude out of you. Real shit."

Playfully reaching between her thighs, Kush acted like he was trying to grab at her womanhood until Brenda giggled and squirmed out of his way. He knew how to push the right buttons to get her attitude straight, and it had seemingly worked. That was, until she glanced across the room and saw Tonya rolling her eyes.

"I gotta pee," she announced, standing suddenly.

With her fingers grabbing at the edge of her tight, little shorts, she pulled them down over an exposed chunk of booty meat, doing a little wiggle that made her thighs gyrate in a way that almost made Kush's eyes bug out of his skull. Brenda didn't catch Kush's lustful stare, but she did catch the way that Tonya had quickly made herself and her luscious curves the center of attention. She glared at her with disgust as she walked away with an extra twist in her hips.

"I can't wait until that bitch gets out of here and finds her own shit. It's too crowded in here with the three of us."

Kush smirked and looked at Brenda sideways. "I thought that was yo' homegirl. How you gon' say some shit like that?"

"Easy. Just like the fuck I said it." She huffed out her response, aggravated to the max. "I'm tired of her sleepin' on my damn couch, using up all my body wash and shit, eatin' up all my damn food and she don't give me not a single dollar to help with replacin' the shit, but always seem to be able to keep her nails and hair done. Whatever nigga she fuckin' with to give her money for that shit needs to give her money to go towards my muthafuckin' rent!"

At that exact moment, Brenda's phone began to ring and she grabbed it, answering on the first ring as soon as she saw that it was a Gangstress. They didn't call her just to gossip and talk shit, so whatever was about to be said was something important.

"Hey, Myia, what's good?"

Beside her, Kush said something about going into the room to grab something and she nodded, waving him away without really paying attention.

"Yo, B, I'm at White Castle and it's some chick who work here. She's wearin' a necklace that looks like the one Star's sister is wearing in her Instagram pics."

"Ebony? She's wearin' Ebony's necklace? You sure? Did you check?" Brenda fired off a mouthful of questions, wanting to make sure that Myia was positive about what she was saying before she passed the info on.

"Yeah, I pulled up one of the pictures and checked for myself. You want me and the girls to grab that hoe up and bring her down to *The Spot?*"

Brenda shook her head, thinking. "Nah, we can't take her there. Polo said the block is too hot 'round there right now. Just watch her for right now. I don't wanna do—"

She stopped talking and sat alert and at attention, thinking that she picked up on the sound of talking and movement coming from down the hall. When nothing else was heard, she continued her conversation.

"I don't wanna do nothin' that will have the police out there and fuck shit up for us before we can get to the bottom of this. Just keep eyes on her but try not to let her catch y'all watchin'." There was another sound and, this time, Brenda stood to her feet to go investigate. "I'll meet you up there in a few. Call you when I get there."

Pressing the button to end the call, she bent her brows and was about to turn towards the hallway when Tonya suddenly scurried from out of the hallway in a rush. The sight of her made Brenda pause, watching her hard as she stormed by and returned to her seat. She kept her head bowed the entire time, like Brenda hadn't even been standing there.

The wet, cherry red gloss that Tonya wore on her lips was smudged slightly around the corner of her mouth and Brenda immediately took notice of it. An idea came to her mind and she took off, continuing down the hall, stomping through with purpose until she came to her closed room door. She wasted no time before barging in on Kush who was fumbling with the drawstring on his sweatpants.

"Man, what da fuck wrong with you?" he asked when Brenda rushed up to him and clutched his chin tightly between her fingers as she inspected his face. If she saw any hint of Tonya's cherry red lipgloss on his face or neck, it was about to be on.

Unbeknownst to her, she was checking his face when she really should have been checking his dick which Tonya had just been rolling around between her jaws.

Once Brenda was satisfied that she didn't see a trace of lipgloss on Kush's neck or face, she released him, sighing deeply.

"I'm good," she said, still frowning slightly at him. "I'm 'bout to bounce though. Got some shit to tend to regarding Star's sister."

Her words were like sweet music in Kush's ears. It had been a couple of days since he really had a chance to sample Tonya's sweet pussy. The short slurp job she'd given him while Brenda was handling her call was a tease that only left him wanting more.

"I'm prolly gon' head out, too," he told her, lying his ass off. "I got a lot on the agenda."

Brenda nodded slowly. She was hesitant to believe what he was saying when, only a few minutes ago, he was walking around the apartment like he didn't have a thing in the world to do. Without responding, she turned on her heels, feeling like she was being played for a fool in some way that she had yet to discover. She wasn't sure whether it was for a good reason or if Ki-Ki's warnings were driving her crazy.

"You goin' somewhere?" Tonya asked, looking at her under one brow when she walked into the living room holding her sneakers in one hand.

Brenda nodded her head. "I am, and so are you."

With a frown, Tonya pointed her index finger into her chest. "Me?"

"That's what I said. Go get dressed. Myia told me that she saw some bitch down at White Castle wearin' a chain that looks like the one Star gave her sister. We 'bout to run up on that hoe and get some answers."

If Brenda had been looking up, she would have caught the way that Tonya's entire body froze, along with the stricken expression on her face. Thankfully, she was busy tying her shoes and it gave Tonya just enough time to get herself together.

"Oh hell nah, I don't wanna be part of that shit."

She shook her head and turned around to recline on the sofa, holding her phone steady in her trembling hands. Mentally, she prayed that the girl they'd found was not Jazmyn because she had already made it clear that she was taking the fall for nobody and would snitch on both Tonya and Assassin the second she thought that she was in trouble. Could she really be wearing Ebony's necklace? For someone so scary, you would think she'd know better. Then again, it was obvious that Jazmyn wasn't the sharpest tool in the box.

But that bitch can't be that *damn stupid*, Tonya thought.

Thinking back to her previous encounters with Jazmyn, she was doubtful. The girl hid burgers in her panties so that she could eat them later. She was nobody's genius; Assassin was dumb as hell for bringing her in on their plan and Tonya was dumb as hell for letting him do it.

"You ain't got a choice," Brenda argued. "All the Gangstress gotta stand behind Star on this so you need to put that lil' personal shit you got with her to the side and do what you gotta do. You took an oath so now it's time to uphold that shit and prove you ain't got shit to do with this."

Tonya nearly leaped to her feet from out of a full recline.

"What you mean? People think I got somethin' to do with her sister bein' kidnapped? Why would anybody say that?"

Something about the way that Tonya responded and the utter fear on her face made Brenda look at her sideways.

"I'm just sayin' that it ain't no secret that you don't like Star. If you sit this one out, it ain't gon' look good."

"Well, it just ain't gon' look good because I ain't goin'."

Brenda balled her face up into a tight scowl.

"Yes, you are. You already don't pay for shit as it is. You not 'bout to sit on my muthafuckin' couch, suckin' up all my air while I'm out workin' and shit. Get yo' ass up, get dressed and let's go."

"She ain't gotta go if she don't wanna, B," Kush inserted, walking into the room. "I'm 'bout to leave and if both of y'all leave, the house gon' be empty. I heard they been robbin' niggas' spots up here and if Tonya stay, she can keep an eye on my stash."

Tonya smiled, grateful for Kush's help, even though she knew that he was only looking out for his own interests.

"Nigga, what stash?" Brenda snapped. "You got a couple dime bags of weed and a little ole stack of money hidden in there. Niggas ain't 'bout to run up in my shit over you."

With his pride wounded, Kush scowled to himself and muttered something inaudible under his breath before walking away to leave Tonya and Brenda alone.

"Now hurry the fuck up and get some clothes on. We ain't got a lot of time."

There was nothing that Tonya could do but follow orders, being that not only did Brenda outrank her in the Gangstress organization, but she also outranked her in the apartment, being that Brenda was the one providing her with the roof that was over her head. She did as she was asked, changing into something that could cover as much of her as possible without making her melt away in the Chicago heat. It was her hope that she wouldn't be spotted by Jazmyn among the other Gangstress and could just blend in until she had a chance to figure out what to do.

"Let's go," Brenda said, and Tonya reluctantly began dragging her feet behind her. Suddenly, she remembered something she desperately needed.

"Wait, I gotta get my purse!"

"Hurry up!"

Reaching on the side of the couch, Tonya snatched up her purse after checking to make sure that her pistol was stashed in it, the same one she'd killed J-Rock with. She didn't want to carry around the dirty weapon and risk having an unsolved murder pinned on her but, right now, she had no choice. If this situation with Jazmyn called for her to use her gun in order to save herself, she would have to shoot first and answer all questions later.

CHAPTER 15

WITH HER HEART RICOCHETING IN HER CHEST, SHE STRUGGLED TO breath, legs like rubber. Star unlocked the door with a pistol concealed behind her back, determined to take on her most formidable foe. She took one last glance back at Kato and he gave her a tacit nod, an affirmative that blood shed was about to start.

Star opened the door just as Kato aimed both pistols. The mantra of the hood was to always shoot first and aim carefully. Not an easy task when you're under the influence of lean and weed while also leaking with enough bullet holes to make you look like Swiss cheese.

The door opened and there stood a gang of Gangster Disciples, a hallway full, along with the faint odor of alcohol, cologne and cigar smoke.

In the middle of the fray, Yesman spoke first, his voice like rolling thunder.

"What's good, Star? What you gon' do? Shoot me?" he said, peering at the hand that she was hiding behind her back. It was as if he could see through her. She sucked in a deep breath and took a timid step back. She didn't have a clue what was going on.

"And damn, nigga," Yesman continued. "So this is what it is, Kato? I came a long fuckin' way for you to be holdin' two bangers lookin' like hell done frozen over. What kinda respect is that?" He spoke with a smile but his eyes were obsidian and cold as steel.

"O.G. I'm sorry. Shit been crazy. I'm shot the fuck up. Feel like I'm losing my mind." Kato threw up both his hands and Yesman nodded his head with sympathy as his troops stood around looking stern, like war-tested soldiers.

"I apologize. Come in, I forgot I sent word for you to meet me here," Kato said apologetically and hobbled forward.

It was obvious that he was in extreme pain by the way he grimaced, biting down on his lip. Frowning, as he came forward, Star looked at his bandages. They were sanguine red, in desperate need of changing.

Then her eyes went back to the man—Yesman. Where had she heard that name before? It was like a riddle that was on the tip of her tongue but she couldn't solve it.

Yesman was a tall, austere older man in his late 40's with a slight potbelly. He stood about six-foot-four and still possessed the muscular build of an ex-football player. His brawny shoulders and arms were huge and he had a barrel chest that stood out just as pronounced as his potbelly. His skin was swarthy, and he had intelligent eyes that shimmered with mischief and enigma.

Beside him was his Chief Enforcer JaJa. He had long, skinny dreads with a bad case of acne and deep-seated hawk eyes that penetrated the soul. He was tall and willowy with long arms and legs. He wore a green army coat in the blistering heat even. JaJa was known for carrying a Mac-10 and an Uzi as well as grenades on him at all time.

Many years ago when JaJa was a teenager, the Federal Marshalls had a warrant out for his arrest for guns; however, he was so violent with a string of murders they couldn't pin on him, they were fearful of apprehending him on the street. He was too dangerous. They actually planned an air strike to take him out in the event he resisted and had an armored vehicle on standby.

On the other side of Yesman was his trusted Chief Advisor, Keith. He was bespectacled, with skinny rim glasses, and had short cropped hair. Light skin with freckles, his features were handsome; he was like catnip to the ladies but his pretty boy features were like a mask covering the deadly gangster hidden within. Keith was the mastermind to a slew of murders and the engine force that got the Disciples into politics and city council position. He was the brainchild and one of Jimmy's secret weapons.

"Y'all wait for me right here," Yesman said with authority. He was dressed in a blue Nike sweat suit and a huge, six-point, gold-encrusted pendant on his Cuban link chain shimmered.

The other men all waited outside the door like security, except JaJa and Keith. They escorted him everywhere.

Without waiting to be asked inside, Yesman walked in and smiled. What could have passed for a devilish grin flashed across his face when he began to comment.

"Damn, you look just like your daddy, Star. His spitting image. And, from what I hear, you're a fighter like him, too."

Star took a step back and watched him with awe as he passed gracefully with his men and it suddenly dawn on her who he was: Yesman Butler, the man her dad had told her to get Kato to contact when she was at the prison.

She followed him with her eyes as he passed. He had an aura of mystique about him that she had never seen before in her life. The light skin guy standing to his side wearing glasses reminded her of an older version of Drake. He seemed so out of sync with the rest of the crew, she couldn't help but think.

Yesman entered in cautiously but as if he owned he place. His men, without even asking, searched the apartment as Kevia stood tongue-tied. She knew power when she saw it and her life on the rough streets of Chicago had taught her that you live a lot longer when you see with your eyes, ears and mouth shut while around real gangstas.

"Clear!" JaJa said as he came back in from the bedroom.

He was holding an Uzi machine gun with a full banana clip; it could shoot a hundred rounds in six seconds.

"Clear," Keith said also as he walked out the bathroom. He had a huge chrome-plated Glock in his hand.

Yesman turned and watched Kato as he pathetically limped over and took a seat on the couch.

For some reason, Kato wouldn't look the older man in the eye which Star found peculiar. What she didn't know is that though Kato had called Yesman over, he knew that nothing good would come of him being there. He'd called him because Jimmy requested it but now that Kato had the blood of more than a few Disciple soldiers on his hands, he knew punishment for his crimes would soon follow.

Yesman looked for something and JaJa must have read his thoughts; he walked over and got the older man a chair which Yesman then straddled backwards.

The entire time, Kevia looked on like she was watching a film. Until Yesman looked up at her.

"Is she 'Folks,' part of the family?"

"No," Kato said and massaged his temple as Star spoke up.

"Yes, she is. She and I were brought in together and she's my best friend."

"But I have no problem leaving!" Kevia announced before turning to walk to the bedroom. She glanced at Star in silent communication that she wanted no problem with this gangsta and his hoodlums.

As soon as the bedroom door was shut, Yesman turned to Kato and frowned.

"Do you know why I am here?"

"Yes."

"Why?"

"Because Jimmy had me contact you about things that were not going well with the organization."

"Correct."

"I swear, I did nothing wrong," Kato declared before starting to ramble off the Disciple oath. "I'll die and dedicate my love to all nation causes like the blood oath I made—"

"Shut up!"

Silence.

Yesman began again, but this time slow and methodically like he was trying to control his anger.

"The last time I was here and there was shit like this goin' on, Disciples killing each other, do you remember what happened?"

For the first time Kato looked up squarely at the older man.

"Yes," he said and had a flashback.

. . .

THE BLACK STONE RANGERS, *a branch of the Disciples, in a fight for power and money ambushed two Disciple bosses along with their girlfriends at a movie theater on 47th Street and King Dr. They were gunned down with Mossberg shotguns, shot multiple times in the head and face. It was a grizzly killing but they knew that by killing the top two heads of the organization, it would cause chaos on the inside which is what the needed to launch a takeover.*

There was internal strife in the organization and that was when the Black Stone Rangers took advantage of the moment and waged war on the entire Southside using brute force, mayhem and murder. They seized hundreds of millions of dollars in drug sales and other illegal activities before they were through. That was until Yesman, only second in command to Jimmy, was ordered to take back control of the city and restore the Disciples back under the stronghold they once had.

The year was 2016. Yesman, dressed as an undercover narcotics cop along with eight other Disciples, rolled up on eighteen Black Stone Rangers in a section of town that had been infamously named 'The Hole'. Normally the Black Stone Rangers would have been armed to the teeth and always on high alert but when the cops came in, they thought it was more police harassment bullshit and followed all orders, eager for it to be over.

With their backs against the wall, Yesman and his crew unmercifully massacred all eighteen gang members in one of the most hideous bloodshed crimes Chicago had ever known. The news media named the massacre, "The 2016 Most Brutal Gangland Killing."

Yesman took things a step further. Thirteen Disciple members accused of assisting the Black Stone Rangers were also executed. Two of them had their heads and hands chopped off and strung from a street light pole on 59th and Normal Avenue, the same territory they sold drugs on without paying fees to Jimmy.

This was done to set an example in the organization: there would be no tolerance for crimes against the gang by its own members. Yesman was both judge, jury and a hand with an iron fist in the execution.

"YOUR FIRST KILL, who called for it and what did you do?" Yesman asked Kato nonchalantly.

Kato looked up at Yesman like his mind instantly took a trek down memory lane, then he looked at Star. She could tell he wished she wasn't in the room, that she didn't have to hear the gory things that he had done to people.

"I cut off a dude's dick after I had sliced off his fingers. Put them in a box and left it outside the door of the people he had conspired with. You called in for me to perform the hit."

"And why did I have you to do that?"

"Because he was disloyal," Kato said with a strained face.

"Correct, now look at you and the things you and Polo have done—"

"But I didn't do—"

"Stop!" Yesman raised his voice and that was all it took. Both of his henchmen advanced upon Kato with pistols drawn. Star shuddered, horrified.

"This is like the same situation we had before. If you create bedlam and strife, the structure of the organization crumbles and our adversaries are able to advance, taking possession. The Four Corner Hustlers are eagerly watchin' as you both kill each other so they can make an attempt to occupy our illustrious throne on the streets. Am I not correct?"

Kato held his head high and maintained the stern expression on his face as he spoke through his teeth.

"That was not my intent. I feel like Polo is stealin' money and doin' fuck shit. He tried to kill me first. I had to defend myself."

Yesman's eyes narrowed as he continued speaking.

"You killed a lot of men. Some of them were experienced, valuable hittas that are going to be hard to replace. If Polo has done wrong, you should have come to me."

Kato scoffed and tried to throw up his hands. He flinched due to one of his injuries to a shoulder where the bullet went in and out.

"You did too much. There has to be retribution. Normally I would have the both of you pay with your life and next of kin but because of your track record, I won't allow it. A man cannot rule with good conscience if he is not a servant first to his people."

"But that don't apply to me!" Kato's nostrils flared.

"Yes, it does. You are both leaders who have failed to lead. And as for Polo, there will be severe punishment. Heads will roll," Yesman said and reeled back in the chair. He looked at Kato as if considering his thoughts carefully.

Just then Star's phone chimed. She looked at the number; it was from Brenda, her Chief Enforcer. She excused herself and walked over to the corner of the room by the window and accepted the call as both henchmen watched her intensely.

"Hello?" Star whispered and removed a lock of hair from her forehead and stole a glance back at Kato. He looked helpless as he bowed under the power of one of the men responsible for making him the man he was today. She let out a sigh, wishing she could help even though there was no way she could.

"I'ma make this quick. There is some bitch at White Castle, not the one we do the drops at but the one on 66th and Halsted, who got a gold chain with a medallion just like the one your sister Ebony had. It may belong to her. She may have stolen it from her" Brenda was talking a mile a minute, not even coming up for air.

Star narrowed her eyes. "What you mean she has my sister's gold chain, and why y'all didn't bum rush that bitch?"

"She works there and they didn't want to chance ruining shit by causin' attention with the cops if shit go wrong. Or it may not be your sister's chain for that matter, feel me?"

Nodding, Star exhaled a heavy breath.

"Right. That's true."

"I got Tonya and some more Gangstress with me. We gon' be about forty deep in whips. We gon' slide through and pick you up before we head up there."

"Alright, but don't give nobody my address. I'll text it to you. I'm 'bout to get dressed now."

After Star hung the phone up, she turned around to hear Yesman asked, "Any luck with your sister?"

She wanted to but didn't even bother asking him how he knew. It seemed like Yesman was the type to know everything about anything.

"Yes, I have to get ready because they may have found somethin'."

The older man nodded his head. "If there is anything I can do to help, let it be known."

"Thank you," Star whispered, feeling a ball of suppressed emotion lodged in her throat.

With that said, Yesman then turned back to Kato.

"Both you and Polo will be sanctioned and punished, you both will be stripped of your rank, you will also receive corporal punishment—"

"Stripped of my rank?" Kato shouted.

"Trust me when I say you are getting off easy."

Kato didn't respond, he just sat with a grim frown on his face.

Yesman stood. "That is all. I will visit Polo next. I am sure this is not going to go well for him and his crew. Also, nothing that has been said leaves this room or there will be severe consequences." He turned and looked directly at Star. Instinctively, she knew he was putting emphasis on her too.

She responded, "Yes, sir."

"Kato, you look like shit. Stop with the drinkin' and drugs, eat organic and get your rest."

And with that small bit of advice given, Yesman and his team left as quickly as they'd come and without a trace.

"I'm off count," Kato muttered once they were gone, frowning with contempt.

That was the same as being kicked out the organization. Like Superman being reduced to a peon. To him, gang was family and now that he was off count, it was like everyone he loved had turned their backs on him.

CHAPTER 16

After Yesman and his men had departed, Kevia left directly behind them. She had a doctor's appointment, at least that was what she said. Star suspected that Kevia had experienced enough excitement, drama and near-death experiences for the day.

"Are you going to be okay?" Star asked Kato as she rushed around the bedroom changing clothes.

She was about to put on some blue leggings and sports bra with a simple blue t-shirt and Jordans. These were her 'true blue Gangstress, down to beat a bitch ass' clothes. Brenda and the crew were on their way to pick her up and there was no wonder what would follow next.

"I'm good, ma," Kato said in response.

He was standing in the doorway, and just happened to catch Star bent all the way over putting on the tight leggings. He had a perfect view of her ass and thong lace panties. When she turned, struggling to pull up the tights, her ass jiggled even more. She was so thick you could see it from the front.

Damn, he thought and then shook his head as if trying to rid himself of the thought. She was rushing to check on her sister who, hopefully, wasn't dead and he was standing there thinking about sex. What kind of ain't-shit-ass-nigga did that make him?

"I hope you find yo' sister and she's good," he said, suddenly. "I wish I could do somethin' to help but, right now, I ain't really worth shit."

Star shook her head. "I wouldn't ask you to come even if you could. I can handle this. I got the Gangstress with me and you got enough to deal with."

Without speaking, he watched her closely as she darted around the room, making sure that she had everything she needed.

Then suddenly, he began to speak again, making Star stop in her tracks. The cadence of his voice had changed. When he spoke this time, it was like she saw his passion, his raw interior; she saw something new in him.

"I don't know what I've done to deserve this. You riskin' a lot to have me here and... I don't know. I guess I'm just feelin' some type of way 'bout it."

A small smile tugged at the corners of Star's lips as she stared up at him.

"You're feeling 'thankful'." Her brows shot high when she saw the awkward look on his face. "Have you never told someone 'thank you' before?"

When he bit down on the corner of his mouth and gave her a lip-sided smirk, she had her answer. Rolling her eyes, she couldn't suppress a small bit of laughter as she shook her head at him. Even in the craziest, more terrible situations, somehow, Kato was always able to make her smile.

She liked him—a lot—in that weird way she couldn't explain. At this point, it had to be love. Or was it? It seemed far beyond that even. Something about him felt like she had bonded with his soul. They were connected. She wanted to deny the fact that she could possibly be falling in love with a ruthless thug but she couldn't shove the thought from her mind.

"I have to go," she said and moved to put on her t-shirt.

As she passed by him, he grabbed her waist.

"Stop, please," she spoke softly with her hand on his chest right next to the bloody gauze. "I can't..."

"You made me look at life from a different way, with a different prospective."

Silence lured as he held her in his arms, with her heart pounding fast. He frowned slightly, piecing together his words carefully and with great effort.

"I don't wanna die... I don't wanna leave here yet. I kinda wanna meet this love thing you told me about. Know what that shit's all about, feel me?"

He caressed her shoulder and like a moth drawn to a burning flame, sure to kill her if she fell victim to its charm, she let her head rest on his battered chest and inhaled his manly scent.

There was no need to rush. Brenda was not there yet and most likely she'd spend the rest of her day worrying and praying. At least for now, he gave her peace.

With his nose nestled in her hair, Kato soaked in the fragrance of her, wanting say so much but, oddly, unable to put together exactly what he wanted her to hear. His mind felt like it was caught up in a fog; he felt so much but had no way to convey it. These were new emotions, none of which he'd ever experienced before but he knew he never wanted to let Star go.

Then Star's phone chimed bringing them both back to reality, away from the utopia they wanted to escape into; the fantasy land that they brought to each other.

Fighting her emotions, Star tried her best to pull herself together to speak to Brenda.

"Yeah?"

"We downstairs. This a big ass building, you want us to come up?"

"No, I'm on my way down now."

Disconnecting the call, she looked at Kato. His large hands were back on her waist, and his eyes were pulled down at the corners in sadness. She resisted the urge to caress his handsome face, knowing that she had to go. What she felt for this man was so different from everything she'd experienced with Polo.

With Polo it was all physical, but with Kato, their connection was mental. He had her mind and, once you mastered a person's mind, you forever had their heart.

As soon as Kato walked into the living room, Star pulled one of the duffle bags of money out of the closet and draped the straps over her shoulders. Next, she grabbed her .9 mm, stuffed it in her purse and headed for the door.

It was at that moment that she realized Kato was standing behind her, watching as she walked out the door. With a small smile, she bowed her head to him before stepping outside and closing the door behind her. Before she had even taken a few steps away, she heard him lock the door and then secure the chain locks for added security.

The life of a real goon.

THE PAST FEW days it had been raining and again, the clouds threatened to erupt with rain but still it was a beautiful, clear, gray day.

As soon as Star walked out the front of her building and stepped onto the concrete with her Nike shoes squeaking on the pavement, she saw the caravan of cars, three to be exact. Brenda, her Chief Enforcer, was in the lead car, the blue Benz, next was a blue Tahoe truck and a Cadillac SUV.

As soon as all three carloads of Gangstress saw Star, they instantly started throwing up gang signs, hooting and hollering, showing her mad love. They may have all been in a gang but for the most part, it was bonded with love. It wasn't no secret to the crew that Star had been going through a lot with her sister missing and her relationship with Polo up in the air. With all the drama that had been going on with bodies and pistols popping, for many of the girls, it was just a relief to show solidarity, even for a terrible cause.

Star moved to the car with Ki-Ki and Brenda sitting in the front. As soon as she opened the back door, she was surprised to see Tonya sitting in the back, all smiles, like this was the happiest day of her life. Star's stomach churned. That bitch would forever be a mortal enemy as far as she was concerned.

"Hey girl, you lookin' good in that true blue outfit," Brenda said with glee, and Ki-Ki seconded that with a nod.

"Yeah 'folks', you lookin' good girl," Tonya said as she toyed with her hair and slightly rocked in her seat, uncomfortable.

Star wasted no time showing her discontent when she turned all the way around in her seat and looked at Tonya dead in her eyes

"I don't fuck with you like that and you know, it so let's keep this shit one thousand."

Tonya rolled her eyes.

"That's the past. I'm trying to move on to the future. As soon as I found out what happened to Ebony, it was like fuck the beef. We need to get this shit solved, period, and that is all I care about. You my sister and fuck everything else," Tonya declared, putting on a spectacular show full of lies.

Both Ki-Ki and Brenda chimed in. "Yeah, right now it's about finding your sister."

"Damn right, and getting her back home. So let's squash the bullshit. Kato and Polo already got enough shit going on."

Brenda was doing about a hundred miles an hour driving down Cottage Grove Street.

"Bitch, slow down! You know you ain't got no fuckin' license and this car ain't really legit so stop speeding," Ki-Ki said.

Tonya pulled out a big ass bag of loud and fired up a blunt before passing it to Star.

"I'd give my life for all nations causes," she said, reciting the oath they'd all sworn. "You can hate me but we have to find your sister, that is more important than anything."

Not feeling anything Tonya was saying, Star hesitated. For some reason, Brenda looked in the rearview mirror and frowned, like she was upset about something.

This bitch is layin' this shit on thick, she thought, wondering why Tonya was acting all chummy with Star all of a sudden.

Then something else occurred to her.

"Tonya, I'm tryna figure out how you getting all this damn weed but you can't pay a bill?" she said, putting Tonya on blast.

"Fuck you talkin' about? I found this weed in *'The Spot'* but you ain't have to call me out like that. You could've pulled me to the side and asked," Tonya huffed with a lie.

The weed she was smoking had come directly from Kush; a gift after she broke him off with some bomb pussy. She puffed hard on it, trying to calm her nerves.

At that moment, she was petrified. As soon as all the Gangstress pulled up on Jazmyn, there was no doubt in her mind the girl was going to scream, telling it all, and Tonya would be the first name that came up.

This had to be the most terrifying ride of her life and she spent the whole drive there plotting but no ideas came to her. Suddenly, Tonya realized that she may have taken things too far.

Once again as they road in silence, she made another attempt to text Assassin and then waited.

No answer.

"Shit!" she cursed under her breath and looked out the window watching her reflection in the glass as the world strode by.

When everyone got out the car, she would just get ghost, lost in the shuffle, or so she hoped. That was her only recourse.

THEY PULLED up to the White Castle and instantly Tonya's stomach knotted up like it was filled with rocks to the pit of her gut. To her surprise, there were more cars there, all Gangstress. In fact, there were chicks there that Tonya had even forgot were on count. Polo must have really sounded the horn for Star and the word had spread like wildfire.

Before Brenda could even turn the engine off, a clique of Gangstress walked up; they too were all dressed in true-blue gang colors.

Myia and Andra and several of the girls approached the car, and you could tell they were hype and anxious. Myia's hair was on point. She wore her lace wig in a ponytail with oodles of baby hair curled around the edges of her angelic face. She had a blue sweat shirt with jeans, and you could see the bulge in her pants from the .380 pistol she was toting.

Andra, her sidekick, was the complete opposite. She wore her hair in a bun, all natural, her skin was mahogany brown, and she too was dressed in all blue. She had a gold grill at the bottom of her mouth, and she was also thick with ass for days. They were part of the 48th and Indiana Gangstress and were known for being more aggressive than their counter parts, the male Disciples.

"Hey Star," both Myia and Andra said as they exchanged dap, then Myia went into her spiel.

"So I got a homie that works in there. He says the fat chick, that was spotted wearing the chain, is Jazmyn. She just a gut bucket, starvin' ass hoe that been stealin' shit and don't wash her ass. She quiet and mostly keeps to herself but she smart in that nerdy kinda way. He said today she came to work all beat the fuck up and she been acting antsy the past few days."

"What time she get off work?" was all Star asked.

"She gets off in about another twenty minutes. She catches the bus right here."

Both Myia and Andra pointed as the other girls stood around. Star couldn't help thinking about how well the girls had done their home-work. Now all she needed to do was formulate a plan. If that was her sister's chain, they would have to abduct this Jazmyn chick in broad daylight.

That could present a problem, Star thought as she looked around. There were a lot of witnesses.

"I need to use the bathroom," Tonya suddenly said, making up an excuse to get out the car, hoping that she could possibly escape or maybe warn Jazmyn. Either way it was risky, but she had no other choice.

"No, we need to get this shit over with. Plus, it's been too many Gangstress goin' in and out of there anyways," Ki-Ki said. "We don't wanna get the chick all scared and shit."

"First off, I don't like that attitude, Ki-Ki. And since when you start givin' orders 'cause I sure didn't get the memo that you was head bitch," Tonya sassed.

"It ain't about that just chill!" Brenda shot back, aggravated.

"Hold up, there she go right there!" someone else said.

Star looked up and there were a few people, several of them holding umbrellas to shield from the rain.

"Where?" she asked, feeling her heart beat faster as she searched for the girl they had been talking about.

"Right there! The big bitch with the dirty ass gray jacket and the camel hump in her back, walking towards the bus stop," Andra said, pointing excitedly as she moved around animated.

Star stepped outside the car with quickness and felt a few drops of rain hit her face. As soon as she moved, a sea of blue women moved with her, again, drawing too much attention. Even though in her heart Star was overjoyed that so many Gangstress came to her aid, the very thing that was designed to help her could hurt, their unity. At that moment, she needed to move stealthy with as least attention possible.

"Myia, Andra, Brenda, Ki-Ki and Tonya walk with me and the rest of y'all stay here. If this bitch got on my lil' sister's chain, we abductin' her ass and she coming with us until she tells us everything she knows," Star said with her voice strained, eyes red but intent and focused, full of determination.

Then she stepped into the fray, speaking to the clique of Gangstress.

"I need y'all to fall back, act like y'all on chill mode. Y'all attractin' too much damn attention."

They all did as told and watched from a distance as Star and her crew walked with purpose towards the front of the restaurant.

Jazmyn was standing against the store wall with her hand in her pocket. The bus was late. Feeling anxious, she stared up at the sky as a light rain fell. Her face looked like she had been kicked by several horses. Even with the shades on she looked hideous.

"Hey Jazmyn, what's up?" Star said, looking the big girl up and down.

She was shocked. Up close, the girl was huge and instantly she detected a foul odor from her, like frying grease and funk.

Lost in her thoughts, Jazmyn was chewing on something, then suddenly stopped when she brought her attention to Star. Her eyebrows shot to the top of her forehead, alarmed, as she suddenly stopped chewing and dropped her chin, leaving her mouth partially open.

All the while Tonya stood in the back of the group, shaking badly, trying to hide her face as best as possible. She had never been a religious chick, but that day she prayed like a Catholic priest.

"What?" Jazmyn asked with her eyes bugged. She tried to swallow whatever it was she had in her mouth in one gulp, but it wouldn't go down. Her throat had gone dry.

"Damn, somebody must've thrown that bitch out a three-story window, head first," Myia cracked.

Star gave her the eye to be quiet.

"You got a chain on. I wanna check to see if it belongs to my sister," Star said and walked up, standing right in front of the big girl as if blocking her path. She couldn't help but notice all the horrible bruises on the girl's face as she waited for an answer.

"Yeah, I got on a chain. Somebody gave this shit to me, why?" She challenged back, jutting her chin out.

"Bitch, you better watch the tone of your fuckin' mouth before we tear that bitch out and feed it to your fat ass," Brenda said, never one to back down from a fight.

"You ain't gon' do shit to me. I'll beat your skinny ass," Jazmyn responded taking a step forward.

"Hold! Hold! Hold!" Star threw up both her hands. "If we can just see the chain, we outta here."

Jazmyn looked at all the girls then she glanced over at the parking lot. She wasn't no fool. All them girls wearing blue sureky weren't parking lot pimpin'. They had another agenda and she knew it must have been her.

No wonder all these bitches dressed in blue been staring holes through me at work, she thought.

"Okay, you can look at the chain, but I gotta catch my bus. I gotta go."

Jazmyn was serious; the bus was late and she only had fifteen minutes to make it home to get Ebony oxygen. But at that moment that was the least of her worries. Her concern then was if she showed the Gangstress the chain and they realized that it did belong to her sister, what would she do then?

As soon as she dug into her sweatshirt the girls, as if on cue, began to surround her. That's when she made eye contact with Tonya and nearly bugged out. Her brow furrowed with a scowl, that was easy to pass for a plea for help, but then Tonya gave her a warning glare to keep her mouth shut.

With her hand trembling, Jazmyn reached into her blouse and pulled out the chain, looking directly at Tonya. Her swollen bottom lip dropped to release a small whimper as she stood there, surrounded by all the Gangstress.

As soon as she looked at the chain, Star's legs nearly buckled. She couldn't believe her eyes. Her little sister's face flashed in her mind and she suddenly felt a gut-wrenching feeling. Something was wrong, terribly wrong.

With a calm voice and her legs trembling, Star asked evenly, "Where did you get it from?"

"I... don't know. I found it," the big girl stuttered as she looked around frantically.

Her legs started moving like she was walking in place, shifting her body like she was about to make a dash for it.

"Found it where, bitch?" Brenda yelled as she lunged forward.

"Yeah, hoe, where you find it at?" Ki-Ki was right by her side.

"I can't remember," Jazmyn said and starting moving her legs forward, trying to ease herself away from the crowd and distance herself from the madness. The only voice of diplomacy was Star and that simply was because she felt a terrible vibe about the girl and was afraid for Ebony's life.

"Please, tell me where you got the chain from. It's my sister's. I gave it to her," Star said with tears in her voice as she watched the girl intensely.

"I told ya, I can't remember... I think I found it."

"You lying!" Ki-Ki shouted. "I've had enough with this big bitch looking, like a retarded ass raccoon, with them big ass knots on her head and dark circles under her eyes."

Ki-Ki was ready to swing on the girl, and the other Gangstress chimed in with ruckus, loud and belligerent. They were ready to set it off.

People around them began to stop and stare. Star had to diffuse the situation so she called for them to fall back in a way that was genial, nearly soothing. Shaking like a leaf, Jazmyn looked up at her like she was her savior.

"Suppose I gave you a hundred thousand dollars," Star began. "Would that help refresh your memory? Would you help us find my sister?"

The big girl cut her eyes at Tonya again, who shook her head, giving her a subtle 'No'.

Capriciously, Jazmyn wiggled her head no to Star, her jowly cheeks looking like a walrus. She suddenly got nervous and looked around like she had seen something that spooked her. She started back peddling, moving like a big ox as she tried to run for safety. The Gangstress were on her fast, pushing and shoving; things were about to get ugly fast.

Someone threw a punch and it connected with the girl's jaw, making her sunglasses fly off her face onto the dirty concrete and into the street.

"Y'all stop it!!" Star shouted, and grabbed the girl by her arm with a tight embrace. "I'll give you the money, just help me to get my sister back!"

There was a pause and then Jazmyn looked into her eyes, seeing a small bit of hope. Or at least a bit of care, something she didn't see a shred of when she looked at Tonya.

"Y'all gon' hurt me."

She began to sob, her massive shoulders slouched. Then somebody in the crowd called out her name. She looked up in Tonya's direction and something set her off. It was Tonya who, behind Star's back, gestured with her hand making a cutthroat gesture, a signal to Jazmyn she was about to be killed. The girl panicked. Like a wild beast, she shoved Star with all her might. A group of Gangstress grabbed Star to keep her from falling into the street while the others jumped onto Jazmyn, assaulting her with punches.

"No! No! Stop! Leave her alone! Leave her alone!"

Star was moving fast and, with her eyes petrified with fear, Jazmyn looked at her, shouting out like a deer about to meet slaughter.

"Help me, please! I'll tell you everything!" Jazmyn howled. "But you're runnin' out of time. You have to get to her before—"

Then it started, like watching a trainwreck before it happened. One of the Gangtress punched Jazmyn so hard her head bobbed back. She staggered, legs wobbled, and a hamburger fell from her pocket.

"STOP!" Star shouted just as Tonya rushed up, aimed a gun, and pulled the trigger.

POW!

The bullet struck Jazmyn in her right temple and exited from the back of her head as her legs crumpled like she had been stepped on by a giant. Instantly, people began to scatter, except a few girls. Star's face was dotted with tiny splotches of blood as she turned and looked at Tonya, bewildered.

"What the fuck you shoot her for? You didn't have to do that!" Star was enraged, speaking through her teeth as she tried her best not to wring Tonya's neck.

"Sh... she was tryin' to buck, actin' like she was going to pop off on you," Tonya responded with her hands out like she was shocked. Her face was pale, ashen, she looked around terrified as a herd of people moved across the parking lot. She was putting on a good act.

Brenda, Ki-Ki and a few others stood around loyal to the Gangstress with bangers in their hands, eyes wide, watching, focused.

"Star, we gotta go," Brenda said, knowing that someone would soon call the cops.

Star bit down on her bottom lip and looked down at Jzmyn's dead body. A rivulet of blood spilled into the gutter from the gaping hole in her head as she lay on the dirty concrete with her eyes wide open, staring at a distance place that only she could see.

Bending down, Star took the necklace from around her neck and tucked into her pocket as she wiped away a single tear.

"Bitch, there go twelve!" Ki-Ki shouted, referring to the police. She reached down and grabbed Star just as she was ruffling through Jazmyn's pockets. She pulled out hamburgers, fries, napkins and loose chain until she found what she was looking for: a wallet.

Standing, she looked around at the faces staring at her. She would never forget the expressions of the people looking at her through the restaurant window, horror-stricken with disbelief. To the common eye, it looked like Star had just robbed the dead girl but in reality, it was more.

As soon as Star hopped into the car with the motor running, Brenda took off, burning rubber to escape before the police arrived.

"Bitch, I'ma keep it one billion wit' yo' ass. I was about to roll off and leave you," Brenda snapped with good reason.

Beside her, Ki-Ki folded her arms over her chest and pushed her lips forward with a confident nod of her head in agreement. Her expression said it all: Star was on some dare devil shit.

"Don't drive crazy. I got a pistol on me and I'm still on probation," Ki-Ki said, reminding them of her probation for the millionth time.

"Bitch, I still got the gun that I shot that fat girl with," Tonya shot back.

Brenda sucked her teeth and glanced at Tonya through the rearview mirror.

"That is why you need to get out and run. They might pull us and Cook County jail don't give bonds no more for murders if you Black."

"Y'all be quiet! Act like you relaxed in the seat," Star warned as the car continued to move forward onto the congested streets. "I got the bitch's address. Let's go see if we can find anything at her crib before the police decide to go there."

Tonya leaned back in her seat flabbergasted. She couldn't believe what she had just heard. Star was smart enough to go through the dead girl's wallet and find her address.

"Shit," she cursed and threw her head back onto the headrest.

Things could really get worse if Ebony was discovered alive.

CHAPTER 17

THEY PULLED UP TO THE ADDRESS, AND IT WAS IN THE HOOD, AN OLD decrepit house that looked ancient, as if it had been built in the late 1930s. It sat between two older homes, one of them an abandoned crack den, with its windows boarded up and covered with graffiti. Tall grass covered the landscape on both sides along with discarded trash. In the distance, dogs barked as a rustle of wind toyed with the car windows. A light rain pelted the windows as they fogged.

"You sure this the right address?" Brenda scowled her disapproval.

"Yeah, this is it," Star said, moving for the door handle. For some reason, she could sense that she needed to be moving fast and thinking quicker.

"Hold up, don't go in there. Can you see all those Four Corner Hustlers gang signs all over the area? Them niggas takin' pussy and killin' bitches with no questions," Tonya said, her eyes spread wide like she was in sheer terror.

"And we killin' bitches and fuckin' niggas, Four Corner Hustlers too," Ki-Ki said all animated, waving a gun at Tonya, causing her to duck down.

Both Brenda and Star got out behind Ki-Ki who was hype to get shit started, but Tonya hesitated and it was obvious that this was the last place in the world she wanted to be, and with good reason. This house would serve as her morgue, a hood mausoleum for her burial if things worked out the way she feared.

Brenda turned and discovered Tonya was still in the car and frowned at her.

"Girl, come on," Brenda said as Star walked straight ahead up to the front door and wasted no time knocking on the door.

There was no answer.

The time was 4:47. Jazmyn needed to change the oxygen almost thirty minutes ago, or was it twenty minutes? No one really knew exactly.

Moments later, Star was banging on the front door like a mad-woman and still there was no answer. She walked over to a dirty window on the porch, the wooden deck floor cracked as she peered inside.

"Oh my god!" she shrieked and looked at Brenda and the girls in disbelief.

"The living room floor is covered with blood!"

Star grabbed her forehead with the palm of her hand in exaspera-tion and suddenly pivoted and rushed, kicking the door, not once or twice but several times. She then began pounding it with her fist. All the girls looked at her as if she was crazy.

"Girl, is you okay? If it's that serious, I can just shoot the lock," Ki-Ki offered with apprehension written all over her face as Brenda watched with alarm. She had reached into her panties and removed her gun. The entire time Tonya paced with her arms crossed over her chest.

"No, with no silencer, the police will be called and we'll have to run. I feel like my sister is in there and time is running out. I can't explain it but it's a feeling deep in my soul," Star said pungently with a heavy heart.

"Say less," Brenda said and kicked on the door, so did Ki-Ki and Star. The entire time Tonya stood back and watched, not trying to help one bit.

The door didn't budge. Then Star had another idea.

"Let's go around the back and see if we can get in some way back there without the neighbors seeing," she said and took off before anyone could answer.

STAR NEARLY SLIPPED as she trotted across the tall, willowy, marshy grass and nearly slipped again when she had to make a sudden turn.

There was an old shed with garbage stowed outside along with a lawn mower, an assortment of beer cans and beer bottles. There was also something that looked like a patch of dirt that could have passed for a small grave, except it had some type of tube attached to a tank coming from the dirt.

As soon as they reached the back door, a piece of plywood covered the small window on the door. The door handle was ancient too and weathered with time.

Star wasted no time. She tried the door handle, and it rattled loosely but the door was locked. Without even speaking a word, they all started kicking and ramming the door, then with one powerful shoulder, using all her weight and meager strength, Star was able to get the door open.

As soon as they entered, the stench from the inside was horrible. By then Star had her pistol drawn, eyes alert, mind attentive. She was fully aware she had just committed a felony house invasion but she didn't care.

"It smells like skunk booty, shit and a rotten ass egg up in this bitch!" Ki-Ki said, frowning as she walked behind Star with her shirtm-pulled over her head.

"Ugh!" Brenda muttered with her hand over her mouth.

Tonya stood alone at the front door with a grim expression on her face.

As soon as Star walked into the front room, calling out her sister's name loudly, she knew something was terribly wrong. All the furniture had been turned over like there had been a violent struggle.

Then there was the blood. Lots of blood.

Star walked and stood over it. For some reason, she pinched her eyes closed as if trying to communicate with the essence of the room, its gory past, its formable presence. Then she bent down and stared at something. The rest of the girls stood silently, watching her in awe. It was as if Star was in a trance, her mind was distant, she was reliving a moment in time that had nothing to do with her but it did; her baby sister was missing.

She reached down for the tiniest thing. It was a long piece of hair. She examined it carefully, feeling in her heart that it was her sister's hair.

She then turned and they all searched the rest of the house and still nothing. It wasn't until Star was about to give up that she noticed another trail of blood. Blood that looked like it had started from the living room.

The trail led them surprisingly outside the door and suddenly disappeared into the vast openness of nothing. Instantly, Star's heart was filled with despair and hurt. She felt like she had been so close, her desperation was nearly causing her to hallucinate. She really felt like her sister had been here. As she walked away, ready to head back to the car, her gut feeling was telling her that she was missing something. Stopping, she looked at her watch as she stood in the pouring rain. It was nearly 5 o'clock.

"I'm going to get back in the car, y'all come on. No telling who house this is," Tonya said for the first time, like she was suddenly getting her voice back.

Brenda stepped in front of her to stop her.

"Before you get your ass back into that car you need to get rid of that dirty ass gun you hit up ole girl with."

The two began to bicker back and forth, not even noticing that Star was onto something. She was staring down at footprints, muddy footprints that led in and out the house, like an old trail. She followed them with her eyes and gasped when she saw that they led right to the stump of dirt in the yard with the tube and tank connected to it.

As the girls argued on, she meandered over to it with her eyes wide as if she could sense something. Once she get up close, she saw handprints, lots of them! Whatever was buried under there had been done in a hurry.

Please, God, no.

Fearing the worse, she bent down low and examined the tank next to the mound of dirt. It had some type of clock device on front, about the size of a quarter, enveloped inside a small casing to protect it from the elements.

The clock read 4:15. Instantly Star's mind flash back to the big girl Jazmyn, and one of the last things she'd said before she was killed. Something about time.

But you're runnin' out of time. You have to get to her...

"Oh, God! Noooooo," Star cried out and fell to her knees, digging frantically with her hands.

"Y'all help. Help me please!" she shouted to the others.

Running over to her with confused expressions on their faces, they all looked at her like she had lost her mind. Everyone, except Tonya. She alone knew what was next, her worse fears were about to be confirmed if the girl was found alive.

As soon as Ebony was dug up alive, she would point the finger right at Tonya and tell a horrifying tale that would make national news. Tonya would probably have no choice but to plead guilty to seventy-five years in prison to avoid the death penalty by snitching on Assassin. But not if she could help it.

I'll have to shoot them all, she thought, watching as Star, Brenda and Ki-Ki all dug up the wooden box. *Right in the back of the head and leave them all in the shallow grave.*

She suddenly walked over with her pistol out at her side, ready to start blasting.

The girls got the dirt off the cover of the box and removed the top, praying they wouldn't see what they expected.

"Oh, shit!" Ki-Ki shouted, jumping back with her arm covering the lower part of her face.

There was Ebony, tied up and gagged. Her face was so disfigured, swollen, bruised and caked up with blood and dirt, that, at first, Star couldn't even recognize her own sister. As she gently wiped at her face, she broke down in tears. It was too much to bear. Behind her, Tonya crept up slowly from the back with her gun poised, ready to kill.

"Wake up. Come on, baby. Get up, please. Please!" Star wailed poignantly as she held her sister against her bosom.

No one else said a thing. It was obvious to everyone around that Ebony was dead but they didn't have the heart to say it. Her body was lifeless, her once beautiful skin was the color of burnt charcoal.

Brenda and Ki-Ki couldn't help but sob as they watched Star lift her baby sister from the box. They helped her carry the dead girl into the kitchen and lay her down on the floor as Tonya stood behind them, trying to appear sad. On the inside, she was shouting with joy. There was nothing more for her to worry about.

Feeling a sense of relief, she eased the gun back into her purse and feigned heartbreak right along with the others.

CHAPTER 18

SLOAN SAT IN THE PASSENGER SEAT OF POLO'S RIDE, QUIETLY wondering what new evil plan he was up to. Their destination was a secret; Polo had simply called and told him where to be so that he could pick him up, and Sloan asked no questions. The thing with being a Disciple was that it was easy to be loyal when you knew that everyone was following the same code and believed in the same thing. The problem was, these days, Sloan wasn't so sure that Polo was following any rules other than his own.

Chief and Westin sat behind Sloan, attentive, focused and grateful for their new position. After Kato gunned down most of the Disciples' leading hittas, Polo had to work quickly to refill the ranks of his entourage with all who were left. Chief and Westin were only too happy to jump in those spots and prove their loyalty. Behind them, Trey drove a black SUV filled with more armed Disciples, as if they were headed into war.

"You know what I like about you, Sloan?" Polo spoke up, breaking the silence for the first time since Sloan sat down in the car. "I never have to question your loyalty to me. You bleed true blue and you always keep that shit one hundred percent so a nigga never gotta guess where you stand. I thought Kato was that way, but he ain't. I guess real niggas do change."

Pausing, Polo raised a brow after waiting in vain for Sloan to respond. Unlike Polo and Kato, Sloan had never blurred the lines between friendship and duty. He never interacted with them as if he were one of the homies, and only did what was required of him as a fellow Disciple and second in command to their leader.

"You're right," Sloan finally responded. "Real niggas do change."

His reply was vague, but it worked for Polo who smirked with satisfaction as he bent a corner, entering the suburbs. A text message hit Sloan's phone and he grabbed it from his pocket, knowing who it was before he even checked.

Are you goin' to my appointment today? I might get to see what I'm havin'.

Looking up from the phone, he let out a breath before responding.

I'm with Polo. Idk for how long but I'll try.

Her reply came fast.

K, I'm at Star's, hiding in the room. Some men came by looking for Kato. Yesman was one of their names. The shit scared me half to death. You heard of him?

Hell yeah, I know who Yesman is. What did he say?

It took a moment before she replied.

He was just looking for Kato.

Sloan raised one brow, knowing that Kevia was keeping something from him. Yesman was the type who always laid low and he wouldn't make a trip to Star's spot unless he knew for a fact that Kato was there. He had too many niggas trying to touch him to make moves that he didn't have to.

Is Kato there?

No, was her reply, but Sloan had a feeling that she was lying. Once he saw her at the hospital, he would ask her again. She could do a lot of things but one thing Kevia couldn't do was lie in his face.

"Yo, where we goin'?" he asked and looked at his watch. "Is it goin' to be a long trip?"

"We 'bout to get payback for all of our niggas that we lost thanks to Kato pulling that fuck shit at *The Spot*. I know you ain't think I was gonna let that shit fly."

Brushing his hand over his jaw, Sloan didn't seem to visibly react to Polo's statement; however, his mind was working a mile a second wondering what it was that he was about to be pulled into. He didn't want to go to war with Kato, especially not over what seemed to be some personal shit that he was in his feelings over.

"This still 'bout Star?"

"Hell nah, this ain't 'bout no fuckin' Star!" Polo shot back, enraged at Sloan even asking the question. "This is 'bout the fact that this nigga gunned down some of the organization's top hittas just because he ain't wanna fall in line. What kinda man would I be if I let that shit fly? We supposed to be goin' to war with them Four Corner Hustler niggas, but one of our own men has done more damage than they ever done. That shit can't go unpunished."

"It happened because you called for an unwarranted violation. What kind of man would Kato have been to take some shit laying down that he didn't even deserve?"

"A loyal one," Polo answered without hesitation.

They pulled into a residential area, what appeared to be a middle-class neighborhood, and Sloan's eyes narrowed when he realized that they were in an area that was home to many relatives of key Disciples. When Polo slid the car in front of a nice-sized home, white with blue trim and an expertly manicured lawn, Sloan squinted at the license plate of the car parked in the driveway. The plate read "QT KAY" and the second Sloan saw it, he knew who it belonged to.

"Ma, what da fuck kinda dumb shit is this?" he remembered Kato saying, pointing at the custom tag that his mother had made for the car he bought her. *"You might as well call niggas up and tell them where to find you, if you gon' be drivin' in this shit. Just make it easy for them muthafuckas who tryin' to get at me to come after you instead."*

True to her ratchet nature, Kato's mother had simply rolled her eyes and popped her gum before saying her piece.

"Ain't nobody stupid enough to come at me like that. These niggas out here don't wanna start no shit with my son so I ain't got a damn thing to worry 'bout. Now leave me da fuck alone."

She had been right because nobody ever did a damn thing to her, even though Kato had plenty of enemies in the street.

Nobody until now anyways.

"Aye, y'all ready?" Polo said, looking in the rearview mirror at Chief and Westin who were already holding their weapons in their hands.

"Polo, man, c'mon. You can't do this shit right here. It's not right. What Kato did was wrong but this not the way to handle it. The bylaws state that—"

"Real shit, I'm tired of you always tryin' to check me on everything. I took the same muthafuckin' oath as you and I been runnin' this shit for some time now. You think I need you to remind me of the laws that I swore to uphold in blood?"

"I ain't tryin' to check you on shit but you 'bout to touch this man's mama. Ain't no comin' back from this. Once it's done, it's done, and we officially at war with this nigga until he takes his last breath."

For a moment, Polo considered Sloan's words, knowing that he was absolutely right. His own father had been laid to rest right in front of his face by a rival gang member by the name of O.C. and Polo never forgot his face. He made it his personal goal in life to make sure that his would be the last face that O.C. saw when he took his last breath but, before he killed O.C., he killed his brother and his pregnant wife so that he could feel the pain of losing someone he loved before he lost his own life.

What Polo didn't know was that O.C. killed his father because his father had killed O.C.'s cousin and robbed him. The brutal cycle of retribution and murder seemed to never end once started, and this was what Sloan was trying to get him to understand.

But what Sloan didn't know was that Polo had no intentions of killing Kato's mother; he only wanted to send a message. He'd received word earlier that she had left to go on a short vacation with one of the O.G. Disciples that she was seeing. Although no one else was aware, Kato's mother wasn't in the house and wouldn't be harmed. He would be able to send a message that he wasn't weak or afraid of Kato, get revenge for the men he'd lost and possibly even draw Kato from out of hiding.

"The innocent shouldn't have to pay the price for some shit that don't involve them," Sloan continued, trying to be the voice of reason. "Doing this is wrong."

"What 'bout my dog, Killa?" Chief spoke up aggressively from the back seat. "K Dot was innocent! He ain't have nothin' to do with shit when Kato killed him just because he was followin' orders. *Your* orders."

Chief looked squarely at Polo as he finished his statement.

"K Dot wasn't innocent, none of us are," Sloan said. "We all took an oath and we know that any day can be our last because of it. That's what bein' a Disciple is about. But I can't stand for this shit right here. Ms. Denice damn near helped *raise* all of us in the hood. We was shorties sittin' up in her house playin' video games and shit back in the day."

"My nigga was just doing what he was told and he paid the ultimate price for that. Now you tellin' me that we just gon' let that slide because y'all on some memory lane shit?"

"Shut da fuck up!" Polo finally weighed in, growing frustrated with the conversation taking place around him.

He heard Chief loud and clear and what was coming out of his mouth was the reason that he knew he had to make this move. The other Disciples wanted revenge for the ones that they'd lost and already too many days had passed of him sitting around, waiting for Kato to show his face. If he didn't do something soon, he'd appear weak.

"This what I want y'all to do," he began, speaking to Chief and Westin only. "We gon' pull a twenty-eight and then we out. Move quick —in and out. Trey and his team already got the orders."

With clenched teeth, Sloan watched as both men jumped out of the whip with their weapons of choice in hand, Chief making sure to give him an extra hard look as he made his exit. Chief was reckless with a strong appetite for murder and mayhem that knew no bounds. Men like him, placed in a position of power, could be everything needed to tear the Disciple organization down. He didn't believe in order, had no morals and was bloodthirsty without cause.

"This is wrong, man," Sloan spoke up, trying once again to appeal to Polo's humanistic side; a part of him that was steadily decreasing in size.

One look at him and Polo could see that he'd lost Sloan's respect. Seeing that, he decided to come clean.

"She's not in there," he explained now that the men were gone. "They don't know it but she's not. I got word that she was goin' out of town with JaJa, the O.G. from Yesman's old crew. This shit right here is just to send a message and to get niggas like Chief off my back. They out here thinkin' a nigga is weak and I can't have that shit."

Sloan frowned deeply, thinking back to the text message that Kevia had sent him earlier about Yesman dropping by Star's apartment.

"She's with JaJa?" Sloan asked. "You mean Yesman's Chief Enforcer? He's not out of town."

With widened eyes, Polo sat straight up in his seat, hoping that he'd heard him wrong. Glancing outside, he saw as all of his men moved to surround Kato's mother's house, all of them raising their guns.

"What you mean, he's not out of town? I was told this morning that—"

"I mean that he's *not* out of town. Yesman was seen entering an apartment by some Disciples this morning," Sloan replied, making sure to keep Kevia and Star out of it. "He wouldn't go anywhere unless he had JaJa with him. You need to tell them niggas to back down because Kato's mama might be in—"

Before Sloan could finish his sentence, gunfire sounded off around them like it was the Fourth of July. Chief, Westin, Trey and the rest of the Disciples all emptied their clips into the home, making sure that anything in it that might have been moving would never move again. Sloan looked on in absolute terror as the group of Disciples completely annihilated the home beyond repair. When the shooting finally stopped, he turned to Polo and looked at him with a venomous look in his eyes.

"You better pray to God that she ain't in there."

As the Disciples ran back to the car, Polo didn't say a word. His facial expression was blank, not giving any hint of his thoughts. Deep down, he did hope that Denice wasn't hit but he would never admit it and never let anyone other than Sloan know that killing her hadn't been his true intent. In order to lead an army of savages, they had to believe that the one in charge was the most savage of them all.

Chief and Westin jumped in the car, hype, rowdy and satisfied now that the attack was over. With their hands in the air, they threw up gang signs, celebrating a job well done.

"Long live, K Dot!" Westin shouted, repping his set.

"That's right," Chief added. "My nigga can finally rest in peace now that—"

The ear-piercing sound of a woman's screams stopped him mid-sentence and everyone's eyes turned towards the source of the sound. It was coming from the house. The tragic, excruciating sounds of a woman who had been shot, crying out in agony.

"The bitch is still alive," Westin spoke up. "How the fuck she live through all of that?"

"Want me to go put her out of her misery?"

Sloan cut his eyes to Polo, saying a lot in his stare that he wouldn't let fall from his lips. He didn't need to; Polo could easily read every single thing that he wouldn't say. He sniffed and then lifted his hand to nudge the tip of his nose.

"Make it quick."

Chief ran to do as asked as Sloan and Polo sat in the car silently. Westin, on the other hand, was almost giddy as he watched his friend leave to carry out the task. The screaming stopped abruptly, a signal that the job was done, and in the next moment, Chief was rushing back to the car with a broad smile on his face.

"The bitch didn't even see it comin'," he gloated as Polo mashed on the gas.

"Long live K Dot," was all he said.

Various hoots and howls sounded from the men in the back seat until Sloan couldn't endure it any longer. Pulling out his silenced weapon from his side, he swiveled around quickly in his seat and pulled the trigger twice, letting off a shot in the center of both Chief and Westin's foreheads.

"SHIT!" Polo yelled, nearly swerving off the road. "What da fuck you do that shit for?"

Sloan turned around in his seat, facing forward once more.

"They was already dead."

It was true. Once Kato caught wind of what had happened to his mother, it would be a wonder if any of them made it through the night.

"Fuck! You just shot both of them niggas in my fuckin' back seat. How the hell am I gon' hide this shit?"

Polo didn't expect to get a response from Sloan so he didn't wait for one. Grabbing his cellphone, he called Trey and gave him orders to take a different route to their destination, stating that they should split up in case the police were called. Once Trey made a sudden turn in the other direction, Polo began to drive in the direction of a vacant warehouse that belonged to the Disciples where he could set the car and Chief and Westin's bodies on fire to hide Sloan's crime. With Kato now his enemy, he couldn't risk losing Sloan. Not at the moment anyways.

NOT TOO MUCH TIME LATER, Sloan and Polo were standing in silence watching as the car they'd been driving in went up in flames. Even though it would seem that this was done to cover Sloan from being violated by killing fellow Disciples, he knew the truth and was fully aware that Polo had really done this for his own benefit. Sloan was worth more to him alive than dead, plus the number of men loyal to Sloan was more than the ones loyal to Polo. To violate him would be to risk losing his position and maybe even his life.

"Whose apartment did Yesman run up in?" Polo asked after running his mind through everything that Sloan had said to him earlier. "And which Disciples told you 'bout it? I ain't hear shit."

"All I know is that Yesman was seen earlier and he had his enforcer and second in command with him."

Polo wasn't convinced. His gut was telling him that Sloan was protecting someone and he had a suspicion of who.

"Yo, what's up with ya girl, Kevia. She's pregnant, ain't she?"

Sloan nodded his head and scratched at his jaw, not at all liking where the conversation was going.

"Does Yesman know who she is? I mean, it can't be a coincidence that ain't nobody seen that nigga in a while and, all of a sudden, he pop up when you got a baby on the way with another broad. That shit don't seem funny to you?"

Sloan's body filled with tension. "It wasn't Kevia's apartment that he was seen at."

"How you know?" Polo shot back. "I thought you said you ain't know who apartment he was at. It makes sense to me that he might been 'round there at Kevia's, tryin' to see if the rumors were true that you been fuckin' around on his daughter and now got yo' side bitch pregnant. How 'bout we go check on Kevia to make sure she wasn't the one to get paid a visit?"

There was no need to respond because Polo already knew there was no way that Sloan would allow that to happen, and he also knew that Yesman hadn't come out of hiding just to check on Kevia. It was true that Sloan's wife and daughter's mother was Yesman's daughter, Yasmina. This was an arrangement that Yesman had required of him years ago after Jimmy Johnson was locked up and sentenced to death row.

With Jimmy locked up, Yesman was forced into hiding to stop the Feds from coming after him, too. Sloan was dating his daughter at the time and Yesman asked him to marry her and vow to protect her in exchange for being made Polo's second in command. Sloan didn't like the idea of being offered a high-ranking position as a matter of a deal but after finding out Yasmina was pregnant with his daughter, he agreed for his child's sake.

Now it was years later and the love he once had for Yasmina was nonexistent, but Yesman was still in hiding and refused to absolve Sloan of their agreement unless he was violated and stripped of his rank and removed from the organization. So he moved Yasmina out in the suburbs, stating it was for her protection, and split his time between running the streets and being with his daughter so that he didn't have to deal with her more than he absolutely had to.

Although he was sure that Yasmina knew there was another woman, he'd never given her any evidence of the fact so she had nothing to go off of. Sloan knew that his time was running out now that Kevia was pregnant, but he was hoping that a miracle—preferably

Jimmy Johnson being released and Yesman coming out of hiding—would occur before he had to make a move.

"There is no need to visit Kevia," Sloan said to Polo, more forcefully than before. "She wasn't the one he went to see."

"Then if it wasn't Kevia that Yesman came out of hiding for, who was it?"

With his eyes concentrated on the smoldering flames in front of him, Sloan weighed his options, knowing that he wasn't going to be able to sidestep Polo's questions for much longer. As much as he didn't want to put the heat on Star and Kato, the reality was that they'd chosen their path and would have to suffer the consequences. Kevia was innocent, her only crime was that she was a loyal friend, and she was the only one that he was required to look out for.

CHAPTER 19

THE INSIDE OF STAR'S APARTMENT WAS FULL OF SO MUCH SMOKE IT looked like a gas chamber. With the lights off and the curtains pulled closed, Kato mumbled incoherently under his breath, sputtering broken sentences to illustrate his disdain at Yesman taking him off count. It was as if he was having an identity crisis of the greatest kind. If not a Disciple, what was he? He'd been in the streets, repping true blue, for so long that he didn't know what he would be if he wasn't the person he'd been.

With no other recourse, Kato decided that he would simply just smoke his life away. As soon as he was positive that Star was out of the house and wouldn't be doubling back, he began rolling up and blew his worries into gassy green clouds.

"Da fuck is that noise?"

Kato placed his hand on his forehead and then to his ears, trying to find the source of the ringing noise that seemed to be coming from his head. It wasn't until he sat all the way up that he realized that the sound wasn't coming from his head but from the cellphone that he'd been lying on top of.

"Who this?" he asked, answering the call.

"Hello, this is Dr. Peterson and I'm calling to speak to Kato—"

"Yeah, this is me. What you want, Doc? I already told you that I wasn't payin' that bill but here's the good news. As long as I owe you, you'll never be broke."

The doctor sighed on the other end of the line, already knowing that this conversation was about to be much harder than it should be simply because of the man he was talking to. Kato's situation was severe and the quicker he could get him to understand that, the better. As time passed, the more unlikely it was that Kato would be able to fully grasp the seriousness of his condition. Too much time had passed already.

"Kato, listen, I wanted to follow up with you on the tests that we ran while you were here... the ones that we spoke about during your stay," the doctor began. "Every day your brain is deteriorating at an alarming rate because of your condition. The trauma to your brain is only going to get worse unless we do something about it now. We have already seen evidence of Alzheimer's and it's only going to progress further if you don't continue to undergo treatment. This time next year, you won't be the same Kato that everyone around you knows and loves. You'll be someone else."

Snorting air through his nostrils, Kato began to laugh, for some reason finding humor in the solemn tone that Dr. Peterson was using.

"The Kato that everyone around me knows and loves? Doc, you obviously don't know shit. No one knows and loves me."

"I'm sure that's not true," Dr. Peterson replied. "What about the young lady who was always at the hospital visiting you? I believe Star is her name. Does she know about the tests that we ran and your results?"

Kato clamped his jaw shut tightly as his mind traveled back to the day when he called Star to tell her not to show up at the hospital. It was the same day that she shocked him with news that she was going to Northwestern after getting her transcripts. He had just gotten the results back from the tests they ran on his brain and was told that within another year or two, he wouldn't be able to wipe his own ass. Hell—wouldn't even know he *had* an ass that needed wiping. That day, he remembered feeling like she was both the last person and the only person that he wanted to see. She was the only one who could make him feel better as well as the one person who reminded him of the future that he would never have because his days with her were severely numbered.

"She knows 'bout it," Kato lied, simply because he didn't want to admit that he was afraid to tell her. Of all things he'd faced in his life, he hadn't known real fear until it came to Star. He was afraid to lose her and afraid to let her know that, every day, she was losing part of him.

"That's good. Letting her know what is going on is a good start because she will need to help you through this. The next year can be pretty rough if you don't get treatment soon."

"We both know I can't afford the treatment that you're suggestin' so it's not an option for me. Plus, I don't need no help gettin' to the grave and I'm not 'bout to be pissin' and shittin' on myself before I get there. I'll take fate into my own hands before I get to that point and have to depend on Star or anybody else to take care of me."

"Kato," Dr. Peterson began in a chastising tone, "I hope you don't mean to say that you're going to end your own life because, in that case, I would have to—"

Before he could finish his statement, Kato ended the call and tossed the phone to the side. Already he had been stripped of his rank and his family; he was no longer a Disciple, which meant that he had little left fighting to stay alive for. Star was the only reason he had for living and as soon as he made sure that Polo was no longer a threat to her living her life and that Jimmy got the justice that he deserved, he would go out like a real gangsta, on his own terms. It was said that those who lived by the gun died by the gun, and Kato wouldn't have it any other way.

STAR WAS a complete and utter mess and there was nothing anyone could do to make things better. Her baby sister, the only person in this world who she wouldn't have hesitated to put her life on the line for, was dead and she couldn't help but feel like it was her fault.

"We gotta get her out of here," Brenda said to Ki-Ki, both of them wiping tears from their own eyes. The scene was devastating to see. It wasn't clear how Ebony had died but it was obvious that the young girl had suffered.

"Nobody should have to die like this." Myia, who had been sitting out front as the lookout with Andra, spoke with words that echoed what everyone around was thinking.

Even Tonya, who was standing behind them all, silent as she looked at Ebony's lifeless body. She didn't care about the girl—definitely hadn't liked her and wouldn't have hesitated to kill her to save her own skin—but she had to admit that she'd died a terrible death.

"Aye, we gotta get out of here," Andra said, walking towards them from where she had still been stationed out front as the lookout. "The nosy bitch across the street was on her phone, lookin' over here while she was talkin'. She either callin' the Four Corner Hustlers or them boys in blue. We don't wanna see either one of their asses so we gotta peel out."

"I can't leave her here!" Star sobbed, almost hysterical as she fought against Brenda and Ki-Ki who were holding her back from Ebony's body. "I can't let them have her!"

Star was only too aware of what could happen to her sister's dead body if it were left here for the Four Corner Hustlers. She wasn't sure who Jazmyn was or who she was related to, but she had to be pretty high up to be the one they trusted with watching Ebony's sister. Once it was discovered that she'd been killed, they would mutilate Ebony's body and parade what was left around like a trophy.

"She's right," Tonya agreed, her mind suddenly coming up with a plan that could solve Star's problem as well as save her own skin. "Let's just torch the place. It's better to do that than to allow poor Ebony's body to be desecrated more than it already has."

All of the Gangstress, minus Tonya, exchanged glances. They were unsure of what else they could possibly do to satisfy their leader when they were running out of time as it was.

"We can't stay here too much longer and we can't bring a dead body with us because if we get pulled over, that's a wrap," Ki-Ki said to Brenda. "So you're second in command. What should we do?"

Brenda sucked in a breath and let it out slow. She hated to admit it, but Tonya was right. The only way out of this was to burn everything down.

"She's right," she said, nodding her head to Tonya.

"Noooooo!" Star cried out, trying to fight her way out of Brenda and Ki-Ki's tight hold.

"Star, listen. There is no other way. We either leave her here and hope that the police find her first or we—"

As they went back and forth, trying to find a solution, Tonya made one of her own. With a gas cannister in hand, that she'd grabbed from among the mess strewn about the back yard, Tonya began tossing the liquid all over Ebony's body as Brenda and Ki-Ki continued trying to speak sense to Star, and Myia and Andra ran around front to look out for unwanted visitors. It was too risky to leave if the police were on their way because there was no telling what she could have possibly left in the house after being forced to have sex with Assassin. Plus, Jazmyn had mentioned her diary on more than one occasion and Tonya couldn't be sure that the stupid girl hadn't written an entry about all of their plans.

"No," she heard Star suddenly say while shaking her head. "I want to bury her the right way. We can just drive slow and—"

Tonya rushed to ignite the trail of gasoline leading to Ebony's body with the long barbecue lighter that she was holding in her hand. The flame spread at an alarming rate and, within seconds, little Ebony's entire body was on fire. Star lost it. Ki-Ki had to hold her up as she broke down in loud sobs at the sight.

"What da *fuck* did you do that for?" Brenda snapped, walking up to Tonya with her fists balled. "She was just 'bout to say that she wanted to take the body with us."

"I was workin' fast to get somethin' done because we didn't have a lot of time! You said that you agreed with me and I started movin'. How was I 'posed to know that she would change her mind? We needed to do somethin' before we got caught!"

As if on cue, police sirens sounded off in the distance and everyone froze, except for Star who was still wailing away in Ki-Ki's arms.

"We gotta get out of here now!" Brenda shouted before turning around to help Ki-Ki carry Star back to their car. "Tonya, since you started this shit, you need to finish it. Set the rest of this shit on fire and let's go!"

Without argument, Tonya went to work to do as she was asked and poured the rest of the gasoline outside the window of the room that Assassin had forced her to have sex with him in. If the rest of the house didn't burn, she didn't give a damn. As long as this room was gone, along with any evidence of her presence, that was good enough for her. Thinking quick, she pulled the pistol out that she'd killed both J-Rock and now Jazmyn with and tossed it into the blazing flames as well.

Once she ignited the flame that would do the rest of her dirty work, Tonya ran to the front of the house and jumped in the car, just barely able to slam the door closed before Brenda took off at top speed. Behind them, Myia and Andra took off in the opposite direction. In the backseat, Star seemed like she was on the verge of losing her mind. She knew she had to get it together in case they were pulled over but she couldn't think about anything but Ebony.

"Star, baby, listen," Ki-Ki said, rubbing her back as she held her in her arms. "We gon' get them Four Corner niggas for this. Every last one of them who had somethin' to do with what happened to your sister... we gon' get them muthafuckas, if it's the last thing we do. I know I can't say anything to make it better but just know that everyone who had a hand in this will pay for it."

"That's right," Brenda chimed in from the front, brushing a tear away as she tried to concentrate on the road. She heard Tonya make a clicking sound with her tongue and teeth, as if to disagree with what Ki-Ki had said and she glanced at her, carefully watching the expression on her face while Tonya was unaware.

"We are all here for you, Star," Ki-Ki continued. "Every single one of us, and we feel your pain."

Bitch, please, Tonya thought, rolling her eyes.

The sound of Brenda clearing her throat made her lift her eyes to look at the rearview mirror where she found herself staring right into Brenda's disapproving eyes.

"Yes, that's right. We are sisters. We'll be here for you," she said for

Brenda's satisfaction, sounding more like a robot than anything else. Thankfully, Star was too distraught to notice.

"Oh shit!" Brenda yelled out all of a sudden.

"What?" Ki-Ki and Tonya both asked.

She was too panicked to respond right away. She had driven right through a red light at a major intersection. She hadn't noticed what she was doing because she had been so busy looking at Tonya. She also hadn't noticed the cop car that had been sitting at the corner watching the entire thing.

Not until it was too late.

Chirp! Chirp!

All of the girls froze. It was the sound of the beast.

Brushing tears from her eyes, Star turned her head and, sure as shit, there was a blue and white police car following behind them.

CHAPTER 20

"PULL OVER YOUR VEHICLE!" THE OFFICER SAID OVER THE loudspeaker.

"Shit!" Brenda hissed.

Ki-Ki sat straight up on her seat with her eyes stretched open to max capacity.

"I got a probation violation out on me and a gotdamn pistol in my purse. I ain't goin' back to jail."

"Just chill!" Tonya issued, motioning for Ki-Ki to hush as Brenda pulled over to the side of the road.

Star bit the corner of her lips, hoping that this day wasn't about to go from bad to worse. It was enough that she had to inform her grandmother that Ebony was dead and that there was no body to bury; she didn't want to go to jail too.

"What they doin'?" Star asked, hearing the quiver in her own voice. She knew better than to turn around in her seat. That would look too suspicious.

"Both crackas getting out the car," Brenda narrated as she watched carefully through the side mirror. "One of 'em got his hand on his gun. The other one talkin' on his radio. They runnin' our license plate. Fuck! I hope this car make it."

Star's heart nearly came to a complete stop in her chest. She knew exactly what Brenda meant. All of Polo's cars were stolen and then taken to the chop shop where they would swap the vin numbers with cars that had been sent to junkyards.

"I got a gun and weed on me, plus I'm on probation. I say you just take off and let them muthafuckas chase us. If they catch us, then we'll just deal with it then," Ki-Ki said with a shrug.

"Bitch, that's a dumb ass idea," Tonya shot in. "Then we all goin' to jail if we don't get killed by Brenda's non-drivin' ass."

"Shut up! Just let me do the talkin'," Brenda said just as the cop knocked on the window with the butt of his flashlight. Star stared back at him as he peered inside. His skin was pale; white as a sheet.

Brenda rolled down the window and spoke with the sweetest voice, intelligent and pleasant, like she wasn't a hood-rat driving a stolen car with guns, drugs and felons sitting inside.

"Hi, Officer! What can I help you with today?"

The officer snorted and bobbed his head inside the car, his face frowning with skepticism.

"You can help me by telling me why you ran that light back there. And... is that marijuana I smell?"

The other cop, his partner, was on the opposite side of the car, glaring down at Ki-Ki. He was chubby with hound-dog, blood-red eyes and a disdainful frown on his face like he was having a bad day. He then turned his attention to Star, staring hard. It took everything in her power to give him a polite smile and a curt nod of her head, pretending that everything was fine as she acknowledged his presence. It didn't work. In return, the cop gritted on her, sneering evilly.

"Oh, now we don't know nothing 'bout that. Just cigars," Brenda offered, nudging her head to a leftover butt in the ashtray. "It's a nasty habit. I'm tryin' to stop." She continued to smile painfully through her teeth like she'd been chewing on cracked glass and continued, "And I honestly didn't mean to run that light back there. I... um..." She cut her eyes to Star. "We just received word that a friend of ours lost her sister in a horrible accident and I'm a little distracted by my emotions. That's why I'm tryin' to get home."

"That's no excuse to be reckless," the cop replied snidely. "Let me see your license and registration," he demanded.

He caught Brenda completely off-guard. She had been sure that her excuse would work and she'd be let off with a simple warning. She pretended to search in her purse for a driver's license and registration that she knew she didn't have. She was stalling for time, waiting on a miracle.

The cop began to talk over the car to his partner, giving Ki-Ki a chance to whisper to her from the backseat.

"I got this pistol in my purse. I can't go to prison. Either cut the car on and punch the gas or I can try to shoot our way outta here."

Tonya's brows shot to the sky. She was not trying to be involved in a shoot-out with the police.

I know I didn't hear this bitch right, she thought, fear gripping her insides.

"What did you say?" the cop on Ki-Ki's side of the car asked with his hand on his gun.

"I said 'shit, it's hot in here,'" she replied with a jerk of her neck, her fear obvious. "We need to turn the car back on so we can get some A.C."

A glean of perspiration was starting to form on her shiny forehead. Ki-Ki was paranoid and it made her reckless. Star watched in horror as Ki-Ki leaned forward slowly, discreetly easing her hand into her purse.

The cop watched her, unaware of her real intentions but still noticing some slight movements.

"You sure is antsy," he remarked. "Why you so jittery all of a sudden?"

Star knew that Ki-Ki was concentrating too hard on what she was attempting, to even try at giving him a good enough answer. She spoke up on her behalf.

"Because police be shooting people for no reason. We all scared and she already said this was a simple accident, so can we go?"

"Yes, please, it was an accident but I'm payin' attention now," Brenda chimed in, eagerly following Star's lead.

"Young lady, you need to be showing me your license and registra-tion," the cop on Brenda's side demanded.

To Star's relief, she saw Brenda hand him her I.D. before she responded with an attitude.

"Here it is. Now can you leave us alone?"

The cop glanced at the I.D., his eyes knotting up a tight line across his face.

"I asked for your *driver's* license. This is a high school I.D. card. Everybody out the car, *now!*"

The cop flung the door open and grabbed Brenda by her arm, snatching violently.

"Man, what da fuck!" Ki-Ki scoffed and then eased her hand deeper in her purse.

With the cop on her side temporarily distracted by his partner and Brenda scuffling on the other side, Tonya knew that Ki-Ki's crazy ass was fully intent on grabbing her gun and setting it off right in broad daylight. Things were not going to end well. She actually thought about bailing out the car and running, but she knew that she was slow as a turtle with two left feet. Besides, she damn sure couldn't dodge a speeding bullet. She glanced down at the bag at her feet and licked her lips, knowing that if she could get away with the money that Star had in it to pay for Ebony's ransom, this could quickly become her lucky day.

"Y'all muthafuckas need to be stopped!" Ki-Ki yelled, making the cop on Tonya's side turn his attention towards her.

Snatching open the back door, he violently yanked her out the car. She still had her hand on her purse and was prepared to pull out her gun when he turned away from her and reached for Tonya's door next.

Things were moving in slow surreal motion as cars passed with people gawking at the sight. A crowd of people standing on the street had begun to gather round, pulling out cellphones to record the entire incident just in case things went bad.

"Get out of the vehicle or I'll have to remove you myself!" the other cop yelled at Star after snatching open her door.

She glanced over at Ki-Ki and noticed that her face was twisted up, a determined, menacing expression covering it. Star shot her a warning glare and furtively tried to wag her head 'no,' hoping that Ki-Ki got the message and would stand down.

Then it happened.

With an expression on her face that told Star that she was ready to die if it was her time, Ki-Ki pulled out her gun, prepared to fire. Suddenly, a fusillade of shots rang out and there was a blood-curdling scream that Star hadn't even realized came from her own mouth until she dived down, out of the vehicle and onto the ground. She covered her ears with her hands as a seismic shiver seized her body, like a gigantic iron fist, wrapping around her with sheer terror.

Beside her, Brenda was hugging the asphalt as though it was her lifeline, her eyes stretched wide in fear as Star lay at her side. Their eyes connected and though neither one of them spoke, they could see that they were thinking the same thing: *Today just might be their last day.*

On the other side of the car, Tonya grasped the handle of the duffle bag in her hands and ducked down low in her seat as Ki-Ki and both police officers engaged in a battle of fire outside the car.

"Tonya, grab yo' gun!" Ki-Ki yelled out, using the car door as a shield. "Help me!"

That was the last thing that Tonya had in mind to do.

"Come up here," she told Ki-Ki, shouting over the sound of gunfire. "You'll get a better angle from behind my door."

With her head low, she watched Ki-Ki's face, wondering if she were dumb enough to listen.

"Drop your weapon!" one of the officer's yelled.

"Fuck you!" was Ki-Ki's response before she turned to Tonya. "Okay, I'ma come up there but you gotta cover me."

With a nod, Tonya pretended like she was reaching for her gun as Ki-Ki bit down on her bottom lip, conjuring up what she hoped was enough courage to make her move. She waited for a second to make sure that the police weren't about to fire and then moved swiftly, ducking under the car door to join Tonya by the passenger door so that she could get a better angle to fire on the police.

As soon as she was in place, Tonya grabbed her by her arm and yanked her up before pushing her forward roughly. With a loud yelp, Ki-Ki fell forward in front of the car where she instantly became target practice for the two officers who fired shot after shot into her body.

"Noooooo!" Brenda screamed as she witnessed Ki-Ki's body turn into Swiss cheese before her very eyes. "Ki-Ki, nooo!"

With the diversion she needed now in place, Tonya tucked the bag of cash under her arm and made her getaway with the sound of Brenda's grief-stricken howls of despair providing the soundtrack to her victorious moment.

CHAPTER 21

It was the middle of the night when Brenda and Star were released from the holding cell at the jail. To them, it felt like they'd been locked up for weeks rather than only a couple of hours. Although they occupied the same cell, few words were passed between them. Their thoughts were on the friend that they'd lost.

Squeezing her eyes closed, Brenda brushed a tear away from her cheeks as she walked into her dark apartment, wondering if Tonya had made it home. Of the four, she'd been the only one who had been able to escape. Once the gunshots ended, Brenda and Star were arrested and tossed in the back of the patrol vehicle where they were positioned in perfect view of Ki-Ki's mutilated body. She shivered when the image of what was left of Ki-Ki came to her mind's eye. For the rest of her life, she would never be able to shake it away.

"Tee?" she called out, turning on a lamp in the living room. When she saw that there was no one there, she immediately went for her phone, hoping that nothing had happened to her friend. Although they had their differences, she couldn't toss away the years she'd spent being Tonya's friend.

After shooting her a text letting Tonya know that she had been released and asking her to let her know that she was safe, Brenda peeled off her clothes and stepped right into the hall bathroom to take a shower. With the hot water burning her chocolate skin, she tried to push away the thoughts of everything that had transpired that day. As she lathered her body, she felt a feeling of vulnerability began to seep in and she found herself suddenly craving the love of her man. Moving quickly, she rushed to finish washing herself so that she could curl up in Kush's arms.

Brenda stepped out of the bathroom with a towel wrapped around her body and halted in the hall when she saw that the lamp that she'd turned off in the living room was now on. She took careful, light steps into the room, holding her breath along the way and only relaxed once her eyes fell on Tonya who was lying on the couch, scrolling through her phone.

"Girl, you scared me!" Brenda said, pressing her hand to her chest. "When did you get in?"

Tonya gave her an awkward look before replying.

"Just now. I was almost here when I got your text."

With a frown, Brenda asked, "Just now? Why you gettin' here so late?"

"I was scared. When y'all got arrested, I thought maybe the cops would come here lookin' for me or somethin' so I waited at the corner store across the street until you told me you was home."

A few moments of silence passed between them as Brenda stared at Tonya, working her mind around her story. It seemed truthful enough, yet there was an odd feeling bothering her that she couldn't explain. Almost as if her womanly intuition was urging her to call Tonya on her sit... for what, she wasn't sure.

"Okay, well, I'm goin' to bed. My emotions are fucked up so I'm 'bout to get some Vitamin D therapy, if you know what I mean." She laughed a little as she walked away.

Behind her back, Tonya rolled her eyes and curled her nose in disgust at the thought. She didn't bother turning on the TV, however, because she knew nothing would be happening for Brenda tonight as far as Kush was concerned. That ship had sailed already... over and over again, to be precise.

The second that Tonya walked in the door, just narrowly escaping the shoot-out between Ki-Ki and the police with her life, she jumped in the shower to clean blood spatter from her body and was still in there when Kush came home. After she explained what she'd been through, he rolled up a fat blunt to calm her down and then fucked her over and over until she was too tired to do anything but sleep.

With Brenda locked up and waiting for Kush to bail her out, they thought they would at least be able to share the night together before her return. They weren't banking on someone else posting bail for her which was why Tonya had still been wrapped up in between the sheets with Kush when Brenda arrived home. Thankfully, the text woke Tonya up in time so that she could hide in the closet before she was discovered, but when Brenda decided to shower first, she was able to make her getaway.

Dropping the towel, Brenda stepped over it and slid under the covers so that she could curl up under Kush who was sleeping peacefully with what appeared to be a smile on his face.

"Mmm, you're ready for me, I see," she said when she peeked under the covers and saw that he was already naked with his thick, juicy dick exposed and ready for her to mount. He wasn't totally soft but after a few minutes of her sucking on the fat mushroom head, she would be able to get him right where she needed him.

Reaching out, she grabbed his manhood in her hands and then squeezed, making the head sprout and spread from out of her closed fist. She smiled when Kush began to stir, sliding his arms out to wrap around her body.

"Damn, Tonya, ain't you had enough? We been at this shit all night."

Brenda's entire body went tense and all movement came to a complete stop. Even the air in her lungs ceased to flow once her brain registered the words that had just fallen from Kush's lips. She pressed away from him, abruptly forcing away his arms from around her body.

"Sexy Tee, why you runnin' from me?" Kush asked before yawning wide and then turning away.

He was still half asleep, a hazy, drunken slumber. The type that only came after some good weed and drinks, followed by some good sex.

Crushed, Brenda rolled onto her back and stared at the ceiling, processing what had just occurred. Ki-Ki was right about what she said. Tonya was sleeping with Kush behind her back.

Matter of fact...

She thought back to the feeling that she'd had earlier while speaking to Tonya.

She was in here with him when I came home.

One part of her mind was telling her to grab a knife from the kitchen and commit a double homicide. Through the years, the only thing she had been guilty of when it came to Tonya was of giving her total and complete loyalty. They'd became Gangstress together and she'd been Tonya's right hand while she was queen, not once harboring a shred of jealousy at playing the part of Tonya's do-girl who followed all of her commands without question.

Brenda lay there deep in her thoughts, unable to move, until the sun rose. When she felt Kush begin to wake, she closed her eyes and played like she was sleeping while listening to him move about the room. When he left the room to shower, she kept her eyes closed and listened to the hushed sound of him flirting with Tonya—whatever nonsense he was saying had her giggling like a school girl.

He's probably tryin' to get her to join him, Brenda thought, grinding her teeth against each other.

Once he'd left to do whatever it was that he did all day when she was home, so that he could come back and fuck Tonya as soon as she was gone, Brenda continued to lay in the bed, listening to the sound of Tonya moving about in the living room.

I gave this bitch somewhere to stay when she had no one. She ain't paid for shit the entire time and then got the nerve to fuck my man in my own mutha-fuckin' bed.

At some point that she couldn't remember, Brenda had grabbed her gun from out of her nightstand and was holding it in her hands, staring at the ceiling as she fingered it lovingly. She was on welfare; her rent was *four* fuckin' dollars and neither Tonya nor Kush's ass gave her a dime towards that. Electricity was $26 a month, gas was never more than $15 and her foodstamps paid for the food they shared. She provided everything to both of them and, in turn, they didn't do a damn thing to thank her for it.

With her gun in her hand, Brenda stepped out of the bedroom and began walking down the hall, the image of Ki-Ki's bullet-ridden body in her mind. But this time, it wasn't Ki-Ki's body that she was seeing. It was Tonya's.

"Shit!" Tonya cursed, jumping when she saw Brenda come from around the corner. "You scared the shit out of me. Damn, you walk light."

With her hand on her chest, Tonya let out a burst of nervous laughter as she glanced down at the duffle bag by her side. She had only just finished stuffing it full of all of her belongings as well as the money that she'd taken from Star when she saw Brenda walking up behind her.

Looking at the fury on her face, she darted her eyes down to the duffle bag, wondering if the reason behind Brenda's expression was because she'd seen her dump the bag of money in there.

Damn, she thought.

She had been banking on being able to keep the money for herself and not having to split it, but she would have no other choice but to break Brenda off with at least some of it in exchange for her silence.

"You goin' somewhere?" Brenda asked, holding the gun tightly to her side. Tonya was so worried about saving her ass from being found out about the money she stole that she didn't even realize that, right then, she needed to be saving her ass from her own former friend.

"Yeah, I mean... I think I been here long enough, don't you?" When Brenda didn't respond, Tonya continued, "I wasn't goin' to just bounce without tellin' you though. And I'ma give you some of the money for—"

Not wanting to hear another word, Brenda lifted the gun and leveled it at Tonya's head.

"Bitch, I don't want shit from you! I know you been fuckin' Kush behind my back, you grimy, disgustin', friendly-pussy havin' ass bitch!"

With her eyes stretched wide to the max, Tonya's mouth began to move, although no words came out. She was totally caught off-guard and lost all of her words. Of all the things for Brenda to be stepping to her about, her betrayal with Kush hadn't even been on her radar. They'd gotten away with it so long that she had long ago become relaxed in her indiscretions.

"I—I—I didn't—"

Whap!

Using the gun, Brenda knocked Tonya on the side of her head so hard that she almost knocked a tooth loose. She wasn't dumb; she knew that she couldn't fight Tonya one-on-one and win but the gun in her hand gave her some leverage.

"You lyin' bitch!"

Out of habit, Tonya came up with a fist, ready to pop Brenda in the face, but she was too late.

Whap! Whap! Whap!

Breaking her off with a quick two-piece and a hot, honey biscuit, Brenda alternated between the gun and her fist, trying her hardest to knock the air out of her body. By the time that Brenda pulled back, blood and sweat were dripping from Tonya's brow. She wanted to let her go but the sight of blood only seemed to infuriate her more. Before she knew it, she had pounced on top of the girl and was pummeling her mercilessly with blow after blow, beating Tonya's ass like she stole something from her elderly mama.

"Get da fuck out before I kill you!" she shouted once she was able to control herself enough to pull away again.

She didn't want to admit it, but Tonya had taken more than her own ass whooping; she'd taken the one meant for Kush as well. One that he'd deserved but Brenda wasn't ready to give. In some twisted way, she was used to Kush letting her down but she expected more from Tonya, who was supposed to be her closest friend.

Struggling to her feet, Tonya spewed blood from her lips and wiped the blood from her brow. Her fury at being beat and not being able to fight back caused her more agony than the pain of Brenda's attack, but there was nothing she could do being that she was unarmed. Brenda had the upper hand, but Tonya was willing to give her that because she would have the last laugh.

Plodding over to the duffle bag, she bent down to grab it but stopped when she felt the barrel of Brenda's gun pushing against her spine.

"Bitch, the only thing I'm lettin' you leave with is your life and the muthafuckin' clothes on your back. Now you got five seconds to get out of my sight."

Suddenly, Tonya realized that, for someone who thought the world was at her mercy, right then she wasn't too proud to beg. Briefly she considered rushing Brenda for her gun, but the odds weren't in her favor. She was already weak from the ass beating that she'd just endured. To try to fight now would be like volunteering to be shot.

"Brenda, please! I'm sorry for what I did but I ain't got nothin' to my name but the few things that I brought with me. Don't do this to me!"

"Bitch, please! Whatever trinkets you got in there that Polo gave you, I'm gon' pawn off and put it towards what you owe from stayin' here. Now get the hell on."

"But I made a mistake, I was alone and—"

Click!

The sound of the gun cocking made Tonya swallow her words as her eyes looked down the barrel of Brenda's gun, aimed and ready to fire a hot ball right through her skull. She pulled her lips into her mouth and briefly contemplated whether or not she believed that Brenda would pull the trigger. One glance at the icy, cold look of steel in her eyes told Tonya that the probability that she would was very high.

Fuck! she thought, her shoulders drooping low.

With her head bent down low, nearly hanging to the point that her chin was rubbing her chest, she walked slowly to the front door with Brenda behind her, jabbing the pistol at her back. All the plotting and planning that she'd done led her here to this moment. Once again she was penniless and homeless but her situation was even more grim because now, she was also friendless.

The second she shut the door behind Tonya, making sure to secure the chain lock so that she wouldn't have to worry about her coming back, Brenda felt her knees go weak. With great difficulty, she took heavy steps over to the couch and fell onto it, dropping her head into her hands. She felt like her entire world was crumbling around her. She needed to speak to someone but she had no one. For a moment, she thought about calling Star but quickly pushed away the thought. Not too long ago, she had been trying to slice Star from ear-to-ear over Tonya and now she was the only person she could consider a friend; it was almost embarrassing to think of telling Star what happened right then.

A buzzing sound, like a soft vibration, interrupted Brenda's thoughts and she lifted her head. With her eyes narrowed, darting back and forth across the small room, she tried to pick up on the source of the sound. When her focus settled on the duffle bag that Tonya had been trying to grab, she realized what it was.

"Stupid bitch left her phone."

Brenda let out a coarse laugh as she stood to her feet and walked over to the bag. She couldn't help but be curious about what messages she might find between her and Kush. If they were fuckin' behind her back, she didn't need to be a genius to know they were chatting and texting, too. She felt like a damn fool.

As soon as she opened the bag, her jaw dropped wide open when she saw the bundles of hundred-dollar bills stuffed inside.

"That fuckin' *bitch*!" Brenda couldn't believe her eyes.

When the only belongings they were given were the clothes they'd been wearing and the belongings they'd had on them at the time, she and Star had assumed that the money was going to be disposed of by the police, but they'd been wrong. Tonya's ass had stolen it all!

Pushing past the bundles of cash, she grabbed the cellphone from underneath and keyed in Tonya's birthday as the unlock code. It worked, as she knew it would, and she wasted no time scrolling to the text messages.

"This nigga..."

She sucked her teeth when she saw that the latest message had come from Kush, only seconds ago.

She gone yet? I'm missin' that sweet pussy already.

A sour taste settled in the back of her mouth and she swallowed it down before pushing herself to read their other messages. The more she read, the angrier she became and the more she wished that she had killed Tonya's ass. It was obvious that she didn't care about Kush and was only running game, but Kush was too stupid to see it. Whereas Brenda was stupidly in love, Tonya saw him as a trick and didn't have a shred of guilt about using him for what she wanted.

After she was done reading through every last one of Kush and Tonya's message chain, Brenda scrolled back to the messages and began looking over the other names in there. A chain of messages saved under the single letter 'A' caught her attention for some reason and she couldn't suppress her curiosity. Before she knew it, she'd opened the message chain, scrolled to the top, settled into the cushions of her couch and then began to read.

CHAPTER 22

TONYA HAD EXPERIENCED MORE THAN HER SHARE OF LIFE'S BULLSHIT but the situation she was in at the moment was, by far, the worst. Not only did she have nowhere to go but, thanks to Brenda, she didn't have a single dollar to her name. Not even a cellphone that she could use to call someone for help. In her mind, it made no sense why Brenda had been so mad when it was no secret that Kush had never been faithful. If anything, she should have been thankful to Tonya for showing her just how slimy his ass really was.

Stepping into a seedy corner store only a few blocks up from Brenda's apartment, she eyed the Arab man behind the counter, as he stared back at her, unable to stop his eyes from sliding down her curvy frame. Then again, he was most likely not making any attempts at hiding the lusty gaze in his eyes, but Tonya didn't complain because the more she gave him something to look at, the more likely it was that he would give in to a few small favors.

"Um... is there a phone in here I can use?" she asked, twirling a stray strand of hair around her finger, playing it coy, as she spun her body slightly to give him a good look at her booty cheeks hanging from the bottom of her shorts.

"Yes, we have phone," the man replied, licking his lips. "But it's not for customers."

"Oh," Tonya pretended to groan before tugging her shirt down to reveal a good sample of her cleavage. She looked around to make sure that the small store was empty before walking seductively over to the counter.

"Are you sure there is no way that I can use it?" she asked, pulling her shirt down even more.

By now, all but her nipples were showing of her bare chest. When it looked like the middle-aged man was about to cum on himself just from what he was seeing, she tugged down even more, letting one of the chocolate morsels pop out.

"Oops," she said with a smirk, making a show of fondling herself before she pressed the perky nipple back into her shirt. "I can show you even more if you let me use the phone."

The man was nearly salivating and almost before she could get her sentence out, he was already wagging his head. With her smirk still glued to her lips, Tonya walked around the counter and sat down on a stool, spreading her legs open as the man thrust the phone in her direction. With one hand, she pretended to play with herself as he watched her with his lips slightly parted and one hand groping his swelling manhood.

Thankfully, Tonya knew Assassin's number by heart from when he'd given it to her long ago while she was living with Polo. She didn't have the nerve to save it in her phone so she had to commit it to memory, something she was grateful for now. While serving up a full peep show to the Arab man behind the counter, she quickly dialed the number in her mind and waited for the line to ring.

"Who dis?"

A slight frown crossed over Tonya's face at Assassin's tone. His voice was panic-ridden, almost fearful.

"Um, this is Tee. I need you to come get me from the corner store on—"

"Hell nah, I ain't comin' out there," he shot back quickly. "I can scoop you but you gon' have to at least meet me halfway."

Halfway? she thought. There was no way she could get anywhere near halfway to Assassin's spot without a ride and, right now, she couldn't even afford a pass for the bus.

"I ain't got no money or no place to stay. Brenda kicked me out of her spot and the bitch wouldn't even let me get my shit first."

She purposely left out the part where the reason she'd been kicked out was because she had somehow gotten caught sleeping with Brenda's boyfriend.

"I got some things in mind that you can do to get some of yo' money back and get a place to stay but you gon' have to find a way out here. I don't know if you know it, but my cousin was killed and they found ole girl dead at her house. Word is that it was because Jaz's dumb ass was wearin' some necklace that somebody recognized. Anyways, rumors are that this was a Four Corner Hustler hit and the Disciples are lookin' for us. I can't leave out our territory."

"But you got a whole team of niggas with you!" she argued, thinking back to all the men he'd called over to gang rape her before backing out of it. "Why they can't come with you?"

"You must ain't heard what I said. I ain't tryin' to fuck with Polo like that."

This nigga, Tonya thought, wanting to roll her eyes at Assassin's cowardice.

She was so caught up in the conversation that she'd forgotten all about the man in front of her until, in his impatience, he reached out to squeeze her breast. Popping his hand, she watched as he backed away before continuing her conversation. She had gotten what she wanted so the little show he was getting was over.

"I'll be over there when I can," she said and then hung up the phone.

Jumping up from the stool she was sitting on, she muttered a smug 'thanks' at the man behind the counter and was just about to leave when a customer came in, thrusting a $50 bill in front of his face to pay for a couple cartons of cigarettes. Tonya paused mid-step as an idea came to mind. She watched the man open up the register to count out the change and her jaw nearly dropped at the cash inside. It wasn't a whole lot but it was more than enough for what she needed to do.

Patiently, she waited for the transaction to be over and the customer to leave.

"You think you can spare any of that?" she asked, playing up her sexy again. "I just need enough to catch a bus cross town... maybe get a room for the night."

"No."

The reply came fast, complete with a grunt and annoyed glare that said he had been tricked once already and wasn't in the mood to get played again.

"Your parents own this spot, right? You could just slip me a few bills and they wouldn't even care."

At her mention of that, the man turned towards her and cupped his crotch suggestively, to let her know that she would have to put in more work for the money. Tonya groaned inside, knowing that she was going to have to come harder this time but she reasoned that in exchange for that, she would simply charge him more. Plus, as she stared at what he was cupping in his hand, she figured he couldn't be working with much; a little head might be enough to get him off. And there was no way that he could be as repulsive to her as Assassin had.

"Let's go to the back," he suggested with a pointed eye towards a door behind where she stood.

She hesitated, weighing her options but also knowing that she didn't have a lot of time left. Once Brenda went in her bag, and especially if she decided to check her phone, there was a lot that she would find. Now that she'd discovered what was going on between Tonya and Kush, Tonya could no longer depend on Brenda's loyalty as a friend, and it was a real possibility that she might tell Star. Tonya needed an ally as quickly as possible and Assassin was her only hope.

"Fine," she muttered, dragging her feet as she reluctantly followed the man to the room behind the closed door not far from where she stood.

ABOUT AN HOUR LATER, Tonya stepped off the bus and stood on the sidewalk about a block away from Assassin's raggedy, broken down apartment building. As the bus took off behind, leaving a trail of black smoke and smog in its wake, she folded her arms in front of her chest and eyed the people walking around her. She was in territory that belonged to another gang and, although a truce had been formed between the Disciples and the Hustlers, Polo had called it off months before. She wasn't supposed to be here.

"Where the hell is this nigga?" she questioned under her breath as she looked around searching for Assassin who was supposed to pick her up from the bus stop.

As she swiveled on her feet, she couldn't help but notice a group of girls across the street staring hard at her. One look at the colors they proudly repped told Tonya that they were members of the female component to the Hustlers. There was no question in her mind that they recognized her; after all, at one time, she'd been the Gangstress queen and her long blue mohawk was still very much intact.

The group of girls stood suddenly, and Tonya took off walking down the street as if she had somewhere to go while making sure to keep her eye on them from her peripheral. She'd been a fighter her whole life but fighting one bitch was a lot different from fighting five.

Just as the group took off in a trot, headed in her direction, a red and black Camaro swerved to a stop on the side of the road beside where Tonya stood. She sucked in her breath, her eyes widening as she turned to look in the vehicle. It wasn't until she saw Assassin sitting behind the wheel, with Silk on the passenger side, that she was able to relax.

Once parked, he noted the group that had their eyes set on Tonya and, with one hand lifted in the air, began to wave them away.

"Aye, she good. She with me," he said.

One of the girls, a thick yellow-bone, looked like she wasn't feeling Assassin's interference, but she backed away anyways. Still, she kept Tonya in her line of scrutiny, watching her closely from the moment that she ducked into the backseat of the car until the second that Assassin drove away.

The entire drive to Assassin's apartment, all Tonya could think about were the details to her new plan. During the long bus ride over, she allowed her mind to run rampant with thoughts of what she could do in order to get back the money that she'd left at Brenda's so that she could leave and start her new life. There was a possibility that Brenda hadn't gone through her things and if that was the case, she could easily get Assassin's car, steal one of his guns and run up in the apartment to get it back. Once the money was back in her hands, she wouldn't stop driving until she made it out of the state.

"I got some of my homeboys over here. Hope you don't mind," Assassin said as he led the way up the cracked and dingy steps to his apartment.

Tonya followed behind him, curling her nose at the stench of piss, dog shit and garbage. For someone who claimed to be a 'real nigga,' making big money in the streets, Assassin lived in the slums. Silk walked quietly behind. He hadn't said a single thing since the moment Tonya sat in the car, but he'd been talking a mile a minute beforehand, trying to get Assassin to rethink helping her.

Glaring into the back of her skull, for the first time in his life, he sincerely felt the urge to want to kill someone. Because of her, the Hustlers were at war with the Disciples and, because of her, Star's sister was dead. He hadn't known of the plot to kidnap Ebony and hold her for ransom but, if he had, he'd immediately put a stop to it. Although no one was aware, he'd been crushing on Star since they were six years old.

"Damn, bae, you lookin' good with them thick ass thighs," one of Assassin's friends shouted.

She rolled her eyes and the others began to hoot, whistle and wag their tongues in the air while panting like dogs in response to her sass. Beside her, Assassin laughed at their sheer disrespect before turning to Tonya to shrug.

"What can I say? Shit... you fine."

With a scowl on her face, she grabbed him by his arm and drug him to a room in the back. Not only was this the last place that she wanted to be, but she was also running out of time.

"Listen," she began once they were alone behind a closed door. "I need to borrow your car and a gun. We weren't able to get the money since yo' dumb ass cousin got the girl killed, but I was able to take some money that Star stashed at Brenda's. If I can get back over there, I can get it before she asks for it back."

Twisting up his face, Assassin eyed Tonya with suspicion, wondering how much he could trust her. As it was, the only reason she was here now was because she'd betrayed everyone around her. She hadn't told him, but he was well-aware of the fact that she'd been sleeping with Kush behind Brenda's back. Kush was the neighborhood weed man; not only did everyone know him but he was always running his mouth every chance he got.

"How much money you talkin'?"

"Like 25 Gs," Tonya lied without hesitation. "I can split it with you."

Assassin frowned. "Shit, that's it?"

With a nod, she confirmed her lie, unwilling to budge because she knew that he would settle for that much, even though it was a far cry less than what they'd originally sought out to earn. One glance at his dingy residence told her that he couldn't afford to say no to money, no matter how meager the amount. Then again, she wasn't planning on giving him a single dollar anyways so it didn't matter the amount.

"I'll let you hold my whip and I'll give you a pistol."

A gracious smile spread across her face and Tonya's spirits immediately lifted. That is, until he continued speaking.

"But it's gon' cost you." He grabbed his dick for emphasis. "I been thinkin' 'bout that sweet pussy since the last time I seen you. Them lips, too. So what dat mouf do?"

The disgust that encompassed her just at the thought of doing anything sexually with Assassin again had her considering if it was really worth it. Maybe there was another way to get the money. Maybe she could go back to the Arab and convince him to hand over his car if she gave up more than just head. He wasn't the best that she'd been with but at least he bathed. That fact was still questionable as far as Assassin was concerned.

"C'mon, I ain't got all day and, from what you said, you don't either."

He pulled off his shirt, exposing a soiled wife beater that he wore underneath, and Tonya bristled. An idea popped up in her mind and she decided to give it a try.

"What 'bout doin' it in the shower this time? You bathe me, I bathe you..."

He batted her suggestion away with a wave of his hand.

"Ain't nobody got time for that shit."

With her gut twisting inside her, Tonya began to slowly pull off her clothing as she lost all resolve. Every second, she reminded herself that this was just a means to an end. Once it was all said and done, she would be a hundred grand richer and on her way to start her new life.

The sound of metal banging against something hard made her flinch and she looked up, locking eyes with Assassin's gun which he'd laid on the nightstand next to the bed. Tightened on the end of it was a silencer, used to muffle out the sound of the gunshots. An evil plan began to work through her mind as she stared at the weapon, only able to pull her eyes away when she noticed Assassin's attention on her.

"You ready?" she teased, delaying for time as she took her time wiggling out of her panties.

"Hell yeah, you takin' too damn long already. A nigga coulda bust a nut by now."

Biting down on his bottom lip, Assassin held his dick in his hand and began priming it up, stroking it hard as he ran his eyes over her voluptuous curves. His mouth began to moisten as he looked at her and then licked his lips in anticipation. Tonya had the best pussy he'd ever had the pleasure of sampling.

"Let me get on top," she said, lifting her leg to straddle him. "Grab on to my ass with both hands. I like that shit."

He eagerly agreed, moaning in ecstasy once she positioned her pussy over his erect dick. Squeezing hard on her ass, he kneaded it with his fingers like Play-doh, loving the softness of her smooth skin. Tonya's eyes shot over to the gun on the dresser and she wound her body seductively in front of him, grasping the headboard as she prepared to grab the gun.

"Put it in for me," she told him, cooing into his ear. "I like how you do that shit. Pull on my ass cheek with the other hand while you shove it in. That rough shit gets me so wet."

Drunk off the smell of her and loving the way that she was taking control of the situation, Assassin was only too eager to fall in line with her requests.

"Damn, ma," he whispered after dipping a single finger into her wetness before moving to slip his dick inside of her cave. "You wet as fuck."

Tonya nodded in agreement. She was wet but it had nothing to do with him. Her mind was on how close she was to finally meeting all of her goals. The same moment that Assassin grabbed his dick, she carefully leaned over and snatched up his gun. He was so caught up in the pleasure that he just knew was coming that he didn't even realize when she pointed the end of the silencer right at his chest.

Zip!

She let out one silenced bullet right into his heart, stopping it before his brain even got a chance to register what had happened. Blood began to seep through the hole in his chest from both ends, soaking through onto the sheets under his body as Tonya lifted up and pulled away from him, finally able to let out a long, heavy breath.

She moved quickly to put back on her clothes and then ran through Assassin's pockets, collecting his keys as well as the small bit of cash that he had on him. Outside, she heard the other members of his crew laughing and carrying on as they had before, but she knew that they wouldn't bother Assassin as long as they thought she was in there. In order to buy her enough time to get out and get a good distance away, hopefully into Disciple territory, before what she'd done was discovered, she had to escape out the window.

With her heart beating ferociously in her chest, Tonya snatched back the dusty sheet covering the window and pulled the cord on the side to lift the blinds. The moment her eyes focused on a familiar figure right outside the window, she almost pissed on herself and dropped down so fast that she almost smacked her head against the floor.

"Oh *shit!*"

Polo was outside, accompanied by Trey and some others, and he was heading up the stairway to Assassin's apartment.

With her breathing nearly stalling to a complete stop in her lungs, scenario after scenario began to run through Tonya's mind of what she could do. Every single one that dealt with her staying where she was seemed to lead to the very real possibility of her ending up dead. She had to go and she had to go *now!* Reaching out, she grabbed Assassin's hooded jacket off the floor and pulled it on, not even bothered by the stench as she pulled the hood over her head to conceal her blue hair.

A loud noise, like the sound of the front door being smashed in, startled her to the point that she jumped to her feet and she moved quickly to open the window, praying to God that no one was standing outside to witness her escape.

Her feet hit the ground outside the window with a loud thump and she crouched down low, freezing for a moment to make sure that she hadn't been spotted. Behind her, she could hear the sound of shouting as the terrifying crack of gunshots ripped through the air, creating in her a paralyzing fear. Swallowing hard, she kept her head low and forced herself to run, holding Assassin's gun by her side. It, along with the small bit of cash that she'd stolen out of his pockets, was all that she had available to make her escape.

CHAPTER 23

"FUCK... SOMEBODY GOT TO THIS NIGGA ALREADY," POLO SAID AS HE looked down at Assassin's dead body. "A chick, most likely. The nigga still holdin' onto his dick."

Assassin was lying on the bed with one hand still wrapped around his penis, his eyes stretched wide, staring at some invisible object in the sky. The bloody hole in the center of his chest left no questions as to how he'd been killed. However, it also let Polo know that he couldn't have possibly been killed by a stray bullet. The shot was clear through his chest and, as he saw when he lifted the shoulder up a bit, had gone straight through the mattress beneath.

"Grab the kid so he can tell us who was in here," Polo commanded.

Trey wasted no time following his instructions. Within less than a minute, he was back by his leader's side, holding Silk who was trembling like an autumn leaf in his arms. At the boy's head, he had the barrel of his gun pressed.

Pointing at the body, Polo turned to look Silk in his eyes.

"Somebody did this before we got here," he told him and paused to watch as Silk's eyes grew large with surprise. "I already told you that I wasn't gon' touch you because of who your pops is so now you need to do me a favor. Who was in here with him?"

There really wasn't a need in asking because Silk would have given him the information for free. He couldn't stand Tonya and there was nothing more that he wanted right then than to tell him that his ex-girl and the former queen of the Gangstress had been messing with Assassin for some time now.

"T-T-T-Tonya," he stuttered before taking a breath to steady his words. "She and Assassin been workin' together. They was tryin' to get paid after they kidnapped Star's sister, but they didn't expect her to die."

Running his hand over his mouth, Polo gritted his teeth so hard that they made a scratching sound that made Silk's skin crawl.

"I knew I shoulda killed that bitch," he muttered to himself as he took in the scene. "She can't be far," he said to Trey. "Tell some of them niggas out there to go look for her. They need to hit me up when they've found her."

"I saw her," a voice said, making Trey, Polo and even Silk stop to turn their heads towards the speaker. "I didn't know it was her but I saw a chick runnin' down the street with a hood on her head. I ain't know she came from in here."

Polo eyed the boy, immediately sizing up his deadpan expression and the expressionless stare in his eyes. He also recalled that he was one of the ones who had fearlessly walked into Assassin's apartment busting shot after shot with stunning accuracy. At the moment, he was down more than a few hittas and Polo had room to add another to the team.

"What's your name?"

The boy, no more than maybe seventeen in age, lifted his chin, regarding Polo with respect but also without fear.

"Tony. I've been a Disciple since I was thirteen years old." His pride showed in his tone.

With a nod, Polo said, "With Kato out, that leaves room for a new hitta. Based on how you handled shit today, I might have to see 'bout puttin' you on."

Tony nodded but showed no excitement, or any other emotion rather, at his words. To Polo, that was a good sign. The best hittas were the ones who fulfilled the role out of loyalty and commitment instead of glory and shine.

"He would be perfect for the job," Trey added. "His accuracy is on point. That's why I asked him to ride out with us today. Especially since we ain't been able to get in touch with Sloan."

The look in Trey's eyes at the mention of Sloan's name was about as sour as the taste on Polo's tongue. Not only had he refused to give him Star's address but he hadn't seen or heard from him since after they returned from setting Kato's mother's house on fire. It wasn't a good sign. Although he had wanted to keep Sloan on the team, the more time that passed, it became evident where his loyalty lay.

"That nigga won't be a problem soon," he said, rubbing his hands together. "We need to move on what we discussed tonight." Polo ran his eyes over to Tony who was standing silently next to Trey, appearing to have no opinion at all about the topic of discussion. "Matter of fact, take Tony with you to get it done. It can be his initiation into his new position."

"You want me to handle him?" Trey said, pointing his gun down at Silk who winced under the focus of the barrel. "He heard everything."

Polo shook his head. It didn't matter what Silk heard, the boy was no gangsta. Even now, he was cowering on the floor, afraid to even lift his head to look as Trey pointed the gun at him. He was a pussy in every sense of the word and it benefitted them to have Silk on the Hustler team. If ever they needed to find a weak link, he was it.

"Nah, leave him."

Back in the car, Trey drove and Tony took his place in the back seat as Polo scrolled through his phone, seeing more than a few texts stating that Yesman was looking for him, as well as a text from Star letting him know that she'd been bonded out of jail and had made it home. He ignored the text about Yesman, knowing that it concerned some bullshit that he didn't want to deal with, and then quickly read another text that made him frown.

"Hello? You got my message?"

"Yeah, good lookin' out," he replied, toying with the patch of hair on his chin. "Listen, I need you to send me ole girl's address. I gotta pay her a visit."

There was silence on the other line as Brenda swallowed hard, wondering why Polo would request something like this unless to do harm to Star. She was sworn to obey his orders but her loyalty was with Star, too. She couldn't betray her.

"I—uh, I mean..."

"I'm not goin' to hurt her," Polo replied. "And in exchange for your loyalty for this and for lettin' me know 'bout Tonya, I'll let you keep some of the money she stole."

Brenda shifted uneasily as she held on to the phone.

"Ohhhkaaaayyy," she agreed, simply because she had no other choice. Polo was making nice by offering her money because she knew that if she refused to give him what he wanted, the penalty would cost her life.

"Text it to me. And don't tell Star shit. I want it to be a surprise."

"FUCK!" Kato cursed, nearly jumping five feet in the air when he heard the sound of the front door opening before slamming closed.

Springing forward, he snatched up the can of Febreze sitting next to him and began spraying it liberally around Star's room before running over to open a window. There was no telling how long he'd been locked away in the apartment, cut off from the world, smoking blunt after blunt as he thought about his sordid future. He didn't even know what day it was or how long Star had been gone. Briefly, he wondered if it was the weed that had him unable to recall details or if it was a side-effect of his condition.

After a few moments passed without Star storming into the room to yell at him for having her entire apartment smelling like a marijuana farm, Kato frowned. His fingers flexed next to where his gun should have been, stashed at his waist. Its absence was a quick and sudden reminder that he'd left it in the living room, where he'd been before he took it upon himself to trade out the sofa for Star's bed.

"Ebony, nooooo, please God, nooooo."

The weight of Star's pain could be heard clearly through her tormenting wails and Kato immediately relaxed the tension out of his body. Dropping his head, he stood still for a moment, listening to her cry out for her sister. He didn't need to ask any questions; it was more than obvious what had occurred.

He had no words in mind of what to say but knew he had to be near Star in that moment. Seeing her sprawled out on the couch, crying into the cushions as he stood there feeling helpless, ignited a feeling inside of him that he couldn't explain. He'd created this feeling of grief and torment in so many others but, besides inflicting this sort of pain, he had no idea as to how to deal with it. His mind was telling him that she needed him—he knew that she did—but he had no idea how to be there for someone who was experiencing a loss. In his lifestyle, people died all the time, but it was just part of the game. There was no mourning because that outcome was expected.

Reaching out, he placed a hand on the back of her head and ran it through her hair, hoping that, if anything, he could show support by simply being there.

"My baby's dead," Star cried out to him once she was aware of his presence beside her. "They killed her. Buried her alive... I just had to tell my grandma that my fuckin' sister was buried alive! I had to tell her that there is no body to bring home... I can't even have a funeral for her."

Damn, Kato thought, wondering who would be as heartless to do something like that to a child. That was beyond even the things he'd done.

"You should have told me. I would've come with you. You shouldn't have had to deal with that shit alone."

"It was my fault. I knew that somethin' was goin' to happen to her. I knew I should've made her stay with me." She cried harder, becoming almost hysterical.

With his high now gone, Kato felt the re-emergence of the migraine that he'd had more often than not since leaving the hospital.

"Star, you gotta calm down," he asked, but she was too caught up in her own sorrow to hear his words.

He pushed his hands to both sides of his skull, wincing in pain. The more she cried, the more his head began thumping, like a sledgehammer was beating against his skull. His vision blurred and the pain became almost unbearable. Though she wasn't even as loud as before and had started to quiet down, the acute throbbing in his skull was no less.

"Shit, I told you to shut the fuck up!" he almost growled out in anger, holding his fists in the air as if he were going to hit her. He threw a punch and it landed on the wall behind her, forming a fist-sized hole not too far from her face.

Both of them were equally shocked at his outburst but the way that Star jumped away from him, her moist eyes filled with fear, made Kato wish he could take it back. He tried to reach out for her but she recoiled from his touch while wiping tears from her narrowed eyes. She wasn't the same weak person that she had been with Polo and, though it was partly thanks to Kato, she refused to take from him the same abuse he'd saved her from.

"You need to leave. Now! I should have never let you stay here from the beginning."

Kato felt like shit. Star was the only person he had, the only one left who believed in him.

"I would've never hit you for real."

"It wouldn't be the first time," she spat out in response, referring to the night they both wanted to forget, in her grandmother's apartment.

Something about her mention of that night made a wave of some emotion Star couldn't read pass through his eyes and then his gaze dropped, staring at the gun—his gun—that she was holding at her side. When he lifted his head back to her face, there was a blank expression there and Star couldn't help but wonder what he was thinking.

"Let me get my shit and I'm out," he said, not waiting for her to respond before turning back to walk down the hall.

Letting out a heavy exhale, Star dropped the gun on the couch and sank into the cushions, feeling a new kind of devastation in that moment. She didn't want Kato to leave and she had to admit that she knew there was no way he would hit her. Something had happened to make him react how he did and the fact that he'd been holding onto his head right before it happened was a clue that it was something very wrong.

Standing up, she began to walk to the hallway to stop him.

"Kato, I—"

Before she could finish, a whooshing sound—the sound of a silenced bullet being shot—interrupted her, followed by a thump as the handle of her door fell off on to the floor. Star turned to snatch up Kato's gun only to find that it had fallen through the middle of the couch cushions. Before she could go for it, her front door was pushed open and in walked Polo, with two other men by his side, all staring at her as she stood in the middle of the living room, frozen in place. Only a second later, about a dozen others piled into the apartment behind him and Star swallowed hard, trying not to look down the hall toward Kato who was only a few feet away in her bedroom.

"Polo!" she intentionally yelled, hoping Kato heard her. "What are you doing here? And why do you have all these Disciples with you?"

Standing with all the poise and confidence of a gangsta surrounded by a legion of goons, Polo simply smiled back at her.

CHAPTER 24

WHEN THE FRONT DOOR WAS BLOWN OPEN, KATO WAS IN THE bedroom, filling his pockets with the only belongings he had to his name since his apartment was under surveillance: a few baggies of weed, rolling paper and one change of clothes. His vision was doubled, and he was in no condition to be out on his own, being that he was a wanted man, but there was no way that he would stay in Star's apartment if she didn't want him there. However, after hearing Star yell Polo's name from the living room, he realized that there was a very real possibility that he wouldn't make it out of there with his life.

Once more out of sake of habit, he reached to his side for his gun before remembering that the last place it had been was in Star's hand when she asked him to leave.

Fuck! he shouted in his mind.

Walking carefully, he took quiet steps over to the door to listen to the conversation coming from the other side.

"I'm sorry 'bout what happened to your sister but it's time for me to put an end to this shit," Polo was saying. "That nigga Assassin is dead. I laid down about a dozen Hustlers today to deliver a message. Now it's time for you to do your part."

Star's heart tightened in her chest and she couldn't resist glancing down the hall, praying that Kato wasn't able to hear the conversation. She knew that her prayers were useless. There was no doubt in her mind that he was hearing every word.

"You said that you would help me set that nigga, Kato, up and now is the time to do it," Polo continued.

Silent, Star didn't say a word. There was nothing she could say. Even if she wanted to, to admit that Kato had been with her was to admit that she had been helping him hide. It was a death sentence. She decided to take her chances and play dumb.

"I don't know where he is and he's not answerin' my calls," she lied with a shrug. "I haven't heard from him."

"Really?" Polo said, not really asking. "Because I smell somethin' familiar in here. Trey, you smell that shit?"

Curling his lips into a smile, Trey nodded his head.

"Yeah, I smell it. Smells like somebody been smokin' some fat ass blunts."

Star's breath caught in her lungs when Polo nodded and looked back at her, waiting for an answer.

"You know I smoke every now and then," she shrugged again.

"Oh yeah? Well, who put that big ass hole in the wall?" he nudged his head in the direction of the hole Kato had made with his fist.

Star dropped her head to lie, shifting from foot-to-foot as she tried to keep her nerves in check.

"I—I... I did it. I haven't been myself after Ebony..."

Her words trailed off as tears came to her eyes. The reaction was genuine but Polo couldn't let go of his suspicions and began walking around the apartment inspecting everything as he spoke to her in a threatening tone.

"That's right... your sister," he began. "You told your grandmother what happened?"

Sniffling, Star nodded her head.

"So she pretty much all you got... her and Roxy, anyways. It would be pretty fucked up if somethin' happen to yo' grams over some shit you could have dealt with yourself."

Lifting her eyes, Star frowned deeply at his words. "What do you mean?"

Polo was only too eager to explain further.

"I mean, when I'm not focused on shit, accidents happen. And I haven't been able to focus on shit with Kato runnin' 'round. You may not know it yet, but an accident happened yesterday and that nigga's mama got caught up with a bullet to the brain. I'd hate for another accident to happen to Geraldine before I can find him."

Fresh tears filled up in Star's eyes as she processed what Polo was saying. He'd had Kato's mother killed and, most likely, Kato had just heard it for himself.

"Tell me you didn't."

Even as she said it, she knew that he had.

"Didn't what? Kill that nigga's ole lady?" Polo's brow shot up on his forehead as he stopped to look at her. "Yeah, I did. Sloan was with me and helped me do it. Yo' girl ain't tell you?"

He was gaming her and Star knew it. There was no way Kevia knew anything about this but that didn't make Polo's revelation hurt any less.

"I—I'll do it," she said, brushing a tear from her eye. "I promise. I'll let you know as soon as I hear from him."

Still not totally satisfied, Polo gave her a long look before turning around and heading down the hallway, opening doors along the way with his .45 mm pointed ahead of him and a couple of his Disciples trailing behind. Star took a step to walk after him but was stopped by Trey.

"You got somethin' to hide?" he asked maliciously.

Without responding, she snatched back from him and stood firmly in place, appearing as calm as possible. On the inside, her mind was raging with alarm and fear.

Polo vigilantly observed his surroundings as he took steps down the hall of Star's apartment, poised and ready to bust his gun on anything that moved. His gut told him that she was lying; that not only did she know where Kato was but that he was right there in the apartment with her.

The only thing that boggled him was he knew for a fact that if Kato had heard him about having his mother killed, he wouldn't still be in hiding which was one reason Polo had mentioned it. He was counting on Kato to have heard it and come out of hiding so that the ensemble of Disciples could quickly fill his body with bullets.

Motioning to a Disciple behind him, he urged for him to open the door to Star's bedroom and stepped behind him to use him as a shield in case Kato popped up and popped off with shots. He stood on edge as the door swung open and let out a breath only when he saw the room was empty.

"No one's here," the Disciple in front of him said after checking the closet.

Polo eyed the open window and tightened his fist around his gun. "But someone may have been."

EVERY MUSCLE in Star's body was tense and remained that way long after Polo and the last of his Disciples left, but still she couldn't relax. Her breathing was heavy and labored as if she'd run a marathon and her skin burned as if her blood was pumping acid in her veins. She had an unsettled spirit. After losing one family member, she was now in a position where she had to decide whether to betray the man she loved or risk losing another.

Sulking, she collapsed onto the couch, dropped her head into her hands and squeezed her eyes closed, feeling as hopeless as one possibly could. When she opened her eyes, she flinched in surprise when she saw two shoes positioned in front of her. With a sharp gasp, she lifted her head and was greeted by a strong hand around the neck, squeezing so hard that her windpipe was closed off. Like a fish out of water, she gasped without air, making her mouth gape in anguish as she tried to sip air into her lungs. Her eyes bugged out of her skull from the struggle but once she saw who was clutching her by the neck, they bugged even further in surprise.

"I heard everything," Kato said, his voice low and rugged with deadly intent.

His eyes were cold and heartless, just as they had been the night that she almost killed him. She tried to utter a sound, a word, anything to stop him so that she could explain but his grip was so tight, she couldn't get anything out.

"That muthafucka killed my moms and you've been workin' with him the entire time... Using him to find your sister and agreein' to have me killed as soon as you got your needs out the way."

Clawing at his hands, Star felt herself grow weak as he squeezed the life out of her body. Tears spilled down her blurred eyes as she began to panic, fighting with everything in her to force him away. Baring his teeth, Kato only applied more pressure, fighting through the aching of his own heart that was telling him that he was making a mistake. In his rage, he was unfeeling but his affections for Star were so deep that he couldn't ignore how he felt about her. He was both mourning her death and egging it on at the same time.

Out of sheer desperation, Star began kicking and squirming with the last of her strength. At some point, her fist connected with the side of Kato's head, sending a radiating pain through his skull that started at the exact place where he'd suffered the gunshot wound.

"Fuck!" he shouted and released her to clutch the side of his head.

Star collapsed onto the couch, gasping in gulps of air to sooth her burning lungs. In between ragged breaths, she forced herself to speak to Kato, eager to make him hear her before he attacked her again.

"I—I—wasn't betraying—you," she heaved out and swallowed hard before continuing. "I would have never—given you up—to Polo. If I was, I would have done it then. Or before."

Rubbing the side of his head, Kato turned to look at her with narrowed eyes, unsure of whether he could believe her. Was she telling the truth or was this just a desperate attempt to save her own life?

"After you left, that day at *The Spot*, he made me go with him. I had no choice... my sister was missin', you were gone. He was gonna kill me if he knew I was in love with you."

She was speaking and he heard her, but he was lacking in what was needed in order to decide whether there was any truth in her words. His mind was preoccupied by his anger and there was no way he could reason around it. He had an appetite for murder and the emotions that she was trying to illicit from him couldn't see a way around it.

"Gun," he said, holding his hand out.

Under bent brows, Star hesitated for a moment, wondering if it was a good idea to give him the tool he'd need to end her life, swiftly this time. After realizing that she had little choice in the matter, she pointed between the cushions on the couch. Kato went for it quickly, checking the chamber to count the bullets, and then pushed it in the band of his waist as Star let out an inaudible sigh of relief.

Without another word said, Kato turned to leave, making his exit as quickly and soundlessly as he'd arrived. As Star ran her fingers over the throbbing skin around her neck, she watched him slip away, utterly confused about what she felt. On one hand, she was wondering if it would be the last time she'd ever see him again and on the other, she wondered if she really wanted to.

KATO PULLED up to *The Spot* driving a stolen car that he'd acquired by use of the fully loaded AK that he was holding at his side. The gun, as well as more than a dozen others, he'd gotten after making an impromptu visit to one of the Disciples' storage facilities where they stored their guns. With Polo paranoid to the point that he didn't travel unless he had double the entourage he normally kept with him, the warehouse was severely understaffed and Kato was able to overtake the few men outside with ease.

Tony and a few others sat outside of *The Spot*, keeping watch and making sure that no one started any drama that would make the block hotter than it already was. When they saw the unfamiliar red Corvette turn onto the street, all of the Disciples were instantly on high alert.

"Yo, forks up!" Tony yelled, sounding the alarm, to let the Disciples inside know that he needed them outside.

As the car approached, he stood with his hand at his side, pulling out his pistol when he saw it begin to slow as it got nearer to the trap house. When the door opened, he took off the safety and waited on edge, noting that there was only one person in the car. The person stepped out, and immediately he let out a sharp breath when he saw who it was.

"Kato," he said under his breath before turning to look at the men around him. "Stand down. Don't shoot."

A few fearful glances were shot his way—Disciples who were wondering why he was ordering for them not to shoot when it was clear by the guns that Kato held in his hands, that he was most definitely looking for smoke.

"Don't shoot?" one was brave enough to ask. "What we 'posed to do then? Sit here and help his ass with target practice?"

Tony shot him a strong look. "I'll give the word on when it's time. Just stay ready and wait for my signal."

That said, he turned his attention back to Kato who was standing next to the car, guns in hand, looking into each face of the men who stood before him.

"I already know your leader too pussy to be here," he began, shouting loud enough to be heard. "But it don't matter because, on God, I swear I'ma handle his ass later."

Tony felt the man next to him tense up at the threat on Polo's life and he cut his eyes at him to warn him not to take action on his own.

"Which one of y'all muthafuckas had somethin' to do with my mama bein' killed?"

Kato's question hung in the air as all the Disciples gave him their own version of incredulous looks, Tony included. None of them had heard a thing about Kato's mother being killed. Some way, Polo had been able to keep the news from spreading, hoping that he was able to get to Kato before it was found out. Unfortunately for him, he was too late.

"Listen, man, we don't know anything 'bout your moms," Tony said, stepping up to speak for them all. "This is the first time we are hearin' of it. So whoever had somethin' to do with it ain't here."

A few moments of silence passed as Kato looked at each man, searching for a hint of a lie. He didn't want to fire on his brothers if they didn't deserve it. Yet, he had to get to the bottom of the situation and he knew who he had to speak to. There was one person other than Polo who had all the answers.

"Where is Sloan?"

When Tony hesitated to answer, Kato lifted his gun and fired at the man standing next to him. Blood splattered from his body onto Tony but, although the other Disciples flinched at the sight of their fellow gang member's body dropping to the ground, the center of his chest smoking from the hot ball that Kato had put through it, Tony barely moved.

"I can do this all day," Kato said with a slight curl of a smile on his lips. "Now where is Sloan?"

With his finger on the trigger of his weapon, he was prepared to have to use it again, even fully prepared for another shoot-out if the moment called for it. He didn't regret killing the man whose body lay at Tony's feet because, just from looking at him, it was easily seen where his loyalty lay. The hatred in his eyes as he glared at Kato told him that he was loyal to Polo so he had to go, but Kato didn't want to have to kill the others. However, the choice wasn't his; it was Tony's.

"I'll tell you," Tony agreed before putting his gun behind his back, pressed against his spine.

With a simple nod, Kato tossed his weapons into the open car door and watched him approach. Tony peeped the move but he knew Kato well enough to know that he had more than a couple other guns on him. He would never be caught without one; that was a gangsta rule, one that Kato had taught him himself.

ONLY A FEW HOURS LATER, Tony was still sitting on the front stoop of *The Spot*, this time on edge because he knew that a lot of good men would soon fall. Although he warned Sloan that Kato was looking for him, he knew that there was no way that Sloan would hide. They were Gangster Disciples and both of them took the 'gangster' part of the term seriously. Hiding from another nigga wasn't something that was part of their pedigree.

"Polo still ain't answerin' the phone," one of the Disciples told Tony, walking out from the inside. "Should we just bury the body in the back?"

"Hell nah, what da fuck kinda stupid shit is that?" Tony spat and looked at the man like he'd lost his mind. "Keep his ass in the freezer for now until we can get somebody to clean this shit up."

"Heads up," the Disciple sitting next to him said. "Ya boy's back."

Tony lifted his head and, sure enough, the red Corvette was cruising back down the street, this time at top speed.

"Forks up!" Tony shouted, this time his heart beating wildly in his chest, although he was forcing himself not to show it.

From the way that Kato was driving, he was on some reckless shit. That fact became even more evident when Kato chose not to decelerate until the last minute and instead swerved the car around in the middle of the street. With the back of the vehicle facing them, he rammed backwards, pelting right into the side of the front porch, forcing a couple Disciples to dive sideways to escape from being crumpled under his back tires.

"I got a special delivery for Polo," Kato said, jumping out of the car before it had barely stopped moving.

"Kato, what da fuck, man?!" Tony exclaimed with his hands up, scrutinizing the damage to the infamous trap house. "Yo, this shit ain't got nothin' to do with us and we don't wanna be forced to choose between you and Polo. You brought me up—trained me. Just keep this shit between you, Polo and Sloan."

"I ain't here on no bullshit," Kato replied with a mysterious smirk on his face as he walked to the trunk that was pressed against a column that was struggling to stand. "Like I said, I got a special delivery."

Tony, every Disciple that had been inside, as well as curious onlookers from the street all watched, most of them from a safe distance, wondering what it was that Kato was up to. With a press of a button, the trunk opened and everyone in eye's view of the tragic sight inside groaned at its contents.

"Who is that?" Tony asked with his nose curled up on his face, disgusted at the sight of the mutilated, headless body inside.

Pretending to take a double look inside the trunk, Kato frowned. "You mean you don't recognize him?"

He reached in and lifted one of the lifeless hands, stiff now that rigor mortis had begun to set in.

"It's Sloan." He shrugged. "I guess it's a little hard to tell."

Reaching into the trunk, he grabbed what looked like a wallet and tossed it at Tony's feet.

"I been lookin' for Polo, Trey and the rest of them niggas involved but them pussy ass niggas all in hidin'," Kato continued, his tone now serious. "So I'll leave this with you. Polo wanted my attention and now he got it."

His message had been spoken loud and clear. With his head lifted and his eyes never leaving Kato, Tony watched as his mentor, the man he looked up and promised his loyalty to, walked back down the streets without a care in the world. He walked the hood like he owned it when, in fact, he was in dangerous territory. But Tony would never allow anyone to pull a gun on Kato, if it were up to him. And thanks to Polo putting him in charge as his Enforcer, it *was* up to him.

"You want me to try callin' Polo again?" the Disciple next to him asked with a dopey expression on his face.

Once Tony gave him a look, as if asking him if he were stupid, he went ahead and pulled out his cellphone.

"What we gon' do with that?" another Disciple asked him, pointing at the open trunk and the body inside. "If the cops run up here and see two bodies, ain't shit we gon' be able to say."

He was right. Tony thought quickly about what to do and made a decision, hoping that it would be the right one. Only 24 hours on the job and, thanks to Kato, he was dealing with two dead bodies and, possibly, more to come.

"Drive the car round to the back, put the body in the fridge in the trunk with that one and take it out to the warehouse out west," he said. "Burn them both."

"And what 'bout Kato?" the man asked. "We just gon' let him walk away like that?"

He nudged his head towards Kato who was walking casually down the block, with an AK over his shoulder like it was a shopping bag. Every Disciple at *The Spot* knew that Polo's orders were to kill Kato on sight, but none of them had the nerve to lay down the one they all looked up to. Even now, with the blood of one of their leaders on his hands, none had what it took to decide to take him down.

Knowing this, Tony shrugged.

"Do we got a choice? Who you think gon' volunteer to stop him?"

Not one person spoke a word; instead they all stood in silence, watching in quiet admiration as Kato walked away.

CHAPTER 25

THE SUN WAS BRIGHT WITH AN ARDENT HAZE THAT ENVELOPED THE sky. It could have passed for fog but to the conscious eye it was Chicago smog, latent and potent as it imposed its imminent domain on the slums of the street.

On this day, the streets were bustling with people, cars and buses traversing to and fro. Children frolicked, running wild as they darted in and out of traffic with jovial glee while the elders sat perched on their front porches. All appeared to be natural, the norm in a city that had more murders than most foreign violent countries.

On the corner, hustlers sold dime rocks, weed and just about anything else they could get their hands on. On the side of the building, next to a vacant lot there was a dice game in the midst of twenty or so hustlers, hooligans and gangsters, along with a few hot ass females, eager to entice one of the trap boys with the allure of sex for a price. Commerce in the hood wasn't just dollars. Sex, money, drugs or even a life could buy you a lot.

Yesman, one of the most powerful man in gangland, trying to be incognito as possible, pulled up in a Black Caddy SUV with dark windows. Normally, he would have rode with a caravan of Disciples but that day he didn't as to not bring about suspicion.

Too paranoid to stay in the suburbs where he'd lived with Star, Polo was now spending his nights at his condo in the city and Yesman was too cautious about being seen there so he took his chances on finding him at *The Spot*. Anything with Polo's name attached to it was currently the hottest spots in all the boroughs of Chicago. Due to the recent killings that he was suspected to be involved in, the cops were more vigilant.

As soon as Yesman stepped out the SUV, many around paused their activity and placed both eyes on him. One of Polo's lookouts dashed inside to report what he saw and a lone hitta posted up on the roof leveled his shotgun, downward at the SUV.

With his henchmen JaJa and Khaliff by his side and heavily armed, there was no wonder Polo's security was on high alert. JaJa walked with a severe limp and true hittas knew that the only reason a gangster limped like that was because he had an AK shoved down the leg of his pants.

After being alerted of their presence, Polo met the three men at the door with a gracious smile and extended his hand out to Yesman, his boss and the highest ranking member of the organization other than Jimmy Johnson himself.

Yesman glanced down at Polo's hand, knowing that he was expecting to be greeted with the traditional six-point star embrace but, instead, Yesman raised a fist to give him dap. It was an awkward moment and instantly Polo sensed that something was wrong.

With an aura of authority, Yesman strolled over and took Polo's seat at the head of a table that was scattered with piles of money, drugs and guns. It seemed that he had come at a time when Polo's crew had been counting up.

"This shit is hot as fuck and you still hustlin' out of it?" Yesman spat, his temperament was obvious.

The small room was full of gangstas, about twenty deep. Though it had been many days since Kato had pulled up issuing threats and dropping off bodies, there was still dried blood on the floor. A palm of smoke hung in the air underneath a solitary light bulb as Polo stood in the midst of his team of hittas, looking down at Yesman.

"Me and the landlord is tight, he is on the city council, plus some of the cops in this area on payroll," Polo said and shuffled his feet, looking around.

The tension was so tight you could cut it with a chainsaw. There was a rustle of voices in the background like niggas trying to talk quietly and doing a terrible job of it.

JaJa and Khaliff stood on each side of Yesman like the loyal soldiers they were. When Khaliff opened his jacket, Polo spotted the Tec-9 stuffed in his pants.

"You know Jimmy and I started this organization when we were teenagers, long before you were even a sperm. I got locked up in Joliet Juvenile Detention Center and he continued to champion that G.D. life. When I came home, Jimmy was at war with the Black Gangstas and it was a serious war. When the leader, LaShawn Braxton, came to us and made a truce, we then became on nation, one organization, B.G.D., the Black Gangster Disciples. We made an oath to not let one muthafucka cross or betray us."

The older man paused as if to let what he said sink in. In the back of the basement a furnace hissed.

"Yeah... I know the story," Polo finally answered as he rolled his shoulders. He was wondering where Yesman was going with the subject.

"So essentially what I'm saying is no one is bigger than this organization. Not you, not me, not nobody. You understand?" Yesman said with his deep baritone booming as he glared at Polo.

"I know that, and I did make an oath which I'ma stand on but I ain't done nothin' wrong."

Polo tried to speak humbly but his jaw was clenched tight as he folded and unfolded his hands, fighting his agitation.

"What I am saying is your actions right now don't dictate how this organization is supposed to be run. First off, that shit that happened with you and Kato shouldn't have gone down like that."

Polo flexed his jaw.

"As first in command, I did what I had to," he battled. "He disrespected me—"

"And what you did caused several 'Folks' to get killed for no good reason," Yesman said. "And over some silly relationship dispute."

"That ain't what happened. Kato got out of line. He was disrespecting a nigga. He could have just taken his violation and let it be." Polo said.

"And you tried to have the Queen Gangstress, Star, violated unfairly? Even though it's against our laws?"

Polo took a step forward and said, "I'm just not going to let no nigga or chick beneath me disrespect me."

"And that's how I feel as far as the organization goes. But, to be honest, you've done much worse than this. Your crimes are much bigger than petty violations," Yesman raised his voice, causing his thick baritone voice to roll like thunder as he looked at Polo.

"Wha...what are you talking about?"

Polo frowned, suddenly his hands went still at his side and his face seemed to flush red. There was a ripple of hushed voices in the basement.

Yesman held up his hand and Khaliff passed him an envelope. He unfolded it, never taking his eyes off Polo as he began to read.

"On January 3rd, you were delivered $400,000 dollars. February 3rd, you received just over $500,000 and, for the next twelve months, you took in over $300,000 each month. Yet almost none of this money has reached Jimmy. Where is the rest of the money, Polo?" Yesman asked pointing an accusing finger at him.

"I sent the mandated percentage of everything that I received to Jimmy as required. I swear on God. We've had a few 'Folks' stealin' so—"

Yesman glared at him.

"You talkin' bout the 'Folks' you had gunned down in broad daylight at the barbershop in front of his two children?"

Polo paused and glanced around the room at Tony and a few others who were watching intently before frowning.

"Yeah. He stole from us so I had him whacked."

Disgusted with what he was hearing and the fact that Polo had the nerve to try to back it up, Yesman shook his head.

"There was no protocol. You had no permission. You held no trial and had no right. For this and your other charges, you must be reprimanded."

"Reprimanded?" Polo scuffed and scowled like he had just bitten into something sour.

Yemman looked over and nodded at Khaliff. As if on cue, his henchmen pulled out his Tec-9 and leveled it at his side, staring at Polo.

"You will receive the same punishment Kato. You are being taken off count, during while there will be a full investigation. There is the possibility you will receive a violation of the worse kind if you are discovered guilty."

Suddenly the room was dead quiet, the moment was volatile as everyone in the room looked at Polo. The same indomitable machine that had built him up was now capable of destroying him.

The moment lulled like a clock with broken hands until finally, Polo spoke as he stepped forward.

"I never had a violation before and I'm not about to make no changes to my record. It's true that you an O.G. and you helped build this organization with our Jimmy Johnson but I carried the torch for you niggas and put in major work. I have over a hundred thousand Disciples under my reign, following my every command. The entire Southside of this city wasn't given to me. I earned that shit—"

"So what are you saying?" Yezman barked as he stood up from his chair so fast that it toppled over. Khaliff instantly adjusted the strap in his hands.

"I'm saying protocol has always been to keep you hidden, out of sight sou can duck the Feds. Meanwhile, my head has always been on the chopping block, open for the world to see,. I'm the sacrificial pawn, while you worked in the shadows. I know you're a legend and your homicide game supersedes anything we've ever seen, but for you to just walk in here and tell me to take a violation..." Polo snickered and nudged his nose with his thumb. "That shit ain't gon' be easy."

"Young nigga, you bleed like everybody else. So what the fuck you mean?" Yesman raged with his nostrils flaring. He wasn't used to being tested.

"What I'm saying is this, we prepared for this very moment. Every-body in this room, standing around us lives this shit for real every day while you stand back, thinkin' you can call the shots. Not anymore.

These niggas stand at my side, fightin' battles alongside me. Some of them ain't never even seen you. So when it comes to takin' orders, who you think they gon' choose?"

With that said, Polo gestured with a wave of his and a clique of thugs walked up with pistol drawn. They were all heavily armed. Khaliff glanced at Yesman, fearfully seeing that he was very much outnumbered.

"You can tell Jimmy I ain't takin' no violation but I will continue to take over the Southside, startin' with your territory," Polo declared with hubris.

"Nigga, you done lost yo' fuckin' mind!" Yesman raved with his finger pointed at Polo's chest.

"And you lost your life."

Just as Khaliff attempted to raise his gun, Polo reached for his banger and shot him in the head. His dome exploded like a grapefruit being hit with a sledgehammer. Then Polo aimed for Yesman, emptying his clip, as shots rang out all around them. Yesman was struck in the chest, neck and many other areas as JaJa moved with the quickness.

Thinking fast, he turned over the table, causing money and drugs to go flying everywhere as he jumped backwards and, with athletic excellence, and came up with the AK-47 in his hands. Letting off a barrage of shots, he tried his hardest to aim at Polo who he'd been itching to lay down ever since he'd heard that he was the one who had ordered the hit on Kato's mother, JaJa's new fiancé.

One of JaJa's bullets hit the solitary lightbulb engulfing the room in near total darkness as he struggled to make his getaway. With luck in his favor, he was able to scurry out a back door and as soon as his feet hit the pavement outside, he took off running like a trackstar.

"Find him and kill him! Make sure he don't get away!" Polo shouted.

But he was too late.

By the time Polo's crew made it to the back door, there was nothing but a trail of blood. Right outside the fence, a small group of dope fiends were huddled together around a makeshift crack-pipe.

"He went that way," one of them said, pointing their finger out and hoping that they'd be rewarded for their assistance.

Though Polo was livid that JaJa had gotten away, the fact was that Yesman and Khaliff had died by his gun and he could now make a move to take over Yasmen's territory and take his place.

"Get some light on in here," he ordered and a few Disciples used their phones to illuminate the room.

The scene was gory as both Khaliff and Yazmen lay in puddles of blood, both dead. The sight empowered Polo's; it was like a shot of dope straight to his veins. He felt powerful in a way he couldn't explain.

"From here on out, I fuckin' run this shit! We don't answer to nobody. We gon' take over this whole fuckin' city... the state... the nation. And as long as y'all stay loyal to me, you ain't gotta want for shit."

Polo words were awarded with chorus of approval from all who stood in the room. Everybody except Tony who was utterly disgusted as he stood watching in the shadows.

"Wrap both they asses up in these carpets and take them out back. Put both of their bodies in Yesman's house so they can be found there. Don't tell a single soul 'bout what happened inside these walls. In order to take over, we gotta move in silence, starting now!"

As Polo gave his orders, he was pleased to see the men rush to do as he asked, many of them looking satisfied at the change in command. Niggas loved to see power thrown around and that was everything Polo was about. He didn't bow for shit and they respected that. Slowly but surely, he was rebuilding his new team of trusted soldiers.

CHAPTER 26

With shaky hands, Star took a deep breath and lifted a fist to knock on Kevia's door. Throughout their long friendship, there had been many times when they had to endure hard times together but none as devastating as this. To have to tell her best friend that the man she loved and father of her unborn child, had been killed by Kato seemed like the worst thing she would ever have to do in life.

"I'm comin'!" she heard Kevia shout, followed by the sound of heavy footsteps stomping towards the door.

As Star heard the locks being turned, her guilt weighed her down to the point that she could barely lift her head. Not only had she been hiding Kato in her apartment, but she had enlisted Kevia's help as well. She hadn't known it then but, thanks to her, Kevia had been assisting the man who would later leave her to birth a fatherless child. The weight of the remorse Star felt almost seemed impossible to bear.

"Hey girl!" Kevia said cheerfully as she opened the door to let Star in. "Why you ain't tell me you was on your way? I just got done makin' burgers for the kids to eat when they get outta school. I coulda made one for you."

With a deep breath, Star stepped inside but when she didn't return Kevia's upbeat disposition, it became obvious that something was wrong. Pushing the door closed behind them, Kevia frowned deeply and took careful steps behind Star while racking her mind with a good guess on what could have happened since the last time she saw her.

Ebony, she thought. *This has to be about Ebony.*

Although it had been some weeks since the news had come out about Ebony's murder and Star seemed to be coping with it as best as she could, no one really ever got over the loss of a loved one. Especially a sibling. The fact that Star had been the one to find Ebony's body made it even worse. Thinking on that, Kevia shuddered as if she was cold. Being that she basically raised her own siblings, she knew that there was no way that she could go on had it been her in Star's shoes. They were like her own children.

"You know she's in a better place, right?" Kevia offered, taking a seat in the loveseat across from Star. She pressed her hands on top of her thighs and then shook her head when she thought about how she always hated when she'd heard people say that in the past. How could she know for certain if Ebony was in a better place?

"I mean... I know it's hard but she's not sufferin' anymore. And Polo got the ones who did this to her. He made sure they paid for—"

Star shook her head. "This isn't 'bout Ebony."

Raising her head, she looked over at Kevia whose brows were bent into a deep crease, still completely lost on what had occurred.

"This is about Sloan," Star continued and then paused to lick her dry lips. "He was murdered."

Time seemed to stall, and the entire room went quiet outside of the low humming of the A.C. unit positioned in the front window of the living room. After only a few moments, the sound of Kevia's labored breaths joined in with the hum, growing louder and louder the more she processed Star's tragic news.

"You're lyin'!" she shouted, tears welling up in her eyes. "Why would you play with me like this? Tell me you're lyin'!"

Star knew that she didn't need to answer because Kevia knew the truth. There was no way that she would joke about something like this. She could and would never be that cruel.

"I wish it weren't true but it is and..."

Her words died off when Kevia collapsed into tears and she felt the sting of her own emotions pooling in the corners of her eyes. Standing up, she went over to her friend and wrapped her in her arms, rocking her gently from side to side. They sat there for an unknown amount of time, using each other to assuage their own emotions until Kevia asked the one question that Star wasn't sure she had the courage to answer.

"How did it happen? Who did it?"

Star stopped rocking abruptly and her jaw fell open, although no response came out. She knew what she should say—she'd been prepared to say it but now that it was time, the words wouldn't flow. Sensing that something was off, Kevia straightened her back and pulled away from where she'd been laying her head against Star's chest so that she could look into her eyes.

"*Who* did it?" she repeated with more force. "Was it Polo?"

Star didn't answer.

"I *knew* it! I told Sloan he couldn't trust that muthafucka!" Kevia punched her fist into the palm of her other hand, gritting her teeth in agony. "I warned him to watch out for him but he wouldn't listen—"

"It was Kato."

The second the words left her lips, Star could feel the energy shift in the room. The air became cold and her chest throbbed in pain as if the oxygen had been snatched from her lungs.

"Kato?" Kevia repeated, the weight of that revelation steadily settling in. "*Kato* killed him?"

"He blamed Sloan for his mother bein' killed. He said that Sloan was with Polo when it happened, so he got him first and vowed to kill everyone who had anything to do with it. Trey and his men are layin' low and no one has seen Polo."

Star said the words as if she were a robot, spewing a story that had been rehearsed, rather than telling her one true friend that the man she loved had been murdered because of a war that she'd started.

"This is all *your* fault!" Kevia snapped, speaking through her teeth. At her sides, her hands were balled up into fists as she glared at Star with a deadly gaze. If looks could kill, the hood would be mourning another death tonight.

"You started all of this!" she continued, jabbing Star hard in the chest with her index finger. "If you hadn't been fuckin' with both of them, this war would have never happened. They are fightin' over *you*!"

"That's not true! This started because of Polo stealin' money that—"

Kevia raised her hand as if she was going to slap her and Star ducked out of the way. Of the two, she was the stronger fighter, but she would never put her hands on Kevia, especially since she was with child.

"Don't play me like I'm dumb! That money shit is just an excuse. The real fight is over you!" Kevia's anger continued to grow the more that she thought about it, and Star's common sense was telling her that she needed to make her exit... and fast.

"I should have told Polo where Kato was myself!" she raged on, pressing both of her hands to the side of her head in anguish. "Kato isn't innocent. Why should I give a fuck if he's killed after he's killed so many others without battin' an eye? But because of *you*, I protected him and now Sloan is dead for it. Oh God!"

Dropping to her knees, Kevia cradled her belly in one arm as she used the other one to hold her up from hitting the ground. Star jumped up and knelt down by her side, praying to God that nothing was wrong with the baby. She reached out and tried to touch Kevia but was met with a hand, slapping her away.

"Just go! Get out of here now. I don't want you here. Just GO!"

Star hesitated, not wanting to leave Kevia alone in her grief but when she raised her hand once more and pushed her hard, forcing her away as she yelled for her to leave at the top of her lungs, there was nothing left to do but leave.

"I'm right here in the building... I'll be in my apartment if you need me."

Her words were met with nothing but the sound of Kevia's torturous wails as she cried out in painful howls that sounded every bit as grief-stricken as what she felt inside. With her forehead pressed against the cracked laminate floor, she lay there and sobbed until she had nothing left to give and, with her hand around her unborn child, passed out into a deep sleep right there on the floor.

CHAPTER 27

IT WAS A SAD DAY IN THE HOOD. A REAL ONE HAD BEEN LOST AND everyone felt the pain of it. Sloan was someone who had been revered in the hood, not only to Disciples and Gangstress, but for any and all who knew them. He had respect that crossed gang lines because he was a straight shooter; not just in the sense that he had a gun and he knew how to use it but in the way that mattered. Sloan was all about order, about doing what was right. He joined the Disciples because of all of the reasons that one should: to protect, provide and stand up for the members of his community.

For someone so revered and so loved, there was so much about Sloan that no one knew. There was no word of any funeral plans, no wake or viewing of what was left of his body so the hood mourned their loss in true Disciple fashion by hosting a cookout at the park in his memory.

"There go ya girl," Brenda said to Star, nudging her head in the direction of the park entrance.

Star looked up and felt her chest tighten with emotion when she saw Kevia arrive with two Gangstress by her side, assisting her as she came to pay respects to the man she loved. She was beautiful, dressed casually in a pair of jean shorts and a large t-shirt that covered her growing belly with Sloan's picture printed on the front, but the emotion in her eyes was overwhelming. Star ducked her head and swallowed hard, wanting to go to her best friend's side and comfort her in this moment but also feeling like it wasn't the time. She hadn't spoken to Kevia since the day she had to tell her that Sloan had been killed by Kato, and she was positive that Kevia still didn't forgive her.

"Want me to go get her?" Brenda offered, curling her upper lip as she looked at the two Gangstress assisting Kevia as she tried to find a spot to sit in the crowded park. "I don't really trust them two she got with her. They always tryin' to find a way to steal some shine."

Star shook her head. "No, it's okay. Right now, I'm the last person she wants to see."

Dropping her head to look at Star sideways, Brenda wanted to ask what she meant by that but after thinking for a moment, she guessed that whatever was going on between the two probably had something to do with the rumors that Star was helping Kato. If true, she knew that Star would never admit it because she still didn't fully trust her.

"I just wish my girl was here right now," she said, changing the subject. "She didn't deserve what happened to her. It was my fault. I'm the one who ran that light."

"You ran the light but Ki-Ki is the one who decided to shoot at the police. She could have gotten us all killed. It was a fucked up situation and I hate that she's gone, but she chose to do what she did."

Brenda nodded, nudging her nose as she sniffed tears away. Deep down, she knew what Star was saying was right but it was everything to hear someone say it.

"You know, she was right about Tonya and Kush," she told Star, looking off in the distance as she spoke. "I knew it was true the first time she mentioned it but I didn't want to believe it. I kicked that bitch out of my house the next day. Pointed my gun at her and made her ass get out with only the clothes she had on her back."

Star's brows shot up to the sky.

"What about Kush?"

The expression that fell over Brenda's face after Star's question told her everything she needed to know. But Star was the last one who could judge anyone for forgiving a man they loved for his wrongs. Look at the situation she was in. She hadn't heard from Kato since the day he'd left her house and killed Sloan—the day he'd threatened to kill her until she convinced him that she wasn't working with Polo to set him up. Still, she missed him and prayed each day that he would come back so that they could be together.

"Kush told me that she came on to him," Brenda explained. "He said she was looking for a come up after Polo got rid of her. I mean... I was mad at him and I'm *still* mad, but all men cheat and that's just how it is. Tonya was supposed to be my friend."

Star huffed. "Tonya ain't nobody's friend but her own. You are better off without that bitch."

Heads around them all shifted, everyone looking across the park towards the entrance as if someone important was making an appearance. Chatter ensued and both Brenda and Star shot each other confused stares, wondering what all the commotion was for. With her red cup in her hand, Star stood from her seat and peeked over the crowd to see who had arrived, her eyes tapering into a squint when she saw that it was Polo, walking into the park with a woman and a small child, a little girl, at her side.

"Who is that?" Star asked, frowning deeply before turning to Brenda who shrugged.

She looked back at the woman who appeared to be not too much older than her. She was attractive with a curvy, Coke-bottle shape, wearing a tank top with a picture on it that Star couldn't make out, paired with cut-off jean shorts and expensive sneakers. Standing next to Polo with her head lifted in authority, the only emotion she stirred inside of Star was pure curiosity. She wasn't jealous of her at all; actually, if Polo *did* have his attention on someone else, that would be her greatest joy.

"Myia, you know who that is?" Brenda asked the Gangstress, stopping her as she was walking by.

Myia cut her eyes to Star and gave her an uneasy look and shuffled her feet a bit before answering Kevia's question.

"They sayin' that's Sloan's wife, Yasmina, and their daughter," she informed them. "He kept them in the suburbs to keep 'em safe. That's why we ain't never seen 'em until now."

"*Wife?*" Star echoed, looking from the woman over to Kevia.

She knows, she thought, seeing the devastation on her friend's face as she stole glances at Yasmina. The two Gangstress who were supposed to be helping her seemed more than a little enthused at the drama as they stood around her, doing a terrible job to hide the smirks on their faces.

Star bounced her leg anxiously, trying to stop herself from running to Kevia's side but when she saw Yasmina began to walk in her direction, she could no longer sit still.

"Oh hell nah, we not 'bout to do this here," she said under her breath as she stood up abruptly.

"What are you about to—"

Before Brenda could finish her sentence, Star was off in a mad-strut, focusing in on Yasmina who was now talking to Kevia who had her head bent low in shame. Brenda wasted no time yanking Myia up by the arm.

"Come on!"

"Damn, bitch, do I have a choice?" Myia snapped, but she already knew the answer, so she fell in line.

KEVIA'S HEART felt like it had been stomped into a bloody mess underneath her shoes as she stood in front of Yasmina, who she now knew was Sloan's wife, with her head bowed and tears in her eyes. It was bad enough that she had lost the man that she'd thought of as her soulmate but to now be ridiculed for everyone to see as the woman that he'd chosen to give his last name put her in 'her place'... that was a new low.

He lied to me, she thought as she listened to Yasmina speak. *He told me they weren't together. Never even mentioned that they were married. He lied...*

"So you're pregnant. At least that's what I was told," Yasmina asked, glaring down at Kevia. "Is it true?"

Sniffing her tears away, Kevia lifted her head and forced herself to look into her eyes.

"Yes, I am. Sloan is the father."

Yasmina snickered. "That's not what he told me." She curled her cherry lipgloss stained lips into an evil smirk as she continued. "He told me that you were just the bitch he was messin' around with until you tried to pin a baby on him. I don't even know why you're here, walkin' around like he was your man, wearin' that disrespectful ass shirt."

She narrowed her eyes at the custom-made shirt that Kevia had made with her favorite picture of Sloan and the script 'I Love You Forever' printed below. That morning, Kevia had felt overcome with pride and strength when she pulled it on, but now she just felt like a clown.

"Yo' ass is the only one who is disrespectful," Star snapped, coming up from behind Kevia with fire in her eyes. "This is a memorial to celebrate the memory of a man who we all knew and loved and here you go tryin' to throw bullshit in the mix when you know Sloan wouldn't stand for it. Now I don't know whether what you're saying is true or not, but what I do know is that this is not the time or the place."

"You must not know who you're talkin' to," Yasmina spat, looking Star up and down.

"No, you must not know who you're talkin' to."

With that said, Brenda and Myia took their position next to Star, not wanting to cause a confrontation at Sloan's memorial gathering but ready for whatever if the moment called for it. Standing at a distance behind Yasmina, Polo was amused by the entire ordeal. He knew the moment that he asked her to come with him to the park that drama would unfold at Kevia's expense, but he didn't give a damn.

Now that he had gotten rid of Yesman and Kato had taken care of Sloan, he had his mind set on winning the loyalty of Yesman's team once he made Yasmina his new Gangstress Queen. The past few days, he'd happily provided her with a dick to ride on and once Yesman's dead body was discovered in a couple hours or so, he would provide her with a shoulder to lean on as she cried as well.

"Aye, y'all stand down," Polo said, stepping up next to Yasmina.

"This is not only Sloan's wife but the daughter of Yesman, one of our most revered leaders, second to only Jimmy Johnson himself. Her father was one of the realest ones to ever do this shit and she was married to one of the only men in this world I felt I could trust. We need to show her some respect."

Yasmina's nose shot high in the air as she looked down on Star and Kevia like the garbage she regarded them as. Star bit down hard on her tongue, wanting so badly to let it be known that she was Jimmy Johnson's daughter and pull rank on them all. Polo turned his attention to Yasmina, his expression softening as he looked at her.

"Let me show you around. There are some people you need to meet."

With a nod, Yasmina gave one last pointed look at Star before focusing in on Kevia, eyeing her pregnant belly with disgust, and then left to follow behind Polo.

"For someone who just lost her *husband*, the bitch don't look too torn up," Brenda muttered under her breath while watching her walk away.

"Because she's a liar. I hope you don't believe her lyin' ass, Kee," Star said still looking at Yasmina as she strutted at Polo's side.

When she didn't hear a response from Kevia, she turned to her and let out a sharp breath when she saw that her friend was rubbing tears from her eyes.

"It doesn't matter if it's true or not," Kevia managed to say in between sobs. "The point is, she's married to him and I'm just the chick he had on the side. He couldn't even stay with me through the night because he was always rushin' back to be with her. Who do you think is the liar?"

The corners of Star's lips tugged downward as she fought through her inner thoughts in order to find something to say that could make things right. The truth was, there was nothing that could be said.

"I'm sorry," she whispered, telling her the only thing that felt right in the moment.

Kevia lifted her eyes and settled them on Star's face, seeing the sincerity in her expression. It was wrong to blame her for Sloan's murder and, to be honest, she really just wanted her friend back. She opened her mouth, fully intent on letting Star know that she accepted her apology but clamped them back closed when, suddenly, she felt a small hand tugging on hers. She looked down at her side and her eyes widened in pure shock and surprise when she saw Sloan's daughter standing next to her.

"Hi, are you Ms. Kevia?" the young girl, probably no older than five, asked.

Kevia mired and looked from the girl to Star who shrugged and then back to the girl again.

"Yes, I am."

"My name is Shiloh," the child continued, holding up a small piece of paper. "My daddy told me to give you this."

Star, Kevia and Brenda, who had decided to stay, all froze before looking at each other and exchanging awkward glances. The only one able to find her voice was Star being that Shiloh's statement had Kevia overcome with emotion.

"Um, Shiloh, your daddy—you mean, Sloan?"

The girl smiled and nodded her head. "Yes, he told me to wait until my mommy was gone and give Ms. Kevia this. He said she was the one with the big belly and pretty shoes."

Brenda and Star each bent their head to look first at Kevia's bulging belly and then at the white Nike Air Force's that had been spray-painted with Sloan's name and decorated with glitter and sequins for the day.

"You're sayin' your daddy gave you somethin' for her... just now?" Star asked.

Shiloh nodded.

"But he's dead!" Brenda finally blurted out what they all had been thinking but had enough sense not to say in front of the child. Star gave her a chastising look.

"Brenda!"

"What?" she asked, shooting her hands in the air. "I'm just tryin' to get some answers."

"No, he's not! He's not!" Shiloh shouted, grabbing the attention of a few people standing by.

Star shifted under their attention, knowing it didn't look good for the three of them to be seen speaking to Sloan's daughter who was now shouting angrily.

"Give me the paper and then scram," Brenda told the girl. "Yo' mama don't want you over here and I ain't tryin' to get locked up again for smackin' the shit out of her ass."

She reached out for the paper but Shiloh snatched it away.

"No, my daddy told me to give it to *her*."

Brenda rolled her eyes.

"Well, give it to *herrrr* then so you can go."

Curling up her nose at Brenda, little Shiloh looked every bit like her hateful mother in that moment before turning to Kevia and smiling. She held out the paper and Kevia sucked in a deep breath before grabbing it from her little fingers. With her job done, Shiloh skipped away just as quickly as she'd come, joining with some other little girls who were playing not too far away.

"What is it?" Star asked, her curiosity killing her as she impatiently watched Kevia frowning at the small piece of paper.

"I don't know," she said finally. "There is just a number."

She handed it over to Star who wasted no time pulling it in front of her eyes.

"323? What's that?"

Kevia shrugged. "I don't know."

"I bet it's that bitch messin' with you," Brenda huffed with her arms folded in front of her chest. "And she got her kid in on it. That's just evil."

Star didn't respond and instead looked back at the paper, wondering what it could mean. The more she thought about it, the more she came up with... nothing. With a shrug of her own, she handed it back to Kevia who held it in her hand for a moment before pulling it to her nose. Her eyes closed, she took in a deep breath, feeling a sudden bout of nostalgia when she recognized Sloan's scent. Her eyes jerked open.

It can't be, she thought.

Looking up, she was thankful to see that Star and Brenda's attention was on something in the distance and no longer on her. She put the paper to her nose again and took another whiff, a deeper one this time. The scent was still there; the one that she knew and loved. It was Sloan.

"Somethin' happened," she heard Brenda say.

In the distance, Kevia heard some shouting and other commotion, but her mind wasn't really focused on anything but her inner thoughts.

"I'm goin' to ask Myia."

"Okay," Star replied and then turned to Kevia. "You alright?"

It wasn't until then that Kevia realized she had a goofy smile on her face. She had been thinking about the last time she saw Sloan, when she told him that they were having a boy. She'd been laying on his chest, basking in his presence, delighting in his scent.

"Yes, I'm fine."

Star gave her a sideways look, somewhere between seeming relieved that Kevia was smiling but also questioning whether she'd lost her mind. She looked down at the paper that was still in Kevia's hands and was about to ask another question when Brenda ran back and interrupted her.

"They said it's Yesman," she announced as she returned. "Yasmina's father... he was found dead. Someone killed him."

"What?" Star gasped, covering her hand with her mouth.

She didn't know Yesman all that well and had only met him the one time he came to her apartment looking for Kato; however, she was devastated to hear the news being that Yesman seemed like Jimmy's only hope of being absolved of the crimes he didn't commit.

"Yeah. Yasmina was the one over there screamin' and hollerin'. The only reason you don't hear her now is because her ass passed out." Brenda pursed her lips. "I still can't stand her but I'm glad I didn't have to beat her ass for you earlier. That shit wouldn't look good right now with her daddy dead and all."

Not saying anything, Star let her eyes scan the area as everyone moved about, excitedly spreading the news about the new drama to hit the streets or to crowd around Yasmina who was laid out on the ground with Gangstress attending to her as Polo spoke amongst a group of Disciples.

It wasn't until some time later that her mind went back to Kevia, the childish grin on her face and the paper Shiloh had given her. Turning to her side, she was ready to inquire once again about the note but when she looked at the space where Kevia had been, nothing was there but empty space.

She was gone.

CHAPTER 28

Not long after Kevia disappeared, Sloan's memorial celebration came to an end after news of Yesman's murder came out. Hearing that yet another Disciple that so many cherished and loved, this time one of the original leaders, had been killed put a damper on the party that no amount of weed, alcohol or good food could take away.

Star felt like she had the weight of the world on her shoulders as she passed by Kevia's apartment on the way to hers. She wanted to knock on the door so they could chill, gossip and laugh like old times but, to be honest, she wasn't in the mood. Not only was she unsure about whether Kevia accepted her apology, she felt like she was mourning the loss of a man she loved as well. It had been almost a week since Sloan's death and she still hadn't seen or heard from Kato, wasn't even sure he was still alive. She was still dealing with Ebony's murder and now Kato was gone as well. So much death and destruction surrounded her that she couldn't help but feel that it was only a matter of time before the Grim Reaper came knocking at her door.

After walking into her apartment, Star closed the door behind it and then leaned back on it, closing her eyes, and then inhaled deeply.

"You look sad."

A sharp gasp escaped through Star's lips and her eyes snapped open. She was neither scared or alarmed because she knew who the voice belonged to as soon as she heard it.

Kato stood before her, so close that when she breathed, he could feel her breath on his chest. He looked down at her, missing her instantly. Guilt burned through the middle of his heart when he looked at the faint outline of a bruise around her neck. He lifted his hands and traced it with his finger with the corners of his eyes tugging downward in sadness.

"I'm sorry."

Those were the only words he could think of to say, even though they didn't seem to accurately illustrate the level of emotions he felt inside. Had Star not been able to defend herself against him, her grandmother would have been mourning the loss of another grandchild.

"I don't blame you. After hearin' what happened to your mother, I..." She paused and looked away, afraid to see the sadness in his eyes. "I was scared that you were goin' to come out when you heard it."

"You had my gun," he said, thinking back as he spoke. "That was the only reason I didn't run up out of that room shootin'. I couldn't do shit and I can't leave this Earth until I make sure that everybody responsible for what happened to her is gone first."

Hearing that made Star flinch.

"But Sloan..." She struggled to choose her words carefully. "He was a good man and I know that he was loyal to you. There is no way that—"

Hushing her by placing his palm against her chest, right between her breasts, Kato shook his head slightly while looking her in the eyes.

"When it comes to everything I do, I need you to trust me. Don't question shit, don't lose faith in me... just know that there is a good reason for everything I do."

Caught up by their proximity, Star nodded her head while staring into his eyes. She was experiencing so many emotions in that moment that it was almost overwhelming. Maybe it was the fact that she'd witnessed so much loss and sadness over one man that day that made her so grateful for Kato's presence right then. Maybe it was because she thought at one point that she would never see him again. Or maybe it was because she knew it was wrong. Whatever the reason, she knew right then that she couldn't hold back the way she felt about him.

As great of a connection that she already knew they had, it only proved to be deeper when Kato locked her body in between his arms and pulled her close to him. It was almost as if he could read her mind and knew right then that she was ready to be his if he wanted her. He rubbed up into her, pressing his hard sex right into her core. Before she knew it, a moan had escaped through her lips and she almost lost herself until she felt Kato's hands roaming over her body.

"I need to shower first," she said, her eyes closed as she relaxed into his body.

She knew that she should have been pulling away but the feeling of being so close to him was intoxicating. Especially after seeing so many people torn up over Sloan's death, she couldn't help but feel relieved to have Kato there with her in that moment. She felt a twinge of guilt over being so happy in this moment when she knew that Kevia was living the worst days of her life. But she couldn't help it, she loved Kato and had feared the worse when he disappeared for the days he'd been gone. Now he was back and she felt like her prayers had been answered.

"Do what you gotta do," he told her, backing away. "I been waitin' this long so a couple minutes ain't shit."

She shot him a look, curious about how he'd given in so easily. The devilish smirk on his face only made her wonder further about what new mischief he was up to. She found out about two minutes after she'd been in the shower, enjoying the feel of the hot water against her body. With her eyes closed, she reveled in the moment, letting the steam relax her mind and push her worries away.

The door opened and she snapped her eyes open, jerking to attention. Funny enough, she felt compelled to hide her body, to stop Kato from noticing the stretch marks across her ass or the rolls of fat in places that only the right outfit could hide. He hadn't seen her naked before and, now that the moment had arrived, she feared it. She looked up, seeing that Kato was about to grab the edge of the shower curtain to pull it open and snatched it first to stop him.

"Aye, what you doin'? Star, let go."

"I'm naked!"

He paused. "Duh, nigga. Who takes a shower with clothes on? What you tryin' to hide?"

Giving up, Star released the shower curtain and instead wrapped her arms around her body. When Kato pulled back the curtain, he found her with her head bowed and her arms strategically placed to cover up her large chests as she faced him. Her posture was humped over, like she was trying to hide as much of herself as she possibly could.

"I know you ain't ashamed to show yourself to me," he said, frowning.

Star didn't answer and instead pinched her lips into her mouth, swallowing back her emotions.

Reaching out, he grabbed her hands and pulled them down, placing them by her side. Next, he placed his hand under her chin and lifted her head so that she could look him in the eyes. The gentle stare she saw relaxed her soul. She took even breaths and watched him as he observed her, allowing his eyes to travel over every fold, appreciating her in a way that he'd never had anyone do before.

"You're beautiful, baby."

Star sucked in a breath as she remembered the dream that she'd once had about the first time she and Kato had sex. A dream that had been quickly interrupted by the squawks of the new bitch Polo had brought in to fuck in his condo while she was sleeping in the other room.

"Don't nothin' on Earth compare to what I'm seein' in front of me right now. You don't need to hide a damn thing," he said, slowly wetting his lips with his tongue once he was done talking.

Like a flower she began to blossom before him, her confidence now on a whole other level. She had always felt like she was a bad bitch but there was something about Kato that had her wondering if she was enough for him. His reaction to her naked glory made her feel magical.

He stripped off his clothes and she watched him the entire time, never letting her eyes leave his body. She couldn't help but admire his sculptured, chest and six-pack abs, all brawny muscles; even his legs were muscular. His entire body was covered in tats but what really turned her on was when her eyes roamed down the V-shape of his waist to his throbbing dick. It was big and thick, like a mini arm. Before even putting a hand on her, he had her wet and open.

"Let me get in there with you."

She didn't answer him because there was no need. Before even giving her the chance to respond, he was already welcoming himself into the shower, running his hands over her wet body as he moved to join her. Turning her around so that her back was to him, he cupped her in his arms and pushed his manhood against her ass before plucking the soapy loofah from her hand.

Kato was romantic in ways that she wasn't prepared for. And, if he were being honest, he'd have to admit that he was surprised his damn self. Picture a street goon bathing a chick in the shower, while trailing kisses down her neck. The thought was foreign to him but the act was like second nature and he couldn't help but enjoy every bit of Star's luscious body.

He bathed her with care and precision and then once he was finished, she did the same to him. Although he felt uncomfortable at first and tried to stop her, she begged for him to go with it and he did. As she covered his body with soap, she marveled at every bit of him, every gunshot wound, marks from where he'd been stabbed. He was a beautiful man with a body full of scars that told so many stories, many she would never know.

The dried their bodies and Star was just about to exit the bathroom when she saw Kato grab a bottle from the counter. It was baby oil.

"What's that for?" she asked, the edges of her lips curving into a smile.

"You'll know soon enough. Bend that fat ass over on the bed and close your eyes."

The thrill of it all had her stomach filled with jitters. Without a single word, she followed his instructions to the letter, diving onto the bed belly first with her ass in the air and her eyes closed. Giggling a little at how silly she felt, she was overcome with the giddy feeling that newfound love gave. This moment felt almost like her first time. She was no longer a virgin but damn if he didn't have her feeling like one.

Kato walked into the room and had to pause to appreciate the sight before him of Star bent over with her ass high.

"Damn," he growled, feeling drunk off of his want of her.

Never before had he ever wanted a woman quite like he wanted Star right then. She didn't even know how beautiful she was to him, how much he adored everything about her. But then, in the next moment, he bit down on his bottom lip, thinking twice about what he was going to do.

This is wrong.

The truth was he could never have Star like he wanted her. She wanted to be his, but he couldn't let that happen. Not with the tragic future that he had waiting for him. He sighed heavily, suddenly feeling guilty about taking her body when he knew their relationship wouldn't last.

Star felt his eyes on her, and a playful feeling hit her. Suddenly, she wanted to give him a show. His reaction to her naked body gave her confidence a high. Bending even lower, perfecting the arch of her back, she spread her legs, pink pussy galore.

"That's some sexy shit," Kato couldn't help but say.

There was no way he could leave her now. With his dick in his hand, he gave it a few strokes as Star giggled, winding her ass in circles in the air. She made her booty jump seductively, only stopping when she felt him pull a thin, silky material over her eyes, blindfolding her.

"Mmm," she moaned, anxious for whatever was coming next.

Kato poured the oil in his hands and then stood behind her, his face right above the curve of her round ass as he began to rub it over her body. He started at her neck, massaging her gently while pressing his body into her backside. She moaned louder at the feel of him so close to her mound. She tried to arch her back further, opening her flower up to him in hopes that he would stop teasing her and push up inside, but he didn't

"I wanna take my time," he told her and, even though she was feeling anxious, she decided to enjoy the wait.

Kato rubbed his hands along her back, covering her with oil in a way that was so seductive, her nipples hardened like pebbled rock. When he got to her ass, he kneaded her skin like dough, spreading her cheeks apart, making cold air blow against her clit. She gushed honey that made her pussy lips shine as if he'd covered it with the oil.

Bending down, Kato placed his face right in front of her open ass, his lips only inches away from her open mound. Puckering up, he teased her even more by blowing his breath on her clit. Star groaned in sheer ecstasy as she gushed even more.

"Please... I need to feel you in me. Oh God..."

He had her so caught up that she was begging, her clit was popping and flexing, needing to be touched so badly. Kato was trying to take his time but his patience was almost about to run out.

"I'm not done yet," he said, grabbing the bottle of oil in his hands.

He licked his lips, staring at her pussy as he rubbed his hands together, preparing to massage her feet. Before he could get the chance, Star decided it was time to take matters into her own hands—literally—and reached back between her thighs. Spreading her ass even further open to ensure that he had a good view of what she was about to do, she opened her hips and dipped her middle finger deeply into her moist cave as deep as she could.

Kato's lips parted as he watched her finger disappear into her wetness. His dick grew to its fullness, pass the point of where he could continue to suppress its desire to feel the inside of Star.

"Don't you want this?" she teased him. Before he could answer, she stuck another finger inside, pulling her hole even further open. She worked it around, moaning in absolute pleasure.

"I'ma fuck that shit out of that sweet pussy," he said, more to himself than her.

Pulling her fingers out, he took a moment to observe the juices covering them before dipping both into his mouth, sucking all of the sugar from her fingertips. Once he was done, he wasted no time pushing his face into her ass as he ate her from behind, locking his mouth over her hardened clit, causing her to shriek from sheer plea-sure. She moaned like an old song and couldn't help pressing her face into the bed sheets.

The more she moaned, the more excited Kato became and the more his hunger from her multiplied. He sucked on her pussy like he'd been starving and she was a buffet meal. Running his tongue through her folds, it was like he couldn't get enough. He thumped his tongue against her clit and suckled on her pearl until she felt like she couldn't take any more.

With the entire bottom half of his face covered in her feminine juices, Kato pulled his face from inside of her, eager to get what he'd been waiting so long for.

"Turn around," he told Star, smacking on her ass. "I want to look you in her eyes."

She did as he asked and he couldn't help but to think that this was the first time that he'd had sex with someone in such an intimate way. He wanted to look into her eyes and gauge her reaction to him as he rocked inside of her thighs. With his love for Star in the picture, this whole act was different. It wasn't fuckin', it was definitely love.

"Oh God," she cried out, squeezing her eyes shut as he pushed inside of her, spreading her into two. "Kato... damn, you're goin' so fuckin' deep."

She gasped but he went deeper still; not only did he want to feel all of her, he wanted her to have all of him. He filled her to the brim and watched her expressions change as she adjusted to his girth and overcame the pain. When she began twerking her hips against him, he knew then that she was ready for him. He began delivering long strokes straight to her center. She was his hostage, held in place by his hands on each of hers, pushing them above her head, down into the mattress as he stroked her with excellence.

"I love this..." he whispered against her skin as he nestled his face into her neck. "I love you..."

The declaration came so quietly that Star wasn't sure that she'd even heard it. He pushed hard into her, thrusting with intention and her body jerked as he tapped on her g-spot, making her so wet that her pussy began to make a smacking sound.

"God... this feels so damn. This is so good."

The emotions he was stirring inside of her were so overwhelming. All she could do was ride the wave of his body, giving up to him what he was putting down inside of her, working her hips against his long, thick and rock-hard dick.

They came against each other, fucking up the sheets with all of the evidence of the love they made. Star rolled over to her side, exhausted and satisfied in ways that she could never explain. She thought their moment was over, until she felt Kato's manhood pressing through the opening of her ass. With her back arched, she allowed him to enter her from behind, welcoming him into her pussy from an angle that was just as enjoyable as the first.

"Fuck, this pussy is so muthafuckin' good," Kato growled as he jerked into her with a rhythm that set her sex on fire.

Star cried out in a language no human ear could comprehend as she took him in. Again and again, Kato took her body in different ways each time, bringing them to utter and complete ecstasy before changing up the position so they could come again. He didn't get tired of her and, even when her body was aching and her pussy was swollen, she still wanted more.

Once they were done, he ran a bath for her and washed her once again, hoping that it brought some relief to her throbbing muscles and swollen body parts. As he rubbed her down, only his discipline stopped him from asking for more of her love. While he was in the shower, Star lay in the bed, running her hand over the tenderness between her legs as she thought of him and listened to the running water.

Kato gave her the sweetest kind of love. The tenderness in which he pleasured her body was such a contrast from the harsh, aggressive personality that he was known for. The fact that Star was able to bring out a side of him that he hadn't even known was there made it clear that what he felt for her had to be love. Whether he wanted to believe or accept it, his true emotions were clear to the both of them.

"Do you ever think about the future?" Star asked all of a sudden as she lay in between his arms, resting her head on his bare chest.

He frowned, something about her question alarmed him in a way that he couldn't quite explain.

"Think about the future?" he repeated in a tone like the concept was foreign to him.

Star giggled. "Yes... like kids and having a family. I always wanted to buy a cat."

"Hell nah, not happenin'. I hate cats."

The smile on Star's lips deepened at his response.

"What does me havin' a cat gotta do with you? You tryin' to be my man or somethin'?"

The answer to her question was simple. In his mind, he wasn't *trying* to be her man because he already was. But there was one problem: with his current medical situation, there was no guarantee that he'd even know who she was around this time next year, and she had no idea. How could he claim her, make her fall in love with him, when he knew that there was no chance of a happy ending?

"We shouldn't have done this shit," he said suddenly and sat up, forcing Star to pull away from his chest.

Standing to his feet, he began searching for his clothing so that he could get dressed. He had no clue where he would go but he had to leave from here. When he was around Star, he wasn't able to think clearly or make sound decisions. As it was, the only reason he'd come back was to apologize and then explain that he had to leave but the moment he saw her, nothing went according to his plan. They couldn't be together and he knew it, but her presence was so addicting. She was like a drug and the moment he was near her, he couldn't suppress the desire to ride the high.

"What did you just say?" Star asked, standing as well. "And what are you doin'? Are you leaving?"

Without giving her a response, he sat down on the edge of the bed and began to pull on his shoes. She couldn't help but be reminded of the first time she'd had sex, when Polo had taken her virginity, and how she awoke the next morning only to find that he'd left. That day, he had made her feel cheap, worthless even. It was the same way that Kato was making her feel now.

"I know you heard what the fuck I said!" she shouted.

Kato bit down hard on his tongue as he clenched his jaw, forcing himself to not respond. There wasn't anything he could say that would make it better so silence was all he could give. Things had gone too far and he knew that she was hurting but it was better to hurt her now and break things off than to hurt her later on when they were too deeply involved and he couldn't even remember her name.

"So this is what you do, huh? Fuck me and leave?" Star continued, getting in his face to block him as he began to walk towards the bedroom door. Sidestepping her, Kato pushed past and left out the door, focused on doing everything he could to get out of her apartment as soon as possible before things went south.

"This is what you do but I guess I'm stupid for thinking I'm special. You treat me just like I'm any other basic bitch that you done fucked with around here. Muthafucka, you ain't shit! I shoulda killed your ass."

The words were out of her mouth before she knew it. It was just something that she was saying out of anger but once it was said, Kato stopped suddenly in his tracks, not moving a single muscle. Breathing evenly, Star stood behind him, just as still as he was, mentally praying that she could rewind time and take the words back. He turned to face and the fire in his eyes made her take a fearful step back, suddenly wanting to create as much distance as she could between them.

"You shoulda killed me?" He narrowed his eyes. "You know how we do, Star. We don't live life with regrets."

Reaching to his side, he pulled out his gun. Star's lips parted to scream but before she could get out a single sound, he snatched her arm and placed the handle of the gun in her open palm.

"Here's your chance," he said, standing squarely in front of her. "Do what you want to do. Finish the job you started."

Star sucked in a breath and her eyes widened.

The job I started?

It felt like every hair on her body was standing up on end. Did this mean that he knew she was the one who had shot him? That she was the reason he'd almost lost his life?

"Hold that gun up and point it," Kato ordered, now frowning deeply. "Do the shit! You said I ain't shit, right? That I'm just like any other nigga... do what you wanna do!"

Star dropped her head as tears ran down her face. By her side, she limply held the gun that he'd given her between her fingers. Moments of silence passed and for each second of it she could feel Kato's hard stare. All she could do was wonder what he was thinking and pray that he didn't hate her.

"Give me that shit," he said, snatching the gun from her hand.

He placed it on his body, while keeping his eyes on Star who refused to look him in his eyes. When she lifted her hand to brush away a tear, he questioned himself for leaving her in this way. Briefly, he considered just coming clean and telling her what was happening to him so that he understood why he had to go.

But in the next moment, he shook his head and pushed the thought away. If he only had a few more months of being himself, he didn't want to spend that time with people pitying him for his future. It didn't matter if one day he would forget it, he would rather see anger, hurt and hate in her eyes before sympathy.

With his pistol secure on his waist, Kato turned around and began again to walk towards the front door, this time without Star raving and stomping behind him. However, something else was off. After taking a few steps, he stopped as he exited the hallway and paused to lean on the edge of the couch, blinking his eyes. Sporadic dark spots appeared in front of him and his head felt heavy as a splitting pain shot through his skull.

"Shit," he whispered as he held onto the couch for dear life, struggling to keep the strength in his legs. It was like his body functions were slowly shutting down and the more he tried to fight it, the weaker he got.

"Kato? Are—are you okay?" Star asked, easing up behind him.

He wanted to wave her away, to tell her anything to make her leave so she wouldn't see him like this but his mouth wouldn't move. His tongue felt heavy—his entire body did, and he was powerless to fight it.

Looking at the panicked expression on Star's face, the last thought that crossed his mind before he drifted away was that if he had to die tonight, at least he'd spent his last moments with the only person in the world he loved.

CHAPTER 29

A BLINDING WHITE LIGHT BLINKED OVERHEAD AS STAR SAT IN THE waiting room of the hospital, wearing nothing but a pair of tights, flip-flops and a robe that she'd managed to pull around her just as the paramedics entered her apartment. She bit on the corner of her mouth as she waited for someone to come with word on what was happening with Kato.

Her nerves were a mess and she was plagued by her guilt. She couldn't help but wonder if the fight she'd started was what put him here. Kato had been unconscious all the way to the hospital and had remained that way until the moment they took him away. The last time that happened, he'd spent the next few months in a coma. Now he was back and, once again, it was because of her. What would happen this time?

Star heard footsteps in her direction and she lifted her head, her body tensing slightly when she recognized the person heading her way. It was the nurse's aid who she had seen at the hospital many times before, tending to Kato's needs and assisting him with therapy. Though they'd never really spoke, she was a familiar face and with her came hope that Star would hear something about Kato's condition soon.

"Hi, I don't know if you remember me," the young woman began. "My name is Taymar."

"I remember you," Star replied fast, not wanting to be rude but desperate for any information related to Kato. "Can you tell me what is happenin' with Kato?"

A small smile crossed Taymar's lips. She was happy to see that Star was so eager to hear of Kato's condition. Now more than ever, he needed someone in his corner who truly cared.

"Being that he has not designated a next of kin and I can only give information to his family, I'm goin' to assume that you're his..." She paused and gave Star a look, suggesting that she fill in the blank.

"Wife," she responded, surprising herself as well as Taymar.

"His wife." Taymar repeated, her smile deepening, although the edges of her eyes pulled downward, as if she was sad. Star noticed it and straightened her back, mentally preparing herself for what would come next.

"Kato has suffered severe brain trauma, as you know. During his last stay, he was told that he would need therapy, which he refused. He was told to take medication, which he was refused, and he was also told that he would need another follow-up surgery and ongoing treatment, which..."

"He refused," Star finished with a sigh. Taymar nodded her head.

"Foregoing that treatment is causing damage to his brain that will kill him if it's left untreated. Nothing we say is making him change his mind about it but he has to do this or it will end his life. What happened today lets us know that this condition is progressing at an alarming rate—much faster than we expected. You may have noticed him acting erratically, forgetting things?"

Star took a deep breath and let it out before answering. "Well, he's always acted erratically..." She let out a sad chuckle. "But I have noticed him forgetting things. But I thought it was because he smoked a lot of weed."

Taymar couldn't help but smile a little in spite of the topic of their conversation.

"Yeah, Kato got busted plenty of times smoking in his room. That's his way of self-medicating and dealing with the pain. But it's not going to cure him. He *needs* professional help. You have to talk to him and make him understand that. The reason I'm telling you this is because I know he won't and the doctor can't... but I like to think that I became his friend while he was here and I just can't let him do this to himself if I can help it."

A single tear fell down Star's cheek and she brushed it away before sniffing the others back.

"Is he awake?"

Taymar nodded her head. "He's awake and the doctor should be down in a little while to let you know that and tell you when you can see him so I'll have to go. Please don't tell him I came down here to talk to you because I could get in trouble. But I just had to try to help."

Star nodded and sighed heavily. "I understand."

THE WALK to Kato's room felt about as long as the walk a deathrow inmate made to the electric chair.

What am I going to say? Star thought, nibbling on the edge of her bottom lip.

It was obvious that she knew something Kato never wanted her to know but, on top of that, she now had to figure out how to talk him into doing something he didn't want to do. If she could allow anyone to take her place, she would jump at the chance.

As she stood outside of the room door, marked 352, she bowed her head to say a quick prayer and drew in a breath, letting it out slow in an effort to calm her nerves. When she lifted her head, there was no change. Her nerves were still in an uproar but there wasn't a thing she could do but rise to the occasion.

By way of some miracle, she was able to force herself to walk into the room, though she was fearful of what would happen next. The moment she stepped inside, the first thing she saw was him. Kato was standing directly in front of her, across the room with his back facing her direction as he stared out the window. Outside was a view of the city he grew up in, the city that he wouldn't remember that he ever lived in as time passed.

The sight made tears come to Star's eyes. With the new knowledge that she'd been given about his future, she could only imagine what he was thinking.

"You're still here," he said without turning.

He knew she was close by before she had even entered the room. It was almost like he could feel her near him. Before she walked through the door, she had suddenly come to his mind. In fact, in the few moments before she made her entrance, he had been daydreaming what it would be like to have a family with her, to spend the rest of his days by her side. Things that didn't mean shut to him before... a wife, kids, the family life, these were all things that he now prayed to God for.

"Of course I'm here. I wouldn't have left," Star spoke honestly. "I had to know that you were alright."

He didn't say anything but he loved her even more in that moment.

"I know about your diagnosis." She licked her lips and sighed heavily, fighting through her next words as well as the tears in her eyes. "Why won't you get treatment? Why would you give up when you can live your life?"

Kato gritted his teeth in anguish before dropping his head.

"Taymar ran her mouth, didn't she?" He snickered a little, knowing that he was right even though Star wouldn't answer. "You don't have to admit it because I already know. You sound just like her."

"Why? Because I want you to be healthy? Because I want you to live a full life and be in your right state of mind?"

"Right state of mind?" Kato swiveled around so fast that the wind from his body knocked a piece of paper off the table next to him. Fire burned in his eyes as he charged to her.

"What right state of mind is that? The Kato who is killing muthafuckas that I used to ride out with in the middle of the street or the Kato who slapped yo' grandma? Which Kato do you prefer? Which one do you want to stay?"

Star's lips parted as she blinked in quick sequence, trying to find the right words to say.

"You're not that person, Kato. You're changing. You're becoming a better person—Polo pushed you in a corner. You had no choice—"

"I had no choice then but I do now," he said, running his hand over his face in distress. "I'm not doin' that shit. Ain't no point. I'm not a Disciple anymore... I ain't got shit to live for."

Star stepped up, invading his personal space.

"What about me?"

He eyed her. "What about you? What chick your age wanna spend her time goin' through the shit they wanna take me through? That's bullshit. Go and live your life. Go to school... do all the shit you be whinin' to a nigga about."

She shook her head, not fully understanding what he was saying or why he was saying it.

"And leave you here? Are you crazy?"

He gave her a blank look. "Not yet. At least, that's what they tell me. Give me a couple months."

"Kato, stop. This isn't somethin' I want to joke about. There is no way I can go to college and live like you don't exist anymore. There is no way I can stop wonderin' what's happenin' with you."

"You don't have no choice because I don't want you here."

His words were so cut dry and said so emphatically that Star thought that she hadn't heard him right. What he was saying was so opposite from how she knew he felt about her. There was no way that the man she'd spent months getting to know on a level no one else had could say something like that to her and make it sound like he meant it.

"I know what you're doin' and you don't have to do it," Star said, shaking her head. "You're tryin' to push me away because you think I'm givin' up my dreams to be with you. But what you don't understand is that my dream *is* to be with you. I don't want to do anything unless you're a part of it."

Her words affected Kato deeply; in a way that was both happy and sad. On one end, he loved to hear her profess her love for him. On the other, he hated that she was making the same mistake so many other women made when it came to men. No man should be a woman's everything; she shouldn't sacrifice her life for his because if the shit went south between them, what would she have then? Just a broken heart and unfulfilled dreams. He couldn't let her live a life of regrets, especially when his future was so unclear.

"You don't know shit. Just like you didn't know shit when I first spoke to you and you thought Polo loved your ass." He forced air from his nostrils in a belittling way that made Star flinch. "You so hungry for a nigga to want you that you can't tell what's real and what's fake."

Turning to face her, he forced himself to look her in her eyes, almost losing his nerve when he saw them wet with tears. He clenched his jaw, wanting to seem authentic because he knew that if he wavered in any way, she would pick up on it. Star was smart in general but when it came to him, she had a third eye that saw beneath the surface. She picked up on things that no one else could.

"You fucked wit' a nigga who I considered a friend and now I can't wait to off that muthafucka. The last thing I want is to make his old bitch my new bitch. Not just that... I ran into Roxy one day and she started talkin'. You seen yo' mama lately?"

Star bristled and her muscles grew tense. She didn't respond because he already knew the answer. Roxy was nowhere to be found; didn't even show up after word got out about Ebony.

"She gave me a little insight on what happened the night that I was shot. I didn't want to believe it... thought that it was just a junkie pulling tricks, pretending to know somethin' I wanna hear in exchange for a bump. But the more I think 'bout that shit, the more it got me lookin' at you different."

Kato paused and looked her over, his upper lip curling slightly in disgust. He walked in close to her, invading her space and creating a shadow over her face as she cowered under his height.

"You wanna tell me who shot me? Who *really* killed Mink?"

The question came out more like an accusation than an inquiry. Like he already knew the answer. Star didn't make any attempt to answer him. With her teary eyes glaring into his hateful ones and the hurt he was inflicting showing vividly on her face, she kept quiet.

"Let me drop this on yo' head right quick," he continued again, stepping closer still so that her nose almost touched his chest. "I ain't need nobody to tell me shit because I already remember exactly what happened that night. You all up in my face pretendin' to be concerned and shit 'bout what I been through but we both know you the reason for all this shit."

Unable to hold them back any longer, Star blinked and allowed the tears to fall down her cheeks.

With her lips trembling, she said, "If y-you knew, wh-why did you have sex with me? Wh-why have you been with me?"

Looking down on her, he delivered the final blow, speaking with enough venom to kill every last hope that he was the man she thought he was.

"I heard you had good pussy. Guess I wanted to see for myself. Shit... you let me fuck and I fucked. I did it and now I'm done. I'm over this shit and I don't want to see yo' fuckin' face ever again. I said that I was gonna bust my gun on everybody who played a part in tryin' to end my life. You need to leave before I decide to make good on that promise."

With that last word said, Kato turned around and put his back to her, once again looking out the window, his hands clasped behind his back. Star felt compelled to plead to him that she had made a mistake, never expected to fall in love with him and that she had only been defending her family. But these were things he already knew.

Dropping her head, she turned around and took the heaviest steps she'd ever taken in her life. The walk away from Kato's room was even longer than the walk to it because, this time, she was making her exit out of his life.

CHAPTER 30

STARING AT THE GLOWING RED DIGITS ON THE CLOCK IN HER ROOM, Kevia felt nervous energy coursing through her body with so much intensity that she thought she was going to be sick. Pressing her lips together, she looked down at the crumpled piece of paper between her fingers and read it again, for what felt like the millionth time.

323

She thought she knew what it meant and she prayed that she was right.

Time seemed to pass on forever until, finally, the glowing numbers went from 3:19 to 3:20 and she pushed away the covers from her body and rolled out of the bed to stand on her feet. After tugging a sweater around her body, she grasped it closed with one hand and slipped out of the apartment quietly, careful not to make a sound and wake her mother or siblings who were still asleep. She licked her lips as she rushed down the hall, walking with purpose towards the back exit of the building that led to an outside secluded staircase where she and Sloan would sit, hold each other and talk under the stars.

At night, when everyone else was taking up space in her mother's small, crowded apartment, Sloan would swing by to see her before making the drive to the suburbs where he stayed. He would text her with a time and she would slip out to meet him on the staircase when the time arrived, stealing a few cherished moments of his time before he had to leave.

Kevia opened the door and walked out, her eyes searching around her as she descended the staircase, taking short breaths. A burst of movement across from her made the air halt in her lungs and she gasped softly, blinking her tear-filled eyes in disbelief, when she saw Sloan standing before her eyes.

"Oh my god..." she whispered, taking slow steps forward with her hand covering her open mouth.

She couldn't believe what she was seeing. Even though she'd been praying all day for this moment to come true, now that it was here, she couldn't stop thinking that she was stuck in a dream.

Sloan grabbed her arm and pulled her into his body, hugging her tight with his jaw clenched to control his emotions. He'd struggled with the decision to allow Kevia to think he was dead because he hadn't wanted to hurt her in that way, didn't want her to have to endure the thought of being left to live without him and raise their child alone, but, in the end, he made the choice that he felt he had to.

"I can't believe you're... why would you..." So many questions filled Kevia's mind, she had no idea which one to ask first. Finally, she simply shook her head and gave up.

"You need to explain this to me. Right now."

Pulling the skull cap on his head lower to cover his face, Sloan raised the hood on his sweatshirt and tugged it down over his head before nodding.

"Take a seat," he said, lifting his arm to point at the staircase.

Stubborn in her anger, Kevia shook her head and folded her arms across her chest.

With a sigh, Sloan gave in and began to speak.

"Kato came to me 'bout what happened to his moms and I explained the shit to him. Told him that I didn't want anything to do with it—didn't even know what was happenin' until it was already done. I tried to talk Polo out of it but he wasn't hearin' me. Kato already knew 'bout it because a kid, a young Disciple he had with him, told him 'bout it and also said that Polo was plannin' to have some niggas run up on me that night."

Kevia frowned. "What? Polo was tryin' to have you killed?"

"He saw me as a threat. He already had Trey ready to take my place, but Kato handled him. That was his body that he had in the trunk... not mine."

Kevia's head dropped. It wasn't a secret that Polo was ruthless and moved quick to extinguish any threats to his power but for him to actually plot on Sloan, someone who had been loyal to him since the beginning, was just ruthless.

"Damn."

Then she remembered how she had spent the last few days mourning his death, how much pain that had caused and how hopeless she felt once she realized that she would be raising their child alone. She thought of how angry she'd been at God for taking him away and how much she hated Kato for being the one to do it. And Star... she'd blamed her own best friend for a murder that never even happened. She'd said things to her that she never would have otherwise.

"How could you pretend to be dead though?" she fired at him, her eyes blazing with her fury. "Do you know what that shit did to me? Do you know how much I've suffered behind this?"

Dropping his head, Sloan couldn't do a thing but give her a simple nod before he spoke.

"I didn't want to do it that way," he admitted. "That was Kato's doing. I went to Indiana to take care of some shit concerning Jimmy Johnson and when I came back, I found out I was dead, and a memorial was bein' held at the park." Running his hand over the facial hair on his beard, he chuckled a little before continuing. "I slid over there to see what was up and saw the stunt Yasmina pulled on you. The shit pissed me off—I don't give a fuck 'bout anybody thinkin' I'm dead but I didn't want the two people I love most to be caught up in it. That's why I contacted my daughter and had her send a message to you."

Kevia leaned back on the stair behind her and shook her head as she stared into the starry night.

"So Kato fake killed you and didn't even let you know." She clicked her tongue against her teeth. "I feel like I done heard it all."

"He said he needed Polo to show his face and knew he'd plan a memorial so it seemed like the perfect place to put hands on him. But he never showed up and I haven't heard from his ass since I got back in town, so I don't know what the fuck is up. I'ma just lay low for now."

Cutting her eyes at him, Kevia added to his sentence. "Until you're resurrected from the dead."

A blank expression covered Sloan's face before he burst out laughing at the insanity of the statement. Before long, Kevia joined in as well. With his arms wrapped around her body, he held her close and kissed her forehead sweetly as silence fell over them. They sat there for what felt like hours of bliss, enjoying each other's presence. It was different being with the one you loved after knowing that it was a real possibility that this moment could have been stolen away from them. Kevia had spent the last few days mourning his death and Sloan had just barely escaped Polo's murderous plot on his life. Both of them cherished this time together like never before.

"She said she was your wife," Kevia said finally, speaking of Yasmina and the things she'd said at the park earlier. "And that you said all this stuff to her 'bout me bein' a jump-off and the baby not bein' yours."

A grunting noise escaped through Sloan's nose, as if he were agitated but was trying not to show it.

"She is my wife but not by choice and not once I can figure out how to get rid of her. And I don't even gotta say shit for you to know that last part is a lie," was all the response he gave her but, the second that Kevia saw the look in his eyes, his few words became more than enough.

With her head rested on his shoulder, she forgot about any and everything happening in the world around them and all the people in it, concentrating only on the present moments they shared. They talked as long as they could, catching up on the past few days as if they'd been apart for a lifetime.

"I need you to stay in the house until I tell you it's safe to leave," he suddenly said after a brief pause in their conversation. "Some changes are gonna take place and I need to make sure you're safe until I can move you."

She nodded her head and then her thoughts went to Star. If she needed anyone right then, it was her friend, but first she had to apologize for all of the things she'd said.

"Can I tell Star that you're alive?"

She held her breath as Sloan took a few moments to think, but then let it out sharply the second he nodded his head.

"Yeah, you can tell her," he said, adjusting his baseball cap and hood on his head. "Not on the phone though. Make sure she comes here."

After a few additional stolen moments together, Sloan began to prepare to leave before the sun rose and activity in the neighborhood increased. For the first time, Kevia wasn't watching him go to be with another woman while wondering what her real role was in his life. She was certain of her place and she knew that his leaving was only temporary. Sloan had already promised her that the next time they were together, it would be the beginning of their forever.

CHAPTER 31

WITH A BLUNT HANGING FROM HIS LIPS, POLO WATCHED AS TONYA slipped out of her room door at a Motel 6, looking both ways before backing back inside and closing the door. She was looking for her next trick, a man she was expecting who would never arrive because his body was stuffed in his own trunk. As big as Chicago was, word traveled fast, especially when it came to a former Gangstress queen turned prostitute.

Tonya fell into the lifestyle accidentally; not knowing that it would become her new norm. After the money she'd stolen from Assassin ran out, she went back to the Arab man at the convenience store, willing to do whatever she needed in exchange for a favor. She was desperate; her plan to get back the money that she'd left at Brenda's fell flat when she caught Kush home alone only to discover the bag was gone. Now, not only was she left empty-handed but, thanks to the part she played in both Ebony and Assassin's murders, she was an enemy of the streets as well. Both the Disciples and the Four Corner Hustlers were offering rewards to anyone who had word of her location so they could end her life.

With the hood of his jacket pulled over his head, Polo slid the silenced .45 caliber handgun from his side and held it in his hand, loving the weight of the metal. He was on a mission to take out his enemies and Tonya was the next in line.

Even though he rarely traveled without his entourage, this time he was alone. His paranoia was at an all-time high and had him second-guessing everyone and everything around him. Trey had disappeared off the face of the Earth, Tony's action when it came to Kato had him looking suspect and, being that he'd failed in killing JaJa, there was only a matter of time before it came out that he was the one responsible for killing Yesman. There were too many people hunting him and until he was able to covertly get rid of every threat, he was forced to lay low.

"Game time," Polo whispered when he saw a text come through on the dead man's phone.

Um... are you still coming?

He rushed to send his reply.

I'm here but I don't want nobody to see me. Unlock the door so I can just walk in.

There was a brief pause before Tonya's response popped up on the screen.

Fine but hurry up.

Evil intentions curled the edges of Polo's lips, forming a sardonic smile as he stepped out of the dead man's car, gripping the gun in his hands. It was Star's fault that Tonya was even still alive; she was the one who had stopped him from doing what he knew he should have the second he stripped her of her rank. Tonya was too much like him, she didn't take kindly to anything she perceived as disrespect. She wasn't satisfied unless she had the upper hand and she was incapable of resisting the urge to do everything she could to take revenge on her enemies. Polo knew this about her because it was how he'd trained her to be. It was also why he knew she would continue to be a problem if he allowed her to live.

Her back was turned when he entered the hotel room and for the brief moment before she turned to him, he considered ending her then, before she even got a chance to know what had happened to her. The option was quickly taken away when she swiveled around on the balls of her feet and faced him, her eyes stretching wide with surprise when she realized the man in front of her was the last person she'd been expecting.

"Surprise. You miss me?"

Polo smirked devilishly. In his insanity, he found pleasure in the way that her eyes clouded with tears as the realization that she was living her last moments began to sink in. With her lips parting slightly, she tried to beg for her life as her eyes eagerly searched the room for an escape or some way to protect herself. She had a gun that she kept in the drawer of the nightstand next to the bed in order to protect herself from the random men she entertained, but there was no way Polo would slip up long enough for her to go for it.

"Polo, I—I..."

She had no idea what to say to him. What *could* she say? She didn't waste any time praying that he didn't know of her exchanges with Assassin where she promised to help him take down Polo, by robbing him first and then killing him after. The very fact that Polo was here with his gun pointed right at the center of her chest said that he knew all about her plans and was ready to bring down her judgment, whether she had actually intended to go through with them or not.

"Last words?"

He pressed the gun into her chest, right on her skin. Letting out a sharp breath, Tonya didn't move away and gave up on trying to run. There was no way out of this situation unless Polo decided to show mercy; a trait she'd never seen any evidence that he even had.

Thinking on any possible last words, she knew right away that she wouldn't waste them pleading for her life. There was no use in that. However, for some strange reason, her mind did go to Star and then finally to Ebony. She had few regrets but, in that moment, being part of the reason why Ebony was dead became one. In all of this, she was the one who was innocent and she'd suffered the most. It seemed almost a blessing that she would receive a quick death by a single bullet to the heart when Ebony spent her last moments gasping for air as she suffocated in a shallow grave.

"I just hope God forgives me," Tonya whispered and hung her head.

Looking at the regal way in which she was ready to accept her fate,

Polo couldn't help but feel disappointed. She wasn't begging, wasn't crying, wasn't even making an attempt to put up a fight for her life. Somehow that took away all of the pleasure in killing her. With the butt of his gun, he clubbed her so hard across her head that her knees went weak and she dropped like a rock to the ground. He then leaned over her, noting that she was barely conscious, and cracked the gun against her skull several more times until it broke through the skin and she was out cold.

A knot the size of a golf ball began to form at a shocking rate across her forehead as blood leaked out from the gash on her head, onto her face and matted hair. She wasn't dead but that's how he preferred it for now, until he was able to get her to a secluded place, an abandoned warehouse that the Disciples had long ago stopped using.

Polo had plans to give Tonya a slow and painful death that he would use to send a message to anyone who thought about challenging him once Kato was dead and he regained control of his throne. He would also use Tonya's murder as a way to form a truce with the Four Corner Hustler's and ensure that they would back him as the leader of the Disciples. Not only had he spared Silk's life, but he also took out the woman responsible for killing Assassin.

Peaking outside of the motel room, Polo saw no one around other than dope fiends, prostitutes, pimps and others who didn't give a fuck about the law and damn sure wouldn't want to call the police. He wrapped a sheet around Tonya's body and cradled her in his arms, struggling slightly under her dead weight, and then slipped out the motel room, walking with a steady pace. As he bent a corner towards his car that he parked on the side of the building, he nearly ran into someone.

"Damn, baby, where you goin' so fast?"

Polo looked up into the face of a hooker who appeared to either be a transvestite or a very ugly woman. As if she smelled money on him, she tossed him a wide grin, showing off an entire bottom row of missing teeth, not even noticing the body he was holding in his hands. Polo winced with disgust; it was a hideous sight.

"Fuck off. I ain't got no money on me." He'd said the magic words and, in seconds, the hooker went on her way.

Once she was gone, Polo picked up his pace eager to put some distance between him and the motel in case he was being watched. Balancing the body, he pulled a lever to pop his trunk before tossing Tonya inside. Next to her was a backpack that his paranoia wouldn't allow him to travel without, filled with all the ingredients needed to commit the perfect kidnapping or murder without leaving a trace. He snatched out a few zip ties to secure her arms then feet and, once that was done, he shoved a lemon into her mouth to gag her and was about to secure it with tape when she began to wake up. Lifting his fist, he pounded her skull as hard as he could and finished the job once she was out again.

"Whatever you got goin' on don't look good," a voice said just as he was about to close the trunk. He stalled and glanced up, seeing the hooker again.

"But you can buy my silence for $50," she continued with a playful smile.

"What 'bout a hundred and a feel on that fat ass?" Polo countered, giving her a smile of his own. She took the bait and nodded her head, twisting from side to side as if she were shy.

"Come get it," he said and reached into his pocket.

Pulling out a piece of paper that the hooker mistook for cash, he held it up and waited for her to walk to his side. The second she was close enough to grab what she thought was money, she made the mistake of glancing in the trunk and opened her mouth to scream when she saw Tonya's body inside.

Zip! Zip!

With his gun concealed between them, Polo unloaded two silenced bullets in her back and she fell forward, diving headfirst in the trunk. It was a struggle but once he was able to shove the rest of her body inside with half of her sprawled out over Tonya, he slammed the trunk closed and jumped in the driver's side of his ride.

IT WAS risky driving with not one but two bodies in the trunk, but Polo knew how to play the game. He drove with the attentiveness of a sixteen-year-old during a driving test with both of his hands on the steering wheel and both of his eyes on the road. When it was time to turn, he used his turning signal, he drove five under the speeding limit, checked all of his mirrors before switching lanes and when the traffic light turned yellow, he slowed. He'd even swapped out the hooded jacket he'd been wearing for a collared Ralph Lauren Polo and placed fake glasses on his face, perfecting his version of full nerd swag. In his mind, there was no reason for a cop to even pay him the slightest attention, much less, pull him over.

For this reason, he was surprised beyond reason when he glanced in his rearview mirror and saw the all too familiar blue and red lights flashing behind him.

"What in the *fuck?*" he grumbled and then switched to the next lane, hoping that the patrol car would pass him by.

When the car followed behind him instead, he cursed once again and slowed to a stop on the side of the road, cutting his eyes over his surroundings. He was back in Chi-Town, in Disciple territory, although he wasn't on the side that he controlled. Strategically, he made sure that he stopped right under an overhanging bridge that would be useful if he had to pull out on the cop behind him. There was no way he would take the punishment for being caught with two bodies in the trunk, one dead and the other nearly there. They would toss in prison for life.

The cop car opened at the same time that his cellphone chimed with a message. He dropped his head to his lap and frowned when he saw the message from an unsaved number on the screen.

Time to make amends for your sins, was all it said.

Polo's nose curled as he stared at the text, utterly confused.

"Da fuck does that mean?"

Light taps on the window next to him took his attention off the phone in his lap and he reached out to press the button to let it down.

"License and registration, please," the cop said, not bothering to bend so that he could look inside the car. That fact was peculiar to Polo but he didn't delay in doing as he was asked, not wanting to cause any issues that would delay in being let go.

With his best version of a proper accent, he pulled out his wallet and asked, "May I ask why I've been stopped?"

"Oh, because we got a call 'bout some fuck niggas in the area. We just want to make sure you ain't one of them."

An icy sting passed over Polo's spine and he froze, holding his license in hand.

"What?"

"Fuck niggas, you ain't never seen 'em?"

The voice was so familiar.

Turning towards the cop, he looked up and found himself staring at the badge on his uniform. Something about it jogged a memory in him, like he'd seen it before.

Mason, he thought. *Where do I know that name?*

He quickly scanned through his mental rolodex, knowing for certain he'd seen it before, until it finally came to him. Officer Mason was the mohawk wearing officer that he'd bowed up on at the hospital the day he'd visited Kato. He was the one who had been staring at Star's butt and also the one who had showed up to *The Spot* the day that Star found out about her sister's kidnapping.

As slowly as he could, he moved his hand to his side to get his weapon but stopped when he saw movement from the corner of his eyes and heard a familiar *click*.

"Caught you slippin' huh, bruh," Kato said with a fiendish scowl as he bent down just as a truck passed followed by several cars; they were on a desolated street on 59th.

As soon as Polo recognized who the other cop was his eyes flashed with rage then, something that was hard to discern as his hand made a futile attempt to inch for his gun, only inches away, right there under the armrest.

"Don't do it. Don't fight it, my nigga. Just let it go," Kato warned as the two stared at each other.

Kato had an AK-47 concealed at his side, and he leveled it at Polo to show he meant business. Polo's brow knotted up as his fingers continued to inch for his weapon.

"Fuck ass nigga, I said just let it go!" Kato growled with his top lip feral, eyes slanted in murderous rage. Losing patience, he let loose with the assault rifle.

BLACKA! BLACKA! BLACKA!

The first shot took a large chunk of flesh out of Polo chest, big as a football, and tore a hole out the back of the car seat the size of a cannon. The other shot completely severed Polo's right arm from the shoulder, leaving it dangling by his shirtsleeve only; however, it was the last shot that was the most grisly. It was to Polo's abdominal, causing his guts to come spewing and blood to splash the windshield. The cop with Kato looked on in shock as his uniform was sprayed with blood and gore.

Mercilessly, Polo was still alive with his left hand trying to push his the guts on his lap back into his stomach. His eyes frantically darted around like he was going into shock or perhaps being rudely introduced to death's door beckoning him with urgency.

Mason was calling for Kato to hurry up as lone cars passed. Kato stood defiant, his clothes spotted red with blood, his face too. For some reason Kato was sweating as he looked down and watched Polo, a nigga he had once taken an oath to sacrifice his life for. They had been friends since the first grade in the Cabrini Green projects. As Kato watched him struggle to breathe, fumbling with his bloody hands to push his guts back into his stomach, he leaned down into the vehicle, close, only a whisper of a distance away from his face.

"Yo, it didn't have to come to this. But here we are," he began, speaking his mind. "Money, greed and hoes and what you mistake for power, brought us here. You fucked up and made me fulfill my oath. In this life, I expect to be betrayed but I never thought it would be by you."

For some reason Kato nodded his head somberly as Polo made a heavy and painful gasping sound that made him pause for a moment to look at him. The end was near. The stench of blood and death was heavy in Kato's nostrils as he looked at Polo, his body torn to mincemeat like he had been butchered with a hatchet.

Falling back from the window, Kato allowed room for Officer Mason to take his place.

"This is for Yesman Abdul Shabazz," the officer said before pulling his trigger and releasing a bullet into Polo's skull.

It wasn't a known fact and Kato had only discovered it during his hospital stay, but Devin Mason was a Disciple who had grown up under Yesman and Jimmy Johnson's reign. Disciples who managed to keep a clean record and were able to obtain diplomas or degrees often took on jobs or positions in society where they could benefit the organization. Devin was one of them and used his influence as a Chicago police officer to the organization's advantage by accidentally 'losing' evidence that could implicate a Disciple in a crime or even plan drug raids on their enemies so that he could then take what was found and turn it over to Yesman. Over the years, he had to pull back after a close call almost got him discovered but he was still on count, still loyal and proudly represented his gang.

Once Devin had finished the job, Kato began to take off the uniform that he'd pulled on top of his street clothes and prepared to jump in the back of the patrol car so Devin could drive him into the city. He was securing the AK-47 at his side when he stopped suddenly after hearing a thumping sound coming from Polo's trunk. Thinking twice, he pulled the weapon back out and held it in his hands.

"Shit, I think someone's inside," Devin said, although there was no need. Kato was already three steps ahead of him and was tugging at the lever to lift the trunk with his gun in hand. With his finger on the trigger, he was ready to bust a shot but stopped short when he recognized the person inside.

"Is that ole girl that Polo used to fuck with?"

Kato nodded slowly, frowning as he looked at Tonya who was squirming hysterically, moaning and groaning as she tried to force out a scream around the lemon that was taped inside of her mouth.

"That's her, but I don't know who that other ugly bitch is."

"What you gon' do with her?" Devin asked as cars passed and the pedestrians were starting to stare at them.

"She's seen me," Devin said, suddenly paranoid, and with good reason.

With cold eyes, Kato glared at the pitiful sight in front of him, thinking about Star and how devastated she had been after discovering her sister's dead body. His mind was so caught up in the memory, it was almost like he could hear her agonizing howls in his ears right then. It didn't matter if she'd seen Devin or not, he would've never allowed her to live.

"I've got an idea," he said.

Devin watched curiously as Kato walked to the driver's side of Polo's car and pulled on his body until it fell out of the seat and onto the ground. His intestines fell onto the concrete causing the cop to frown. After giving it one last glance, he stepped over it and sat down on the bloody leather seat.

"Follow me," he said to Devin. "Just to make sure I don't get pulled."

With a curt nod, Devin agreed and jumped into his vehicle, forcing himself to avoid another look into Polo's haunting eyes. A tormenting stare was held inside of them; as if he was already serving out his sentence of everlasting torture and pain in the afterlife. Though Devin had seen many dead bodies before, none would haunt him more than this one. He was only too eager to leave the scene and, as soon as Kato began to drive away, he wasted no time falling in line behind him.

Polo's body was left undiscovered for many hours until, eventually, a teenager skipping class nearly ran into him as he rode his bike.

"Shit!" he cursed as he swerved to a stop, almost colliding with a large cement column that supported the bridge overhead.

Cutting his eyes behind him, he checked over his shoulder before greedily licking his lips as he stared at the gold chains around the dead man's neck. He didn't waste a second before rushing to lift the jewelry off the body. After collecting two gold, diamond-encrusted chains, a diamond bracelet, the diamond studs in his ears and the thick wad of money that was in his pocket, the boy rode off at top speed, with the biggest grin on his face like he'd just won the lottery.

With Devin riding behind him to make sure that he wasn't pulled over, Kato drove to the same warehouse where Polo had been headed towards, one they'd killed many people at together in the years before.

At the warehouse, Kato set the vehicle on fire, cremating the remains of both Polo and the mystery woman in the trunk. For Tonya, he had other plans.

With Devin's help, they dug a shallow grave and lumped Tonya's body inside as she struggled halfheartedly for her life. He kept her hands and feet bound but once she was inside, he removed the tape and the lemon from her mouth. She wasted no time and began to scream, cry and shout for mercy, pleading for Kato to save her pitiful life but, in the back of her mind, she already knew that there was no use. When he returned to her side, kneeling down over her, her eyes widened and tears pooled in the corners when she saw the object he had in his hand: a straw.

"No! N-n-n-no, please. No!"

Kato worked quickly, squeezing her throat hard until she didn't have enough air to even let out a sound and forced the straw in her mouth, securing it in place with Gorilla tape. Once that was finished, the only thing that could be heard was Tonya's sorrowful whimpers as Kato began to cover her body with dirt.

"You good from here?" Devin asked as the radio on his waist began to crackle before turning into voices, speaking of a homicide. In some neighboring town, a man's body had been discovered in the trunk of his car which had been parked at some sleazy motel.

"Yeah, I'm good," Kato replied as he leaned over to observe his work.

Tonya's final resting place was complete, the only evidence of the body that lay underneath being the single white straw sticking out of the ground. For a few moments after Devin made his exit, Kato sat there and listened to the sound of her sucking in breath after breath through the straw, struggling for each breath through her cries and whimpers.

"Rest in peace, baby girl," he said before muttering a quick prayer for Ebony.

With that done, he lifted his hand and pressed a single finger over the top of the straw, plugging the hole. As he waited for Tonya to cross over, his thoughts were on Star and the last time he'd seen her, the day he made her feel like she was nothing to him. She would never know about what he was doing in this moment or that he was doing it for her but, in his mind, it was his way of making amends with the woman he'd always love after breaking her heart.

EPILOGUE

"They tried to stop her, but they failed miserably. They overlooked her, tried to discourage her, and sabotage her, but she persevered through it all with her head held high. They talked behind her back and plotted against her, but they didn't realize that they were messing with an unstoppable, resilient Black Queen. She's ambitious, intelligent, self-confident, and bold. She's a Phenomenal Black Queen that didn't have to compromise her integrity to get ahead. She's genuinely happy, successful, and free to be herself. She can, she does, she wins!"

— **STEPHANIE LAHART**

MANY MONTHS LATER

A STAR IS BORN

"Are you sure you want to leave?"

The question was one that Star had asked herself so many times before but every single time, she came up with the same answer.

"Yes," she replied. "There is nothing left for me here."

"What?!" Kevia snapped, feeling slighted.

Star rolled her eyes and laughed.

"I don't mean it like that, Kee," she explained. "All I'm sayin' is that I'm not on count no more. Ebony is gone, my grandmother told me I need to go and live my life and..."

And Kato doesn't want me, was what she wanted to say but she stopped herself before she did. Instead, she bent her head down and kissed the forehead of the small infant that she was holding in her arms.

Sloan Theodore McKenzie, Jr., or S.J. as they called him, was only a month old after being born a whole month and a half premature, but he was the perfect child. With Kevia's smooth, brown, chocolate skin, thick, curly hair and Sloan's peculiar expressive eyes, he was like a doll. Star kissed him again, hating that she would have to leave him but once she made it in the corporate world and was living the life of a true boss bitch, she would make sure that her godson never wanted for a single thing.

"And what else?" Kevia asked, with a mischievous smile. "There was somethin' else you were gonna say."

Star shook her head, keeping her focus on S.J. Although the secret was out that Sloan wasn't dead which meant that Kato wasn't guilty of his murder, it was still hard for her to talk about her feelings about him to Kevia. Then after how he'd treated her the last time they'd seen each other, it was hard for her to think of him at all. He hated her and she loved him. What was the use of thinking about something she couldn't change?

"I was just gonna say that my life is different now... or at least I want it to be," she added before turning to Kevia, sporting a wide grin on her face. "Promise me you'll visit me. I mean, I know that you'll be busy now that you have a new baby and you're the queen G."

With a sharp roll of her eyes, looked away but Star could see the smile on her face.

"Yeah, whatever, bitch. I'm the same ole Kee."

Kevia didn't want to admit it, but she was happy to be named Queen. Now that Polo was gone, Sloan was in charge of the Disciples and Kevia was his queen. Finally it seemed that the organization had a ruler worth vowing their loyalty to, one who would follow in the steps of Jimmy Johnson and all of the founding fathers, pushing for the progression and protection of people in the hood, young boys and girls who weren't born with a silver spoon in their mouths but were worthy of the same opportunities of the ones who did.

"I gotta get goin' if I'm goin' to make it to orientation on time. Just tell Sloan that I said bye. I'll see y'all when I come back for Thanksgiving."

After giving him one last kiss on his chubby cheeks, Star held S.J. close to her chest and took a long inhale of his fresh baby scent before handing him over to his mother. Kevia's 5-carat diamond ring shined brightly in the natural sunlight coming from the window behind them as she reached over to grab her son.

"Damn, you gon' blind a bitch with that big ass ring!" Star joked and waved her hand in front of her eyes as if she were shielding them from the bright light.

"You just make sure your thick ass can fit into your dress when it's time for the wedding. I heard that when girls go to college, they gain fifteen pounds in the first year from eating all that take out and junk food. Don't go over there and lose your waist, bitch. I need my pictures to be on point."

As they walked together to the front door of the mini-mansion that Sloan had copped for his new and growing family in the suburbs, Star couldn't help but to marvel at how quickly things had changed. She was no longer a Gangstress and was about to leave to head off to attend the college of her dreams while Kevia was now living in the suburbs with her new husband, her new son, her step-daughter as well as her sisters and brothers. Sloan was a great man and he knew that Kevia lived and breathed for her siblings, that there was no way he could have her without making sure that they were straight, and he didn't hesitate to bring them into their home. He copped a spot big enough for all of them and treated every child the same—like his own.

"So... have you heard from Kato?" Kevia couldn't resist asking before Star left. She'd been dying for her to bring up his name the entire time but since she didn't, she decided to do it herself. Instantly, she regretted it when she saw the somber look on Star's face at the mention of the man who used to bring her the purest joy.

"No, I haven't. Not since he made me leave the hospital. And now that he knows what I did, I can't blame him for not wantin' to see me. He probably wants to pretend like I don't exist."

"Or maybe he's *forgotten* that you exist," Kevia said with raised brows. "I mean, I'm not tryin' to make you sad but didn't the doc say that's what would happen? Or maybe he pushed you away before it could get to that point. Maybe he was tryin' to protect you."

Sucking her teeth, Star shook her head, doubtfully. She knew that Kevia wanted to make her feel better about what happened but she was a big girl; she could accept the truth.

"You weren't there and you didn't see the look in his eyes," she said, feeling her own eyes well up with tears. "It was like he hated me. But I'm okay with that. I'll be alright."

With nothing left to say that she felt would be enough to ease Star's guilt, Kevia forced a small smile on her face and nodded her head.

"You'll always be alright," she said. "You're a star."

THE DRIVE to Northwestern was only an hour and a half from Kevia's house but Star took her time and enjoyed the trip. She let the top down on her convertible Benz, allowing her thick, long hair to blow in the wind as she drove down Lakeshore Drive with her radio on high, blasting some new song by Cardi B.

Lying on the passenger seat was a letter to her father, Jimmy Johnson, who was still on death row but would hopefully be able to be released now that he had the best attorneys in Illinois on his case, thanks to Sloan. Jimmy also told Sloan about a storage unit that he and Yesman used to store their savings when they were hustling, which now belonged to Star.

She had enough money to cover her tuition as well as support her while she went to school and even slip her grandmother some money to live a good life; she was even able to move her out the hood.

Star didn't know it but Sloan had also set up a trust fund in her name with some of the money that Polo had been stealing from her father. If she played her cards right, she would never have to work a day in her life. But of course... Star would work. She couldn't wait to make her own money make a name for herself.

As far as the eye could see, life was more than good where Star was concerned, but there was one thing missing.

Love.

Not having Kato in her life left a huge gaping hole in her heart that she wasn't sure any man could fill. Forever and always, he would be that one who got away; the one who made a mark on her life that no other man could ever erase. He was the one she would always love and, no matter who she ended up with, a small part of her would always belong to him.

LOVE SURVIVES

Joy.
Bliss.
Absolute and total excitement.

THOSE WERE ONLY A FRACTION OF THE EMOTIONS THAT STAR FELT AS she wrote her name on the top of her completed final exam paper and packed up her things. Her first year of college was officially done and she didn't even need to know the results of this exam to know that she'd finished with a perfect 4.0 GPA.

"Finished already?" Professor Smithson asked, observing her from under one lifted brow.

With a smirk, she nodded and slapped the exam answer sheet down on his desk.

"Thank you for a great semester," she said and then bowed her head slightly to pay her respects before walking out the lecture hall.

With her backpack hanging over one shoulder, she dug through one of the pockets, searching for her phone, when the sound of a voice told her that there was no need to look further; the person she had been about to call was standing right in front of her face.

"How'd it go?" Sean asked, shooting Star a sexy smile.

Before she got a chance to answer, he wrapped his arm around her shoulders and pulled her in close to his body. Almost immediately, it seemed like every college girl within a three-mile radius shot jealous glares in her direction. Star nestled in closer to Sean, finding it funny. She was the girlfriend of the star football player who had 100% chance of going pro. Everybody wanted to be his girl, but he chose her, most likely because, in the beginning, being with him was the *last* place she wanted to be.

"I aced it. I know I did. Everything you quizzed me on last night was what he covered during the exam."

Leaning in, Sean planted a kiss right on the top of her head.

"You're a star."

Star rolled her eyes. "And you're cheesy."

"Only for you," Sean replied, not missing a beat. "I've got practice tonight, but I'll call you when it's over to see if you feel like going out to celebrate. I can pick you up."

"Sounds like a plan."

Just as soon as she'd said that, her phone began to ring. Reaching into her backpack, she grabbed it and smiled when she noticed that it was her grandmother Facetiming her.

"It's my grandma."

With a nod, he leaned in and pushed his lips against hers, giving her a short and sweet kiss.

"Tell her I said hi. I'm 'bout to head to practice so I'll see you later."

Sean turned to head in the opposite direction of Star as she walked towards the freshman parking lot to her car, rushing to create some distance between them before she answered the call. She knew exactly why her grandmother was calling and, knowing Geraldine, she was about to get cussed all the way out.

Pressing the button to answer the FaceTime call, Star greeted her before the image of her face even came on the screen.

"Hey Granny, what's up?"

"Girl, don't 'what's up' me!" Geraldine snapped back.

Twisting the phone in her hand, Star paused in her steps to squint as she stared at the screen.

"You know you're on FaceTime, right? You ain't gotta hold the phone to your ear. I can see you! Turn the phone around and look at it."

"Oh!"

Star was nearly doubling over in laughter as she watched Geraldine fumble with the iPhone until she began to hold it correctly in front of her face.

"Baby, I don't know what no 'FaceTime' is," she explained. "I saw your name and I just press the button to call. That's why I tell you not to get me all these gadgets because I don't know how to use them. I'm still tryin' to get use to this nice place you got me in. I ain't seen a roach yet! And speaking of, didn't I tell you to stop sendin' me money? You done did enough. I should come down there to whip your natural behind for not listenin' to me but I'm so proud of you, you hear me, chile?"

Forgetting she was on FaceTime, Star rolled her eyes. She was tired of her grandmother's compliments. It was the least she could do to make sure that Geraldine was able to live out her days in a good neighborhood.

"Heffa, I know you ain't roll yo' eyes at me. 'Cause I'ma keep sayin' it. You my grandbaby and I'm so proud of you."

"Granny, I sent you the money because I want to make sure you're taken care of. Just don't let my mama know where you live, please," she added as an afterthought.

"Chile, Roxy is *clean*!"

Star's jaw dropped open.

"What?"

"You heard right," Geraldine continued. "I don't know how long it's gon' last because she only got clean the second she heard that Jimmy might be comin' home soon. I guess she think if she look half decent, he might look sideways at her again. I don't know but he ain't had a woman in all these years, so he can't be too picky, right? She might have a chance."

Of all things for Roxy to decide to come clean for, it *would* be a man.

Typical, Star thought, rolling her eyes.

"What I told you 'bout them eyes, girl? Anyways, I'ma call you later because my stories 'bout to come on. By the way, I love watchin' them on this new FD TV you got me. It make everythin' look real like it's right in front of me."

"You mean HD TV," Star corrected her.

"Whatever, chile. I love you and I'll talk to you later. Send me them grades when you get them."

"Love you too, Granny."

Ending the call, Star almost rolled her eyes yet again as she thought about Geraldine's antics but stopped when it seemed like she could hear her grandmother's own voice in her head telling her that she better not. Giggling to herself, she started walking towards her car, taking out her key from her backpack in the process so that she could unlock her door.

A small piece of paper pushed up under the windshield wiper on the driver's side caught her attention and she groaned loudly, hoping it was not a ticket for some new parking rule she'd violated. Snatching the paper up, she turned it around, frowning slightly when she realized it wasn't a ticket and that there was something written on the other side.

Heart of a lion.

The simple phrase jarred so many emotions in Star's body that she almost felt like her legs would crumple from up under her. Clutching the paper in her hand, she lifted her head and looked around her, searching for the one person who knew how much these words meant to her.

Walking around her, caught in happy conversations with their friends or stuck in the mental ramblings of their own mind, other college students walked about, not paying her the slightest bit of attention. She swirled back and forth searching for Kato as her heart beat a hundred miles a minute, praying that he would pop up somewhere... anywhere... it didn't matter where he came from, as long as when he left, he took her with him.

After standing in the same place for only God knows how long, Star gave up and folded the paper in her hand before pushing into the pocket of her jeans. The devastation that she felt in that moment was as strong as what she'd felt the last time she'd seen him when he told her to go away and never contact him. It was like she was losing him all over again.

WITH A GLASS of wine in her hand, Star lifted the glass and began to drink the last remains of her third bottle of wine. She wasn't old enough to buy liquor for herself, but the woman working at the Jewel grocery store by campus was a Gangstress and, even though Star wasn't queen any longer, she still paid her respect.

On the table in front of her was the crumpled letter that she'd found on her car windshield earlier that day and next to it was her phone that she'd placed on 'silent' as she ignored Sean's calls. Practice was over and he wanted to celebrate the end of another year with his girlfriend, but Star wasn't feeling up to it. Her heart was grieving the loss of another man.

The sound of someone knocking on the door broke through her consciousness, interrupting her from a juicy, drama-filled episode of *Love and Hip Hop* and she jumped to her feet to answer it. In the back of her mind, she prayed that it wasn't Sean. It wasn't like him to show up unannounced but there was a first time for everything. She just hoped that today wasn't the first time for this.

Pursing her lips, she unlocked the front door and swung it open, her attitude already present and ready for Sean if she saw his face. But he wasn't there.

Grasping the door handle in her hand, she leaned outside and looked left and right, trying to figure out who had knocked on her door, but saw no one. She frowned and looked once again.

"Hello?"

"Hello!" someone replied but when Star glanced in the direction of the voice, she saw a group of white boys propped up on a car in the parking lot. When they saw her looking, they all laughed, apparently finding humor in their bad joke.

Grumbling under her breath, Star slammed the door closed and turned around to return to her place of misery, prepared to spend the rest of the night lamenting the nostalgia of her past life. That was... until she realized that she wasn't alone in the room.

"Yo' ass done got too damn comfortable with this college life shit. Ain't no locks on your windows, your back door was unlocked and, just now, you wasn't 'bout to lock yo' door. You sure you from Chi-Town?"

With her eyes shining with tears, Star stood in front of Kato with her mouth slightly parted, wondering if she could trust what she was seeing or if she had slipped into a drunken sleep and this was all a dream. She was in shock to the point that she wanted to break down crying but she hadn't completed accepted the fact that he was there, standing right in front of her.

Kato looked exactly the same as she remembered him, the only difference being that he was a lot more muscular and his hair had fully grown to cover the stitches that had once shown clearly on one side of his head. He still wore long locs on the other side of his head, but they weren't dyed a fiery red as they had been before, but were his natural dark brown and black color instead. Standing before her, she looked him over taking in every bit of his tattooed body, immediately noticing that he had new markings on his body that she hadn't seen before, including a couple more teardrops under his eye.

"You gon' say somethin' or you just gon' keep standin' there actin' like you don't know a nigga?"

"I just can't believe you're here!" Star exclaimed, covering her face with her hands before pulling them away, as if he would disappear.

Kato laughed, humored by her reaction. "This college life got you actin' like a white girl for real. So how you been, pink toes?"

She rolled her eyes before walking over to him, feeling awkward about how she should act towards him. She wanted to kiss him, run her hands over his chest, hug his body close to hers or just touch him in any way to make sure that he was real. However, the things he'd said to her the last time she'd seen him were still ringing clearly in her mind; she wasn't sure what she should do.

One look at the self-conscious expression on Star's face let Kato know that, even after a year, the words he said to her still hurt. He wanted to tell her that he hadn't meant them and that, now that he was healthy, he wanted her to be his for the rest of their lives. But, after watching her during the day and getting a glimpse into her new life, it was clear he couldn't do that.

"Come here," he said, reaching out for her.

Without delay, Star fell into his embrace, pressing her nose into his chest as she soaked up the scent of his cologne. With his chin resting on top of her head, he held her close and looked off into the distance behind her, enjoying this moment that he'd dreamed of for so long but also knew wouldn't last.

Reluctantly, he released her and pulled away, taking his place in a chair across the room. Star bit down on the corner of her bottom lip and did the same.

"How have you been?"

Star smirked and gave him a pointed look.

"I should be askin' you that. You look... healthy."

Kato forced air from his nose, chuckling slightly.

"Yeah, my nigga Sloan came through and dropped the chips needed for me to go through treatment. I wasn't for takin' no handouts but he said he needed me to get it together so I can continue on as his Enforcer."

"Who better to protect him than the man who supposedly killed him?"

Not even Kato could resist laughing at that.

"Yeah, that was some wild shit that we had to do but it worked out in the end. Jimmy should be out in a couple months and Sloan is runnin' shit the way it should be ran."

"And what about you?" Star was unable to resist getting to the things that she really wanted to know. "What do you have in mind for your life? For us?" she couldn't help adding.

His jaw tightened. He knew exactly what she was trying to ask him, but he also knew that he was going to have to break her heart yet again. For a moment, he wondered if it would have been better to not have come. Maybe it was selfish of him to intrude into her life, simply because he couldn't resist stealing a few moments of her time, when he knew that, in the end, he'd have to leave.

"I'm gonna keep doin' the same shit I been doin'," he replied before shooting her a lopsided smirk. "Besides... what's up with you and that fat-headed, nerd ass nigga you been boppin' around here with? Ain't that yo' man?"

Rolling her eyes, Star couldn't suppress her smile. So Kato had been watching her earlier that day before placing the note on her car and he saw her with Sean.

"He's nice but..." She paused to think of her words. "He's not you."

Kato nodded. "And that's a good thing. You don't need someone like me fuckin' up your life. Everything is how it's 'posed to be."

Her eyes shot to him, narrowing slightly as she tried to pick up on his meaning. She fumbled nervously with her fingers before speaking.

"But you came back here so I thought that..." Her words died off.

"I came back here to let you know that I'm sorry for the shit that I said to you the last time. I don't even remember half of what I said because a nigga was buggin', for real, but the doc got me straight."

He shrugged and nudged his nose before looking away. Star didn't speak because she felt like he still had more to say, though she wasn't sure whether she really wanted to hear it. Frowning slightly, Kato let out a heavy exhale before turning back to meet her eyes.

"You taught me a lot of shit, Star. How to love someone, how to forgive. You taught me how to believe in somethin'—how to fight for somethin'. But you also taught me what love isn't. Love isn't puttin' the person you love in a situation that would make them unhappy. We livin' on opposite sides of the world right now, ma."

With tears shining in her eyes, Star pulled her lips into her mouth and bit down on them to stop herself from speaking. She could see the seriousness in his eyes and knew that his mind was made up, but she also knew he was right. There would never be another man that she'd love as much as she loved him, but Kato was part of her past life. He wasn't ready to let go of the streets, and probably never would, and she never wanted to go back.

"Yo' boy is the truth though. All they do is talk 'bout that nigga in the hood, 'bout how he might get the Chicago Bears back on the map if they can get him. You might be a football wife. I might be watchin' yo' ass on the *Real Housewives of Chicago* one day or some shit."

He shot her a teasing grin and she bowed her head as her cheeks began to warm.

"He'll never be you," she admitted in a low tone.

Lifting her head, she locked eyes with him and emotions so raw and pure passed between them. The moment was so intense that Kato had to force himself to look away when visions of the night they'd shared together started to go through his mind. They'd made passionate love like nothing else in the world mattered.

"And no woman will ever be you," he allowed himself to admit.

Before she could stop herself, Star jumped to her feet and moved to him, planting her round ass right in the center of his lap, pressed against his throbbing manhood. She didn't give him a chance to stop her before locking his lips into a deep kiss, but he had no intentions of stopping her any way. With his arms around her body, hands gripping the curve of her ass, he forced away the thoughts of what 'should be' and 'couldn't be' and simply lived in the moment.

He stripped her carefully, gently tugging off her clothing as he sucked on her skin and kissed away the tears that ran down her cheeks. Both of them knew this would be the last time so they weren't in a rush. They took their time exploring each other's bodies, creating memories that would have to last a lifetime.

THAT NIGHT, Kato held the only woman he'd ever loved—the only one he probably would love—in his arms for the last time, battling with thoughts in his mind. Part of him wanted to say 'fuck it' and keep Star for himself, but he knew he couldn't. He had to let her go. The love inside of her for him and that unselfish desire that was natural to women, making them sacrifice themselves for the happiness of others, was something a lesser man would use to his advantage in order to keep her. But Star wasn't someone that needed to be kept—not by him, not by anyone. She needed to be free to live out her dreams, to fulfill her purpose. She was greater than the life that she would have with him and he was man enough to recognize that.

So after a few long moments passed of him fighting the many voices urging him to choose differently, he ignored the noise and did what he had to. With a gentle kiss against her forehead, Kato took one last look at Star before turning away to leave. He slipped off without a sound, like a thief in the night, the only difference being that he took nothing and left everything.

DAYLIGHT GREETED STAR before she was prepared for it to arrive because she already knew that once it came, Kato wouldn't be there. An ache shot through her chest when she stared at the empty space where he'd been, and she closed her eyes tightly as they filled with tears. A heavy exhale was all she needed to force them away once she remembered what Kato had said to her.

Everything is how it's 'posed to be.

It was true, even if it was hard to accept. Kato had given her the closure that she needed and all that she had left to do now was to move on. She slid her legs over the side of the bed and stretched her arms to the sky, yawning wide and squeezing her thighs together when she noticed the ache in her center, leftover sensations from the night before. She smirked as she thought on all of the things that Kato had done to her body and closed her eyes to revel a moment longer in the sweet memories. It wasn't until she opened her eyes that she noticed something on her nightstand that didn't belong. Frowning, she reached out and grabbed it, twisting it around in her fingertips.

"Is this a... bullet?" she whispered, staring at the badly bent and damaged metal.

She looked back on the dresser and saw a note. Placing the bullet down, she grabbed the white paper and held it in front of her eyes.

Star,

By the time you see this, I'll be out. You make it hard on a nigga to leave while you're awake. I'm sure you know that shit, which is why you put that fat ass on me before I could cut out last night (insert me laughing here).

On a serious note though, I hope you don't hate me for this shit. I truly feel like it's the way it should be. Remember everything you told me you wanted to do? Go to college, start your own business, be like Oprah and yada-yada-yada-other-shit? Do all of that. Don't fuck up and don't let nobody get you off track. Remember that day I almost shot you but I didn't? I didn't kill you so let that shit be for a reason.

Rolling her eyes, Star stopped reading to suck her teeth before starting again.

And I know you rollin' yo' eyes right now but I'm serious.

She couldn't help but laugh at that. Kato knew her too well.

P.S. I left a little keepsake on the dresser. Something to remember me by, I guess you can say. It's the bullet they took out of my head when I was taken to the hospital the night I was shot. Getting shot was the best thing that's ever happened to me in my life.

I'll love you every single day that God gives me. You made me understand that every day He gives is truly a gift.

With love,

K8O

NOTE FROM LEO & PORSCHA

Thank you for reading! We know that we say it every time but this was TRULY a labor of love. We spent a lot of time planning out this series to make sure that we not only stayed true to our characters but true to the story of the gang lifestyle as a whole.

If you're connected with us on our social media pages, you'll know that both of us lived in Chicago for part of our lives and, during that time, we experienced a lot of the circumstances and environments described in this book and the ones to come. It's a tale very close to our hearts and very personal.

We hope that, through this series, you understand that everything is not always cut and dry, black or white. Many times people are forced into environments that choose their fates long before they are ever given the option. Some are like Star, lucky enough to have the chance to venture on her own path but others don't always get to choose. Circumstance plays a major part and can sometimes dictate how people spend their life. **But LOVE can survive in the most unlikely circumstances and sometimes it's love that makes all the difference.**

Leave us a review with your thoughts! We read them and we appreciate them.

Special thanks to our loyal readers, our authors and our core supporters. We appreciate you more than you know.

To all authors out there and especially to the urban community of writers—we find strength when we work in harmony **together**. Spread love, not hate. We are all in this book gang together!

Peace, love & blessings to all,

Porscha & Leo

JOIN THE GANG!

Join the Gangland Series Mailing List

READ MORE ON THE LIT READING APP!

Read more books like this one **for less**! Check out some other new releases on the LiT Reading App. Go to www.litreadingapp.com to learn more!

JOIN THE LSP MAILING LIST!

Join our mailing list to get a notification when Leo Sullivan Presents has another release.

Text LEOSULLIVAN to 22828 to join!

To submit a manuscript for our review, email us.